Lying

crying

dying

Lying crying dying

a novel

DOMINIC MARTELL

db

DUNN BOOKS

acknowledgments

Many people helped the author through the perilous enterprise of setting a novel in a country that is not his own. Particular thanks are owed to Julián García, Juan Antonio Madrid, Ignasi Costa and Jorge Prats. Any errors, misinterpretations and flights of fancy that may appear are entirely the fault of the author.

(A) Sants Estació Terminal
(B) Escola Industrial
(C) Bar Manhattan
(D) Hospital Clínic de Barcelona
(E) La Sagrada Família
(F) Font de Canaletes
(G) Plaça Catalunya
(H) Corte Inglés
(I) Le Méridien Barcelona
(J) Police Station
(K) The Palau
(L) Liceu (Metro)
(M) Cafè de l'Òpera
(N) Boqueria Market
(O) Plaça Reial/El Glaciar
(P) Santa Maria del Mar
(Q) Barrio Chino (part of El Raval)
(R) Post Office
(S) Plaça de la Drassanes
(T) Monument a Colom
(U) Moll de la Fusta
(V) Estació de França
(W) Barcelona Zoo

Lying

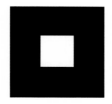

crying

dying

"They came back for the wife, you know. Took an extra five seconds or so, cold-blooded as sharks, just to come back and put a bullet through her head. She might have made it if she'd got out of the car and run, but she stayed with her husband." The words hung in the air for a moment as four Germans waited for one Israeli to speak. Outside the window there was drizzle and cold, the moist dark greens and grays of the Rhine valley halfway to winter. In the distance were the hills.

"Who can blame her?" Hands in his pockets, the Israeli turned from the window, a short square man with a low forehead and an excess of black eyebrow. "I would imagine one's presence of mind is sorely tested at a moment like that."

At his desk Joachim Wirth was trying to suppress the unpleasant sensations in his knotted inner regions. Since Munich, not to mention things that happened before Wirth was born, to lose an Israeli on the very doorstep of the government of the Federal Republic was as bad as it got. "How many gunmen?" asked the Israeli.

"Two," said Jürgen Rahe, Wirth's immediate superior, the senior BND officer present. "One Czech M52 and one nine-millimeter something. Peled died in the first fusillade."

"You had a witness, you said?"

"A lady just unlocking her car at the curb. Considering how badly she was shaken she gave us a hell of a good account." The Israeli nodded, wandering away from the window, eyes on the rug. Into the silence Rahe tossed, "She said she'd never forget the look on the wife's face. She just looked the bastard in the eye, holding on to her husband."

Wirth tensed at his desk; the Israeli halted and glanced up at Rahe. "Yes," he said. "She was probably thinking about the children."

The silence thickened and then the Israeli, perhaps sensing he'd laid it on a bit heavy, took his hands out of his pockets and for no apparent reason looked at his watch. "Well. You seem to have acted with admirable efficiency."

Wirth winced at the word; Rahe soldiered on. "One of them at least is still in the Federal Republic, we think. He bolted out of a Lufthansa office in Karlsruhe this morning when the agent questioned his passport, which was Algerian. The photo was a bit too good and the agent a bit too sharp-eyed. She gave us a good description."

"You found the getaway car, you said."

Rahe nodded, tapping a sheet of paper as he looked down at it through his reading glasses. "It was rented in Mannheim yesterday with a Swiss passport and credit card that the Swiss tell us belonged to a Lugano schoolteacher who recently died of cancer. The customer spoke excellent German but was not a native speaker, according to the clerk. She had no trouble believing he was Italian Swiss but conceded today he might have been just about anything. Anything European, anyway."

"A European."

"So it appears. Probably Mediterranean but certainly not Arab, she said." Rahe's voice scraped the bottom register, full of disgust. "A handsome devil, as she put it."

The Israeli, who was not a handsome man, nodded slowly, looking from the desktop to Rahe's face and back again. "Well. That's good. He seems to have made an impression."

Late at night, in shirtsleeves and with an evil headache germinating, Wirth looked at Rahe across a table scattered with surveillance photos and printouts spilling out of their file jackets and said, "No name, but I'll bet you this is the man. He gets around, doesn't he?"

Rahe looked at the clouded, shadowy figures in the three aligned photos. "What is he then? Italian? French?"

"Spanish, maybe. We don't even know what his native language is."

Rahe straightened with a creak and a sigh. "Thank God he's not German, anyway."

"Yes." Wirth pulled the photos back across the table. "I want this *arschloch*. The Arabs, that's one thing. You expect it. But a European, Christ." Wirth rapped the middle photo with a knuckle. "This is the asshole I want."

PROLOGUE

The woman at the wheel of the stolen Audi A6 sees things in the landscape other people do not see. Beyond that farmhouse, possible cover in the stunted trees straggling up the slope toward the rocky crest; where the wood closes in on the road ahead, a good place for an ambush. She is a city girl and she could not tell you whether that is oak or chestnut, but she could tell you how to get through these hills to the underground *zulo* where the kidnapped banker from Vitoria survived for 147 days in 1993. Six kilometers back was the place where an Ertzaintza officer bled to death on the road in 1992; in the high pasture just shy of that distant summit is the stone hut where Errazkin and Bengoetxea were shot down. This is Guipúzcoa, the heart of the resistance, and the green and fractured topography is a comfort and menace at the same time.

The sky is gray and lowering today. Rain and mist have laid patches of green on the rocky hills. Somewhere beyond them lies Donostia, the sea; she wishes she were there. She has left the road now, following a rough track that meanders up the side of a gully. In low gear she climbs, jouncing over rocks. Vegetation thins and the white limestone skeleton of the land gapes through. Autumn is advanced and the flocks have long since descended; the high pastures will be empty. Ten minutes after leaving the road she reaches the *txabola*. Long and low, windows gaping dark and empty, the hut could be a natural growth out of the earth but for the red tile roof. A plastic jerrican, a discarded auto-mobile battery show that the hut is still in use; there were shepherds here this summer. She halts five meters from the door on the rough stony ground and cuts the ignition.

She gets out of the car. After the noise of the engine the silence is profound. She lights a cigarette and walks away from the car, look-ing at the hills. Behind her, hinges creak and a man comes out of the hut. He is tall and dark, wearing a dark red wool sweater and battered white Adidas shoes. He has not shaved for several days. He smiles as the woman turns.

"Welcome to the Ritz. I trust you had no trouble finding it."

She gives him a long hard look. "No," she says. "But I'm a bit dis-appointed in the staff so far."

"Surprised to see me?"

She shakes her head. "Not really."

He walks to her, slowly, and puts his hands on her arms. She taps ash off her cigarette, head thrown back slightly. He pulls her to him and kisses her, but she will not open her mouth. After a brief struggle he releases her. The look on his face is amused as he steps away. "Your standards are rising," he says, nodding at the car. "That's the latest model."

"It was an easy grab. But I don't want to be driving it tomorrow."

"We'll drive all night. In the morning we won't need it anymore."

"We?"

"That's right. You think anyone still trusts you?" The faint ironic smile is still there.

She smokes. "So where is it?"

The man saunters to the door of the hut. He goes inside and

comes back out after a few seconds, carrying a canvas suitcase. He walks to the rear of the car. "Keys?"

She pulls the keys from her jacket pocket and tosses them to him. He catches them, sets down the bag and selects the key to the trunk. She throws her cigarette away. The first drop of rain touches her face. The man opens the boot and freezes.

He stands very still for perhaps five seconds and then turns, slowly. "Why?" he says. The look on his face is no longer amused or ironic. Now he is very pale.

"Because it's time," says the woman, leveling the Browning Hi-Power at him.

"Katixa," he says. He speaks softly; that could be tenderness in his voice but more likely it is something else now.

She fires three times, quickly, taking him in the chest with all three shots. The shots echo across the rocky slopes. They knock him back into the boot of the car; he sprawls awkwardly, his legs spilling out, one heel digging convulsively at the earth.

The woman puts the gun away inside her jacket and lights another cigarette. She turns her back and waits for him to die, looking at the Guipúzcoa hills.

"Who is Katixa?" asks the widow Vidal, brushing her hair by the window. Outside, morning noises float up from the narrow street: passing footsteps, traffic on the Ramblas nearby, the lonely cry of a lottery vendor. *"¡Para hoooy! ¡Veinte iguales para hooooooy!"*

"What?" says Pascual. He sits up in bed, rubs his eyes. Mornings with the widow Vidal are difficult; there is always a hangover to contend with, as the only way he ever winds up in bed with her is through the intercession of alcohol.

"I said who is Katixa?"

Pascual frowns, swings his feet to the floor. Today the hangover is less severe than it might be; after a certain point last night he had the sense to shove the bottle away. He finds his underwear, finds his jeans. Zipping up, he walks to the window. "When did I say Katixa?"

The widow Vidal sets down her hairbrush and comes to stand beside him. She is smiling. "Don't worry, it wasn't while you were on top of me."

"Well, that's a relief." Pascual forces himself to look at her; he wishes he'd had the sense last night to stay out of the widow Vidal's clutches. She is plump and cheerful and not without her charms, but these loom larger late at night than in the sober light of day. How old is this woman? he asks himself again. She could be an ill-used forty; she could be a well-preserved fifty. Beyond that he shudders to speculate. This happens two or three times a year, and he always regrets it, at least for a few days. He dredges up a smile for her. "Somebody I used to know," he says.

The widow Vidal has stopped smiling and he fears she is about to go melancholy on him. She runs a hand over his stubbled cheek. "You must have had a lot of beautiful women," she says. Her eyes are still dark and alive, but the morning light from the window is not kind to the rest of the widow's face. Forty-five, thinks Pascual.

He shrugs. "A few." He leans on the window frame and looks down into the street. He has remembered the dream now.

"And was she beautiful, Katixa?"

Pascual nods. "She was." Pascual is seeing Katixa in the dream again, lit by a shaft of sunlight in a narrow street between high stuccoed walls; Damascus perhaps. Katixa is saying, inexplicably in French, *"Je te reverrai."* She stands for a moment, trim and feline in black, and goes away, leaving only the sunlight. He remembers now, he struggled to call after her. Katixa.

"Did you love her?"

Pascual snaps her a look and she can tell immediately she has irritated him. The widow Vidal pats his cheek and says, "Never mind. I'm an old gossip, that's all. I'll make you some coffee."

Pascual watches her turn and walk from the room, heavy breasts and broad hips moving under the thin robe. He listens as things clatter in the tiny kitchen. It has been a long time since he has dreamed of Katixa.

God yes, I loved her, he wants to tell the widow Vidal. Now he is the one going melancholy.

Dressed and plied with coffee, he takes his leave. At the door the widow Vidal is in maternal mode, giving advice, talking of everything except the past night. Pascual extracts himself, getting away with a more or less chaste kiss. She watches him out of sight down the stairs before she closes the door, the sound echoing through the stairwell. Pascual knows he will be back; the lure of uncomplicated sex mixed with pity and cognac will ensnare him again someday.

He pauses inside the door, seeing just what he saw in his dream, sunlight playing on the high walls of a narrow street. Pascual has to lean against the wall for a moment, shaken. I will see you again, she said in the dream.

If only, Pascual thinks. But from long experience he knows that people who are gone do not come back.

1

The night Katixa reappears, exploding like a nova into Pascual's cosmos, there is Handel at the Palau. Pascual is in the cheap seats; under the metastasizing plaster and the blister of colored glass, an architect's fever dream, a German chamber orchestra has reached the Allegro moderato in the *Water Music,* and Pascual's eyes are closed because this passage is his life. Beneath the strings and the oboes and the horns stalks the solitary bassoon, inexorable, pitiless. Pascual fears the obbligato like death but it is the most beautiful thing he knows.

Afterward, at the head of the Ramblas, Pascual is almost happy. He has enough pesetas left in his pocket to drink tonight; tomorrow something will turn up. Pascual can feel winter coming; soon the crowds will thin, the tourists will go and the Ramblas will belong to those who live here. Gypsies are drinking at the Font de Canaletes. Pascual drifts seaward down the gentle slope, scanning, waiting: knowing that sooner or later everything will happen and everyone go by.

He is lean and pale, with the tread of a cat and the hungry look of the wolf; there is something in the dark eyes, the long face unshaven for two days, that discourages even the forward German girls from approaching him with their uncertain Castilian and half-folded maps. Beyond that it is hard to say what people see; ask a Catalan and he will say Pascual is Castilian or even Andalusian, something about the eyes that suggests he has long squinted into the sun; ask an Andalusian and he will say Catalan. In Rome he has passed for French; in Beirut once he was taken for American and almost shot for it.

Pascual draws black tobacco smoke deep into his lungs, blowing it up into the cool sea air that is beginning to stir the leaves of the plane trees. When the Ducados run out he will have to cadge. He passes the open-air tables of the Cafè de l'Òpera under their awnings, meets the gaze of a ripe blonde in a long dress until her eyes flick away warily, walks on. Past the Òpera, where the slope begins to level off and the crowd to thin, where the most obtuse tourist begins to step warily, Pascual is nearly home.

The Glaciar under the arcades at the top of the Plaça Reial is full of smoke and laughter and the dark throbbing backbeat of Moroccan *sha'bi*. Pascual slides in next to Baltasar at the bar. Baltasar is ebony made flesh, long limbs and a smooth black face with big cow eyes. "There was an Arab at the pension, looking for you," says Baltasar, shoving a beer along the marble countertop toward him.

"An Arab?"

"Certainly an Arab. I know an Arab when I see one." Baltasar's Castilian is fluent but with a drumbeat accent. He and three companions came to the pension some months ago, political refugees from Equatorial Guinea. The Ajuntament pays the widow Puig a monthly rate to lodge them. One of Baltasar's companions limps badly and Baltasar has been known to wake in the night screaming.

Pascual ponders. "Did he mention money?"

14

"No. I told him the morning is the best time to find you at home. He said he'd be back."

"Let's hope," says Pascual. "Otherwise I don't eat tomorrow."

"Something can always be arranged." Baltasar haunts the Ramblas and the Plaça Reial; he knows everyone and will buy the occasional drink. Pascual believes him to be a merchant of illegal substances on a modest scale. He and Pascual are partners in penury, exchanging cigarettes and petty loans.

The barmaid slaps Baltasar's change on the bar in front of him. He blows her a kiss. "She toys with me cruelly," he says as she moves away, soft curves and black curls. "I am in love with her."

"It's in the air tonight," says Pascual. Pascual prefers Handel but in spite of himself the music has aroused him. He has been watching a table where three women sit smoking, a blonde, a redhead and a pale northern brunette. German? Dutch? Irish? Female and aware of their power, in any event. Pascual watches the redhead go up the stairs to the WC, round hips working in faded denim.

"Viñas had no luck, but then maybe they're waiting for someone younger," says Baltasar.

Pascual laughs. "Or someone with two *duros* to rub together." Viñas sits in defeat by the door, nursing his beer, sketchpad on his knee. He catches Pascual's eye and shrugs, casting a comic look of longing at the women.

"I believe the field is open for you," says Baltasar.

Pascual watches the women smoke. He watches the redhead come back down the stairs. He remembers women from other nights, other bars. "Tonight I don't have the stamina," he says. "Go and work your African charms on them."

15

"No, my heart belongs to Eva," says Baltasar, eyes following the barmaid.

It is nearing midnight and Baltasar has business elsewhere. When the beer is finished Pascual crosses the plaza to sneak out through a narrow lane into the Gothic Quarter. The streets are narrow and empty; Pascual is tired. These black granite walls have been here since Ferdinand and Isabella were in knickers. There are echoes here. Music and beer have washed Pascual up on some far shore but the echoes make him wary. The occasional Moroccan cutthroat can still be encountered in the dark streets beyond the Plaça Reial. Pascual has lost wallets and been beaten senseless. He has no prejudices except against *moros* late at night in the lower Gothic Quarter.

The echoes in the Carrer d'Avinyó are not echoes. Pascual has his key out as he approaches the door, casting a glance over his shoulder. There is a figure there, head down and hands in pockets. Pascual very nearly walks on in search of brighter lights; unlocking the door would be an invitation. Fatigue spoils his judgment. As the man draws close enough for Pascual to make out the North African features, the face of an oversized and undernourished boy, he decides that this shambling *moro* is harmless, as fagged as he is. Pascual unlocks the door and pushes. His last backward glance coincides with the rush of feet. The *moro* is no longer shambling and now the knife is glinting in the lamplight. Pascual tries to slam the door shut but his weight cannot compete with the momentum of the charge. The door bursts inward and Pascual finds himself pinned against the wall at the foot of the stairs, the blade at his throat.

The only light comes from outside; Pascual can just see the whites of frantic eyes and the shine of greased-back hair.

"*Tranquilo,*" says the *moro.*

Pascual has done this before. "You too," he says. "*Tranquilo.* Who reaches for it, you or me?"

In answer the pressure on the knife increases. It is a twitch or an evil thought away from drawing torrents of blood; Pascual can feel his jugular pulsing against the blade through a layer of tender skin. He is very still, hands well away from his body, as the Arab's free hand probes. He has just found the wallet in Pascual's hip pocket when he freezes; a third party is moving in the dark with a rustle of clothing.

There is a click and a faint hiss and then light: a sizzling, crackling sound as blue flame shoots up the back of the *moro*'s head. He jerks away and the little hall is eerily lit as a sputtering blue halo crowns his head. The knife clinks on the floor and his hands are beating at the flames as he slams back against the door, bellowing. A foot comes out of the darkness and kicks him into the street. Pascual has not moved but through the doorway he can see as the *moro* runs, bouncing off stone, screaming, a beacon in the night.

Pascual lets his arms fall to his sides. The cigarette lighter has gone out but Pascual registered a face behind it: female. All he can see is a pale face in the dark, coming closer. Pascual stiffens with alarm and raises his hands again to ward off the attack but it is too late; she is on him.

Still primed for mayhem, Pascual is ill-prepared to respond to a woman's tongue in his mouth. Her hands are on either side of his jaw, fingers in his hair, her body pinning him to the wall. After two or three seconds his blown circuits begin to register wonder. As the kiss begins to ease, softening from hungry to tender, the nova explodes.

She draws back just far enough for her breath to caress his lips.

Stunned, Pascual impels her back toward the door, until lamplight falls on her face. "You," he manages in a hollow whisper.

"Me. I need five minutes."

"What?"

Black eyes gleam in the lamplight. "Give me a five-minute lead and come to the Méridien, on the Ramblas. Room 317. Here's your key card." She slides a rectangle of plastic into his shirt pocket. Before Pascual can react she is through the door and gone; he can hear her heels tap-tapping away on the cobbles.

Pascual feels a shock so foreign it takes him a moment to recognize it as joy. Of all the things that could happen tonight, this one has happened: Katixa has found him.

2

Athens, ancient history: Syntagma Square, where it took Pascual a mere five minutes to make up his mind after he identified the American colonel, the former military attaché in Brussels, sitting with three colleagues in apparent peace of mind at a café table on the margin of the square. Pascual wondered at the confidence the Americans showed, sitting in the open like that; either things had changed in Athens or they were armed to the teeth.

Nineteen eighty-nine, a hot day in June, Athens choking to death on its smog, and by then Pascual had realized that he had done worse than waste his life: he had poisoned it. He sat at his own table, ten meters away, watching the Americans, feeling the seconds tick off the clock and knowing that this was the moment.

The Americans fell silent as Pascual approached; they watched him come with professional wariness. "Could I bother you gentlemen for a light?" Pascual asked, holding up a cigarette for inspection, looking in turn at each of the four middle-aged men in shirtsleeves confronted by a down-and-outer with uncut hair and faded denim. The man opposite the colonel, bald and desiccated, a man who had spent a long time in the sun, tossed a plastic lighter across the table to him.

Pascual lit the cigarette and put the lighter down on the table with a word of thanks. He looked at the colonel, who had light blue eyes under close-cropped hair fading to white. "I was supposed to kill you once," Pascual said, smiling.

He had their undivided attention. The colonel, features freezing in a high state of alertness, watched him for a moment and said quietly, "When might that have been?"

"In Brussels, two years ago. You smoked it out and we called it off." Pascual hesitated for a fraction of a second, an instant, and leaped. "The reason I'm here now is I'm supposed to kill some other people. You find a way to get me safely off the street, without making it look like I want to talk to you, and I'll tell you all about it. I'll be at my table over there." Pascual smiled at the gathering, four stone-faced men, and said, "Thanks for the light." He walked back to his table, slowly.

In a couple of minutes the men left, paying the white-jacketed waiter and drifting toward the lower end of the square, out of his line of sight. Pascual read *Le Monde* and tried hard not to watch what was going on around him. He ordered another beer, wondering what he would do if nothing happened. Twenty minutes later two Greek cops, in uniform, came through the tables to Pascual and asked in English to see his papers. He handed them the perfectly good French passport he had been given at the Hotel Vitosha in Sofia. They pretended to look at it and then asked him, politely, to come with them. Pascual followed them, leaving the newspaper, leaving, he hoped, just about everything.

"Why us?" said the man with the wire-rimmed glasses, late that night in the small, bare room in the third-floor flat three hundred meters from the American embassy. The man had just flown in from Rome; Pascual had stirred the waters.

"Because I don't want to go to Israel," said Pascual.

The man nodded, portly, bald, avuncular. Serene and reasonable. "Any particular reason?"

Pascual drew a cigarette from the pack on the table and lit it, taking his time. "I have the impression the Israelis are not very understanding."

The CIA officer looked like a man who enjoyed a joke. Behind the wire-rims were heavy-lidded eyes that crinkled at the corners. "And we are?"

"That's what I'm hoping."

"How much understanding can you expect for all the things you've done?"

Cigarette smoke curled to the ceiling, above the lamplight. "I never killed anybody," said Pascual, the strict veracity of the statement not quite enough to still his conscience.

"And you're willing to sell them down the river, huh?"

"All of them," said Pascual. He was tired; they had fed him and all he wanted was to sleep; that morning in Sofia he had been a different person.

"Why?" asked the CIA man.

Pascual remembers looking high into the corner of the room. "Because they're assholes."

The CIA man smiled and shook his head, very slowly.

"Surprise, surprise."

"Because I don't buy it anymore," Pascual said, with an uneasy feeling that the hard part had just begun.

"Don't buy what?"

"The whole thing. The idea that shooting twenty people at an embassy party makes the world a better place."

The eyes crinkled behind the glasses and Pascual felt that deep sinking sensation that he would become very familiar with: the concession of undisputed moral superiority to others. "You used to buy it, did you?" asked the man.

It was cool in the room, dark in the corners, and there was distant muffled traffic noise. "As much as anybody does."

The CIA man nodded, looking thoughtful. "They'll want to talk to you," he said. "The Israelis. They'll insist."

"I'll talk. Just don't let them take me."

He shrugged. "We'll see what kind of deal we can make. If you are who you say you are and know what you say you know, they'll move heaven and earth to get their hands on you."

"I guess they're entitled," said Pascual after a long pause.

The hotel room is spacious, decorated mainly in creams, beiges, shades of white. A single lamp by the bed provides a soft yellow light. At first Pascual can only stare: Katixa in the flesh, wicked smile and midnight eyes just as remembered. Eyes to make a man stray from the path, lips to disturb his rest; this is better than remembered. "What are you doing here?" Pascual breathes.

"Running. As fast and as far as I can."

"From whom?"

"From everyone."

"Meaning?"

"Meaning now there are two of us."

Pascual's joy is incendiary. "I never stopped hoping."

"Touch me, you'll see I'm real." They seize each other and Katixa is kissing him again. Hungry kisses; avid, expert carnal kisses; Pascual has never forgotten them. He has never believed in signs and portents, but there must have been a reason for his certainty that the women in the Glaciar were not for him. With Katixa in his arms he believes in destiny.

"Take me to bed," says Katixa.

Pascual is a big man and she has the light trim build of a jungle cat. He lays her tenderly on the counterpane and she pulls him down on top of her. Muscular tension, mouth on mouth: taste of tobacco, faint musky odor of warm flesh. He is absurdly encumbered with jacket, boots and all the rest, and he needs a piss. "Wait," he gasps, ashamed, cutting an oafish figure. Katixa laughs and the sound catches at Pascual's heart. In the opulent bathroom, moving with comic haste, he catches sight of himself in the mirror, a man struck by lightning. When he returns, the blankets are shoved to the foot of the bed and Katixa's clothes are on the floor. Pascual has to stop for a moment and just look. Katixa on her back in the lamplight, legs spread and arms flung out at her sides, chestnut hair splayed on a pillow: breathtaking vistas of flawless skin, convergence of legs, delta as black as the night.

Pascual strips, watching her watching him. Katixa has not moved; only her eyes. When he lowers himself on top of her the warmth of her sends a tremor through him. She moves now, in a spasm, rolling him over on his back. She kisses him again, nails digging into his flesh. Pascual puts a hand to the back of her neck and tries to swallow her. When she pulls away for breath, Katixa's eyes glisten at the corners. Gently, Pascual wipes a tear with his thumb. "Still," says Katixa. "Every time."

Katixa cries when she makes love. The first time Pascual saw it he was dumbstruck. If anyone ever enjoyed sex it is Katixa; he has seen her laugh aloud in delight with his cock inside her. But the tears are always there.

He wound up in Israel after all; Mossad insisted. Pascual's descent into the heart of the Zionist entity was an anticlimax; what he was able to see of the streets as he was whisked through them looked like a generic not-quite-first-world civilization, a crowded nondescript city somewhere on the sunny fringes of Europe perhaps. Most of the time there was no city to see. There was a succession of installations, military and otherwise: air bases, safe houses, midnight transfers in the back seats of cars. There were soldiers, the implacable Zionist foe reduced to bored nineteen-year-olds with negligently slung M-16s, staring at him with contempt. At first there was an endless succession of rooms, sealed off from the sun, with echoing corridors beyond the doors. At night there were narrow beds, a pitcher of water on a table; he slept well most of the time, hearing when he woke in the darkness faint noises of air and road traffic in the remote distance, flights of helicopters through the night.

By day there were relentless, methodical men, speaking English with thick accents or, sometimes, to test him, flawless Arabic, who took his story apart, down to the atoms. Pascual never resisted; he was far down in a well, a deep dark well of suspended life that approximated peace. Finally there was a room with a sunlit balcony crowded with potted plants, overlooking a walled garden, where armed men sat. In the distance was the sea, shimmering blue.

"You're the man who knows everybody," said the case officer. He wore a pale-yellow sports shirt and had a face so seamed it looked like cracked leather. He smoked fanatically and spoke English in a slow accented rumble, Eastern European overlaid with British. Two fingers were missing from his left hand. "You're our unified field theory. We knew there had to be lines from the Provos to ETA to the PFLP and all the little gangs in between, and you've drawn them in. You're an intelligence officer's dream."

"It was the languages, I suppose." Pascual was standing, staring at the distant sea, his back to the table where the Mossad man sat. "I could talk to anybody. So they made me the ambassador."

"Mm, the languages. Let's see. English, French and Spanish you'd have got by virtue of your rather unsettled childhood."

"Catalan, too."

"Yes, of course. And Arabic you picked up during your years in Syria. Which leaves German. How did that happen?"

"I took a course at the university, spent a few weeks one summer hitching around on the other side of the Rhine. I'm a quick learner. And later I spent a fair amount of time in Germany, underground."

"Hmm. All right, they made you a sort of terrorist Henry Kissinger. A security lapse, I'd have to call that."

"Yes. I don't think I was chosen for Athens by accident. To me it didn't look like a mission with a high probability of survival."

"So your time was almost up anyway."

Pascual nodded. "You're wondering how much of my change of heart was just fear."

"It has occurred to us."

"Probably a lot. But the doubts had started before."

"When? When does a fanatic begin to doubt?"

Pascual could have told him exactly when but knew he must not. "When he realizes there is something to go back to," he said finally.

"I see." The man waited in vain for elaboration. "What nationality would you claim, just out of curiosity?"

Pascual shrugged. "My last legitimate passport was Spanish."

"But your father was American."

"A hispanophile and a poet."

The man drank mineral water and said, "Tell me about that unsettled childhood."

Pascual wondered how much they had learned already, and from whom. After seven years of routine lying he was finding the simple truth to be deeply relaxing. "My father left when I was four. My mother and I followed him to New York a while later and I started school there. We weren't very happy. The generational difference between my parents was starting to show and my mother hated Brooklyn. We went back."

"How much older was your father?"

"Twenty-six years."

"That's quite a difference."

Pascual remembered an old man dying, unshaven and in pain, in a crowded hospital ward. "He fought with the Lincoln Brigade in the Civil War and fell in love with Spain. When he was almost fifty and had fumbled one marriage already he went back and fell in love with my mother. She married him to escape a confining family in straitened circumstances. It was the late 1950s and she was a rebel."

"Romantic."

"I think she disappointed him. He wanted a Bohemian gamine and got a nice bourgeois Catalan girl after all." Pascual was tired of standing and wandered to the couch.

"And Paris?" said the man with the seamed face.

Pascual sank onto the cushions, sorting, organizing, remembering. "In the late sixties my mother went north with a lot of other Spaniards. She taught Spanish and gave violin lessons and we lived in poverty, as genteel as my mother could make it. Paris wasn't bad for a schoolboy but it was hard on my mother. By '71, we were back in Barcelona."

In the silence they could hear music, faintly, coming across the garden from a neighboring building. Pascual identified a Bach violin partita and decided it was a recording.

The Mossad man, impassive, as old as rock, watched him listening. "You went back to New York in what, '74?"

"I wanted to get to know my father." Pascual had been speaking in the same calm tone for weeks. "He was sick by that time. I was a disappointment to him, too. He spent his last money to put me in a private high school, which I hated."

They mused together, listening to the violin. In the garden below someone laughed. It was nearly midday and beginning to be hot. Car horns piped and whined not too far away. "He was a poet, you said."

"Not a very successful one. Maybe not even very good. He died poor, anyway."

"No disgrace in that."

"He didn't have to. He lost every job he ever had. He always portrayed them as conflicts of principle but my mother said he was just a crank."

The Mossad man had no notes, never wrote anything down. He merely smoked and listened. "He was pretty far out on the left, was he?"

"He wasn't really a card-carrier or anything. Not a Stalinist. Not much Marxian analysis but a lot of folklore. Wobblies and the International Brigades. McCarthy and all that. I think his politics were mostly nostalgia. He never left the 1930s. I remember war stories, a bunch of old men sitting around a kitchen table in Brooklyn. How he was wounded at Belchite by a fascist who popped up out of a wine barrel. Stuff like that."

"Exciting stuff for a teenage boy."

Pascual wanted to laugh but didn't. "I thought he was full of shit."

"You never went back to Barcelona?"

"My mother had decided to give Paris another try. I joined her when my father died. She had a man there, a painter she met on the Costa Brava, her Bohemian instincts betraying her again. He was pretty good to her but he was another loser, had no money. Somehow I got into the university. The French are pretty generous with things like that. She was run over by a bus on my twenty-third birthday."

"And you went a little off the rails, perhaps?"

The violin music had stopped. Pascual looked the Mossad man in the eye. "It's more complicated than that," he said.

DOMINIC

3

"How did you find me?" asks Pascual.

He has smoked his last Ducado. The sheet and blanket are over them and her head is cradled on his shoulder, her thigh across his abdomen. The lights are out and street noise comes in faintly through double-glazed windows and thick curtains. Pascual is beginning to adjust to the new fundamentals. Three hours ago he was leaving the Palau, ignorant.

"I knew you would be here," says Katixa, murmuring at his throat. "You told me this was where you had been happiest."

"I told you that?"

"In Brussels. You said it was strange that the best days of your life were under Franco."

"I said that? I must have been drunk."

"We went through a bottle or two, I recall."

"It's a big city. How did you find me?"

"Another thing you told me. You said that sooner or later everyone in the world walks down the Ramblas."

"You just watched? That simple?"

Katixa laughs, a throaty musical sound. "You remember the two Chilean guitarists on the Ramblas last week, with their entourage?"

Pascual frowns; unless they are friends, he pays the buskers, beggars and freaks little notice. "Two hyperactive types in ponchos with a couple of wasted hippie girls to hold out the hat?"

"I did quite well for them. The wasted look suits me, I suppose."

"No."

"Yes."

"I looked at them. You. I must have looked at you."

"I saw you walk by twice the first day. On the second day, I followed you to your pension."

Pascual shakes his head in wonder. He squeezes a little, just to feel her shift against him. "Katixa," he says, the first time in eight years he has pronounced the three exquisite syllables: *ka tee sha*. "Tell me about it."

Katixa stirs, rolls away, reaches for the lamp. Light comes on; Pascual puts a hand over his eyes. He hears Katixa rise, cross the room, shift clothing on the floor. There is the scratch of a match, the smell of tobacco. Pascual props his head on a pillow. Katixa comes back to the bed, and Pascual watches her every step of the way. She is still trim, almost lean, the only fat on her the fat that is supposed to be there, perfect and disturbing.

Katixa swings her legs back onto the bed, sits cross-legged beside him and smokes. Pascual waits, looking at her breasts with their small dark nipples. He caresses the left nipple with the back of a finger. Katixa's eyes under the dark straight brows are wide, thoughtful. Her hair is parted at one side and with her free hand she brushes it back across her forehead, out of her eyes.

"I suppose I got tired of sitting on that little door."

"What little door?"

"The one you have to sit on to keep it shut, because reality keeps trying to force it open."

Pascual could have scripted the words for her. "Did it start in Brussels?"

"Maybe." She smokes. "I got tired of everything. Stress, fatigue, mattresses on the floor in empty apartments. And I started to see them for what they are. All the little commissars. Thugs who believe in fairy tales. They cultivate cruelty and think it makes them realists."

Pascual's finger brushes her throat. "That's them. A perfect portrait."

She is distant for a while, smoking. "You certainly betrayed a lot of them," she says.

Pascual's hand drops across her lap. He looks at the triangle of pubic hair; he can still taste her. "Everyone but you," he says.

The sun had doused itself in the sea and night was falling beyond the balcony. Pascual declined a cigarette; he had smoked to the point of numbness. "It started when you went into Beirut in '82. I saw all the footage, the bombing, the slaughter. Sabra and Shatila. All of that. There was a good deal of anger in France."

The man with the seamed face, who Pascual had learned was called Dan, smiled, the seams shifting. "I'm sure there was. The French never lived under a rain of Katyushas."

"I'm just telling you what went through my mind."

"Go on."

"The French students were all sympathizers. Except the Jews, of course. The Palestinians were . . . sexy. The kaffiyehs and all that. And you could always find a way to excuse or ignore the atrocities, the Ma'alots and the Munichs. They were regrettable excesses. The Americans dropped the bomb on Japan; who were they to judge? It was a cause; it was romantic. And after Beirut I suppose I just saw an opportunity to go and become my father."

"Ah. Something to live up to."

"That's right. Go and fight for the underdog. Take on the Israeli juggernaut."

"You wanted to be a hero."

"Yes. No, not quite. I wanted to be an antihero."

"An antihero."

"The last thing I wanted was to do something conventional. I had decided that if the bourgeoisie detested it, there was probably more to it than met the eye. My father's influence."

"How long did it take you to realize you weren't going to get a shot at the Israeli juggernaut?"

Pascual paused, toying with his glass. "Not long. By the end of the first week in Damascus I could tell they had no intention of taking on armed men."

"But you stayed."

"I wasn't going to slink back to Paris with my tail between my legs. What took over then was the desire not to be a coward."

Dan blinked at him, impassive. "A coward? Just what word would you use to describe the actions they planned?"

"I suppose I kept hoping something would change. I wanted to be a guerrilla, a commando. I wanted to be Che Guevara up in the mountains, Mao on the Long March. When I realized all they wanted was Charles Manson with politics, I started working hard at the rationalizations. They're very good at that, providing the rationalizations, helping you suppress the scruples. It takes some effort, but you buy it."

After a moment Pascual drank and looked at Dan. The Mossad man was peering at him with that faintly amused look, black beads of eyes showing through slits in old leather. "So what changed?"

Pascual thought about Katixa, about what he could and could not say.

Katixa leans on an elbow, head on her hand, her face close to Pascual's, speaking softly in a voice full of smoke and secrecy. "I read about the Athens thing in the press. I had no idea that was you until I talked to that ghoul Salem in Benghazi."

"What were you doing there?"

"The usual. Revolutionary solidarity, everyone rolling their eyes as one of Muammar's gangsters makes a speech, just waiting to talk about the money. I was there to talk with the Irish but I spent most of my time keeping the Arabs' hands off me."

"And Salem knew?"

"He had pieced it together. He knew you had to have sold them out. Everyone but you wound up in a Greek jail or dead. You just vanished."

"They told me the Greeks let Farid and Mustafa go."

"And the Israelis got them within a week. You didn't hear?

Mustafa was a bit of a *cause célèbre,* shot like that in the middle of the Kurfürstendamm."

"I was out of circulation."

"They were only the start, of course. You must have been like the Three Kings to the Israelis, bearing gifts. If Jews have something like the Kings."

Pascual watches her, looking for bitterness or reproach; he sees only a faint ironic light. "They had pictures of you," he says.

"Ah, yes?"

"I looked at dozens of pictures. They showed me pictures of myself, taken in Rome, I think. When I saw somebody I knew, I told them everything I could. Names, nicknames, habits, affiliations, haunts. Except for you. You, I had never seen. They knew you had been in Aden but I told them I never saw you there. I think they believed me. They didn't insist, anyway."

Katixa's gaze is far away. "They almost got me in Cyprus. I made it out to Belgrade on my last passport, sweating the whole way. That was when I decided it was time to write off the world revolution and come home."

"I hadn't seen you since Brussels. For all I knew you had already got out."

She is grave then, silent as she runs a finger over his lips. "It wasn't easy."

Pascual searches her face. "But you're out now? You're really out?"

Katixa's eyes flick away again, as if keeping watch in the distance. *"Chaval,* I'm so far out I'm over the horizon."

■ ■ ■ ■

For the first time Dan's face showed something like intensity. Without moving from his pose on the sofa, one leg crossed over the other, listing slightly, he gave the impression of heightened attention, an intense and wary absorption. "Tell me," he said in a quiet tone. "What exactly goes through the mind when plotting something like Fiumicino? How does one discuss the tactics of killing the maximum number of unarmed travelers in the minimum number of seconds?"

Long ago, at the outset, Pascual had resolved to shed all defenses, knowing that only by a complete relinquishing of ego could he survive. At that moment, however, he felt it stir briefly again, the urge to justify. "There was some debate, actually. There were those who wanted only to hit targets that had some military or security relevance, and there were those who thought that simply killing Jews, any Jews, was the idea."

"Not only Jews, apparently. Those people on the floor at Fiumicino were not all Jews, surely."

Pascual swallowed. "For the fedayeen, Jewishness is like a bacterium. You can catch it by traveling to Israel, by failing to condemn Israel with sufficient vigor, or just by being from a certain country the Monday after your government does something to aid Israel."

In the silence Dan peered at him. "And there you were, in their midst, with half the blood coursing through your veins Jewish. Filthy kike blood. Was that why you were there? To repudiate your Jewish father? To purge yourself of the bacterium?"

Pascual shook his head slowly; he had been wondering when this would surface. "I never felt Jewish. My father never made anything of it. For him religion was an atavistic superstition and race was an accident. If anything I felt like a lapsed Catholic."

He could see that Dan did not believe him and that for the Israelis this was a particular source of horror. "Anyway, until Athens I never sat in on the planning of anything like Fiumicino. I was one of the ones who was always pressing for harder targets."

"Like Yossi Peled and his wife?"

"His wife wasn't supposed to be with him." Pascual rubbed at his brow, feeling desperately for the equanimity that had so far not deserted him. "I saw myself as trying to counter what your people were doing, fighting an underground war across Europe. You'll admit, I suppose, that Mossad has shot down a few unarmed men in its day."

Dan blinked, admitting nothing. "What about Athens then?"

Pascual took a long drink of water. "When I saw how nasty Athens was going to be, I started working at those rationalizations I told you about. I thought about dead children I'd seen in southern Lebanon. That kept me going through those planning sessions. Nobody actually says anything like 'aim for the women.' It's just that when they give you a target, a plan, always couched in terminology like 'striking at the diplomatic infrastructure,' you get a fairly clear impression of who's going to be in your gunsights. And even if you don't like those thoughts, you don't want to let the side down. That will carry you a long way."

Dan shook his head, a man looking at dirty pictures. "But it didn't carry you quite all the way. What happened?"

Pascual had an answer for him, one of the few notions that had solidified in the past weeks, an insight. "I suppose I finally realized that courage in the service of atrocity is no virtue."

■ ■ ■ ■

Pascual has a feeling that nothing is going to be simple. He wants to sleep with Katixa in his arms but he knows he is going to have to listen first. "Tell me," he says.

Katixa rolls away, rises from the bed and pulls on an oversized T-shirt. She walks to the minibar opposite the bed and selects a miniature bottle of Scotch, which she empties into a glass. "Drink something," she says. "On me. Quite a step up from the last hotel room we shared, eh?"

Pascual waves off the drink. Katixa comes back, swirling the whiskey in the glass. She sits on the edge of the bed and sips. "I can't do what you did," she says.

Pascual's lips are parted to speak, but she closes them with a finger. "That's not a reproach. They're shits. You did right to shop them. But I can't do it. For me it would be prison time. They'd never do a deal with me like they did for you. My hands are too dirty."

Pascual watches her drink. "That dirty?"

"Dirty enough. I'm not going to get weepy about it. At least the ones I killed could shoot back." The look in her eye is bitter. "The Hipercor bomb here in Barcelona in '87? I tried to veto it. I said I was ready to kill soldiers but not children. That's why I was shipped out to Algiers and wound up in Brussels with you. But I don't expect any credit. I'm afraid the best I can do is retire and hope for good cover and short memories."

"I see. You don't want to wind up like Yoyes."

"I knew Yoyes. I tried to tell her they wouldn't let her quit. They shot her down in front of her daughter."

"And they're not likely to treat you any better."

Katixa drinks and looks far away again. "No. Especially not me."

37

Pascual waits, unable to ask. Katixa's eyes flick back to him. "You read the papers?"

"Every day."

"Then you know the name Bordagorri."

"Of course. It was all over the papers a few days ago. Head of the Zubieta Commando, ETA-Militar. The fellow they think really is dead this time. They called him the 'Cat' because he's had so many narrow escapes before."

"This time he's dead. I killed him."

Pascual's head sags back against the wall. "No wonder you're running."

"Like a rabbit, I'm telling you. They spotted the car after I ditched it in Bilbao, through sheer stupid luck. Apparently they found his blood in the trunk."

"And his fingerprints."

"Yes. The poor bastard can't have been quite gone when I stuffed him in. But he was dead when I tossed him off a bridge, up in the hills. They'll find him when spring comes."

"What happened?"

"Divergences, differences, quarrels. Politics. Over the past couple of years I got tired and he got vicious. There were some fiascos. Finally he accused me of selling them out. I told him I'd defend myself in a fair hearing. He knew nobody would believe it and I got wind I was being set up for the knife in the back, quick and dirty. You heard about the Itarroiz case?"

Pascual has to think for a moment. "The shipbuilder from Bilbao. Kidnapped."

"And released. For a hundred million pesetas ransom."

"Yes, I read about it. I wondered if you had anything to do with it."

Katixa raises her glass. "I planned it."

"Congratulations."

"When we pulled off the Itarroiz business we had the ransom paid in France, via a British firm that specializes in negotiating kidnappings. That's the only way to do it now that the Spanish have made it illegal to pay. The Brits were supposed to deposit it in a bank in Lyon, and we were supposed to wire it around the world so fast nobody would ever catch up with it. But the French have cracked down like everybody else, and what happened was that the go-between got the wind up and opted to deliver the ransom to us in cash, five million francs."

"In cash."

"In unmarked bills, at least that's what they guaranteed. Well, neither the French nor the Spanish can track it now, but on the other hand it's in cash, and that's a problem in itself. It got brought back over the Pyrenees, which I thought was madness, but I was outvoted. And then I got the word Bordagorri was going to use it to set me up."

"How?"

"He was going to catch me trying to make off with it."

"Christ, he really had it in for you."

"Some men turn vicious when you tell them you won't sleep with them anymore."

"Ah, so that's the way it was."

"I was expecting something." Katixa sips; Pascual is transfixed, watching her. "It was self-defense. And after I shot him I carried on with his scenario."

Pascual gapes, takes the glass from Katixa's fingers. There is a little whiskey left and he drains it. "You took the five million francs," he forces out of a constricted throat.

Katixa nods. "Now we just have to get them to a safe place and launder them."

"Five million francs."

"It's a lot of money."

Pascual is reeling. "You have it with you?"

"I hid it. Up in the hills. North of here. It can sit where it is for a while but not forever. I need you to help get it out. Morocco would be a good start. And then wherever we want. Latin America, Asia. Fuck them all, we'll buy an island."

Pascual passes a hand over his mouth, quickly. "Does anybody know you took it?"

"I'm afraid so, now that the car's turned up. I imagine all of ETA will be looking for me."

"How close behind are they?"

"I don't know. There's a network here, of course, and they'll be alerted. Principally I think we have two people to worry about. José Antonio Goikoetxea and Carlos Arrieta. Right bastards, the both of them, and sharp. They'll take over the group now and they'll want their money back. They'll come a long way to get it and they won't leave us around to talk about it."

"But you didn't leave them a trail, did you?"

"I fervently hope not. And then of course there are always the police. Anytime I cross the Pyrenees I'm in enemy territory. We'll have to use all the old nonsense for a while."

Pascual sets the glass on the bedside table. "What are you doing for documents?"

"I've got a set nobody knows about. Bordagorri got them for me."

Pascual lets out a long breath. He puts on a shirt and underwear and finds a cigarette. He gets it going and steps to the window. Parting the curtain, he can just see a slice of the Ramblas. Out there is where he belongs but this is where he is. "So where do we go from here?" he asks.

Katixa pours herself another drink and sits in an armchair, legs crossed, swirling whiskey in her glass. "We want to get ourselves and a fairly good-sized suitcase out of the country, out of Europe, and we don't want to talk to any customs officials. What do we do?"

Pascual smokes and says, "A decade ago I could have given you an answer. But I'm out of circulation. And I never had that kind of connection in this town anyway."

"That's good. We want to avoid anybody familiar. Start with an open mind."

"All right. First of all, why can't we just step on a plane with it?"

"We probably could. The problem would be at the other end. Do you want to take the chance nobody will ask us to open the suitcase when we get off the plane?"

"I suppose not. How were you planning to launder five million francs in the first place?"

"There will be somebody in Colombia or the Caribbean who will be pleased to help us. The problem is getting it there. We need to carry it physically out of the country and we don't want to leave a paper trail. Who do we talk to?"

"I'd have to think about it."

"So think. Who gets things in and out of Spain without going through border posts and talking to customs?"

41

Pascual considers. "The traffickers. But most of that goes on down south. They bring it ashore at Gibraltar or Cádiz or someplace like that."

"Still. Barcelona is one of the great sumps of the Mediterranean. Drugs are not the half of it. There are all kinds of smuggling. There's people smuggling. You can't tell me all these Moroccans come in with papers in order, and you know some of them must have to hightail it home without showing a passport from time to time. Somebody's got a pipeline going. Down where you live, you must know a few of the right sort of people."

"The people I know are at the lowest rung. They're not running speedboats from Tangier."

"But they could tell you who is."

"If I start asking questions, they'll think I'm a cop."

"You must still have the instincts. People have reputations. They're not that hard to find. And they're greedy. A word in the right place that there's money to be had, they'll be interested. It's a problem in human relations. You can solve it."

"I'm not sure how long it'll take."

"You have a passport?"

Pascual nods. "It got me here from Rome and I've never used it since."

"But it's valid."

"So the CIA assured me."

"All right, we may need to get visas, just for cover, for when we want to fly out. Tourist visas, just the usual jaunt to Fez and Marrakesh. Now what about that speedboat to Tangier?"

"I'll ask around." Pascual is thinking of Baltasar.

"We'll need a car. I stole one in Bilbao but had to ditch it after I dropped the money. And the bus isn't going to get us where we need to go."

"Where did you leave it? Under a rock?"

Katixa has not survived twelve years of underground existence by talking freely about her business. She drinks before she says, "We had a certain number of caches here and there for weapons. Remote, secure and dry. There was room in one of them for a suitcase."

"And none of your former colleagues will think to look there?"

"Not this one. The only other person who knew about this one is dead."

"Ah. The late Mr. Bordagorri."

"Late and unlamented." Katixa's look is impenetrable. "You're under no restrictions on travel?" she says. "They're not keeping you on a leash or anything?"

"I'm not on parole. They just wrote me off, wished me luck." Pascual smiles. "I think they were hoping somebody finds me and kills me."

Katixa favors him with one of her cool smiles. "Good thing I found you first."

Pascual nods, looks around the room. "You're making this your base?"

"I wish. It's probably good cover, but it's a fast way to spend five million francs. From now on it's cheap pensions for me, a different one every day or two until we're ready to move. At the end of each meeting we'll set up the next one, maybe have a telephone code for emergencies. We've got to do it this way for a while. There are too many people looking for me."

The realization is finally dawning on Pascual that this is more than a sentimental reunion. He gives it a long look in the lamplight, drifting back to stand in front of Katixa. "Are you sure you've picked the right man?"

Katixa rises and takes his face in her hands. Her eyes are as large and black as the night. Close enough so that he can feel her breath she says, "We shared a hotel room once before. Remember? I won't make the same mistake twice."

Pascual looks into Katixa's eyes and remembers Brussels. "No. This time we won't make that mistake."

4

Pascual remembers rain in Brussels. It was threatening when he stepped off the Sabena flight from Madrid, lowering when he and Katixa met in the safe house on a cobbled street in the down-at-heel district of Marolles, descending in sheets by the time they realized that the operation was coming down around their ears. The Brussels they saw was a gray forbidding city, far removed from the poster prettiness of the Grand Place, a city of bleak monuments to bureaucracy, endless housing blocks, squalid restaurants, sullen Francophones and Francophobes and haggard guest workers. They moved by tram, bus, metro and long slogs through the rain.

They had had three days' briefing in Lisbon with the Action Directe *éminence grise* whose brainchild this was. Pascual had been surprised and delighted when Katixa walked into the villa above the Tagus, but there had been no time for anything but poring over maps and photos, memorizing addresses and telephone numbers, drilling on signs, countersigns, procedures. They had not seen each other since Aden.

In Aden nothing had been consummated; they were merely partners in misery. Pascual remembered Katixa as a stoic: fierce, impatient with the endless harangues, the filth and the heat, capable with

Kalashnikov, Armalite and Heckler & Koch, intent on the proper care and feeding of C-4, disdainful of the febrile and inadequate German women and their whining, vicious in her resistance to Arab sexual advances. Pascual had made none of his own; there was no privacy, no energy left after the enervating routine of hazing and indoctrination. Language threw them together but there had been no opportunity for more than a few stolen moments of private irony. Pascual had told himself sternly he was not there for love; in any event he never expected to see her again.

In Brussels her hair had grown out and she could have been a student, a hairdresser's assistant or a barmaid in a prosperous brasserie. She was clearly not Nordic, but did not stand out in Brussels's long-muddied ethnic mix. She was stunning but did not have the look of an easy mark. In the safe house, a gloomy third-floor flat full of someone's grandmother's furniture, they talked guardedly of Aden, touching carefully on the three intervening years. They compared notes on roads traveled, raised eyebrows at mutual acquaintances. There was no reference to the next day's job until Katixa tore aside a curtain and said, "We're wasting time."

From the start there was something between them other than concentration on the grim imperatives; sheltering at a bus stop opposite the target's apartment block in a prosperous outlying district, Pascual began to fall prey to distracting thoughts, stealing glances at Katixa as she stood at the other end of the shelter, looking intently through the rain at the place where they would kill the American colonel in sixteen hours.

The first signs of calamity came when the car did not appear as promised in the parking area near the Gare du Midi. Pascual had been given two keys in Lisbon, one to the safe house and the other to a red Renault with license number EUR 2437 and two nine-millimeter CZ 75 automatics in the glove compartment, which was to be delivered by 1700 hours on the eve of the operation. Pascual and Katixa combed the area around the station until nearly 1800 hours without finding the car. From a rank of telephones Pascual phoned a contact number reserved for emergencies and got no answer. He and Katixa conferred; they hiked through the rain to catch the bus that would pass the target's apartment block. Through the streaming windows they saw a police car nestled discreetly at the curb opposite.

The rain had not stopped and it was growing dark. They were wet and cold and beginning to feel afraid. Back in the Marolles, Pascual left Katixa at a working man's bar filled with Spaniards making a comforting din and made a pass by the safe house, hooded and hunched against the chill rain. There were dark figures in parked cars and he was careful not to slow or look up at the windows of the apartment. He found a phone and tried the contact number again; a voice answered but could not produce the countersign. Pascual hung up, fast.

In the warmth of the bar he and Katixa traded a look across the table and started sorting options. "We should separate," said Katixa.

Pascual knew she was right. He ordered more beer. "They'll be watching the trains, car-hire firms, bus stations."

"We could try hitching. If we avoid the major interchanges it might work. It'll be slow."

"Tomorrow, maybe. Where do we spend the night?"

It struck them both at the same time that they were assuming no separation. This occasioned a long look over the tops of their beer glasses. "Together, then," he said.

47

"Why not?" Her mouth tensed in the ghost of a smile.

They wrote off the meager luggage they had left at the safe house; there was nothing compromising. With Katixa's shoulder bag they hiked back to the train station and started calling hotels listed on a board outside a closed tourist office. Pascual had flown in on a Spanish passport but had an alternative French one; Katixa's also was French. They had no reason to expect trouble with the documents.

The hotel they chose was not too far off the Chaussée d'Ixelles, a rung or two above the cheapest. They spun a tale of lost luggage and wandering in the rain. The concierge was sympathetic. Pascual confided that it was a poor start to a honeymoon.

The room had a double bed, a cramped bathroom with grout falling from between the tiles, a telephone, a glimpse of traffic hissing along the wet pavements of the Chaussée. Pascual stripped to his underwear, toweled off and stood at the window looking out through the gap in the curtains while Katixa showered. She came out of the bathroom with one towel wrapped around her head and another around her torso and flopped on the bed. Pascual let the curtain fall back. In the light from the bathroom he could see white towels and dark limbs. "I thought I'd never be warm again," said Katixa.

Pascual sat on the bed, his back to her. He wanted nothing more than to step into that shower himself, but practical problems concerned him. "Three days, I think. At least. Then make a run for it. Lie low, hope they don't canvass the hotels. Then try for a frontier, maybe separately."

There was a silence. Behind him Pascual heard springs creak. "I could use the rest," said Katixa.

Pascual turned to see she had rolled toward him, lying on her side. She had removed the towel from her head and her damp hair lay tangled on the pillow. "So," he said. "Which side of the bed do you want?"

Katixa reached for him, hooked the back of his neck, pulled. That was the first of Katixa's hungry kisses he had ever tasted, and at that instant there was nothing on earth he needed more; they embraced until muscles started to give out, making up for Aden, for all the discomfort and dread of the long day. Katixa tugged at the towel and they were belly to belly. *"Querido,* you're freezing," she breathed.

If pressed, Pascual would be able to remember a few salacious details of Katixa's carnal energy, but the main impression that stayed with him was of being warm, as warm as he would ever need to be, and home at last: he had hurtled through black space and collided with the one being that could bring him joy. She cried when he came and collapsed on top of her; she cried at her own climax, his head between her legs. She wiped tears with her fingers and told him it was just a reflex.

Pascual is not sure whether it actually rained for three days and nights or whether his memory is deceptive. There was an afternoon, with room-service dishes stacked on a tray, full ashtrays and a rumpled bed, the curtains open and the gray Belgian sky flinging droplets at the windows. In the morning Pascual had gone out gingerly in search of cigarettes and newspapers. Katixa had been napping in his arms but was awake now, pushing fingers gently through the hair on his chest. Pascual was sinking into depression, staring out at the rooftops and foreseeing only calamity. "Don't think about it," said Katixa.

"How do you know what I'm thinking about?"

"I know. Listen, we could die tomorrow. There's nothing we can do about it now. Now it's just us, just this."

He listened to the rain. Their professional relationship had been obliterated by a night and a day in bed and Pascual thought there were some frontiers it might be safe to cross now. "Are you relieved?" he asked.

"That we didn't have to kill him? Of course."

She really does read minds, Pascual thought. "Have you ever killed anyone?"

She did not answer immediately. Her fingers were entwined in the hair on his chest, gently tugging. "No," she said.

"Me neither. I think I have the courage, but I'm not sure."

"That's why they sent two of us. Always two. Neither one wants to be the coward."

"Smart."

"Ah, yes. They're smart enough."

Time passed; Pascual wanted a cigarette but was loath to disturb Katixa. "This wasn't exactly what I had in mind," he said. "Killing middle-aged men on a street. I wanted to go into south Lebanon and take on the Israelis in a hail of fire."

"It's easier to kill old men."

"I know. Still. I'd rather shoot at someone who can shoot back."

"I'd just as soon not get shot at, thank you. But I have to say I don't give a fuck about NATO. I just want the Spaniards out of my country."

"So how did we get here?"

"Politics. Somebody wants to make a point."

A siren approached in the street outside, warbling, and they were both very still until it passed. Pascual said, "Do you have politics? I'm not sure I do." Katixa said nothing. "I don't think I want the rest of

Europe to look like the DDR or Bulgaria. I'm not sure what I want it to look like, except it would have fewer cops."

Katixa was silent for a time, and Pascual hoped with a sudden chill that he had not misjudged her. "They can all go fuck themselves, east and west," Katixa said finally. "Just let me kill Spaniards."

Wind splattered rain against the panes. "I'm a Spaniard," said Pascual.

"No, you're not."

Pascual said, "Why do you hate them?"

"My father was a Spaniard."

Pascual digested that. "And my father was an American." He mused, listening to the rain. "Perhaps you've got something there. Except, I don't hate Americans, really. Even this colonel, with his little bourgeois life. Their system, their state, their fucking hamburgers. But not the people."

"Well, your father probably didn't rape you," said Katixa, putting a brutal end to Pascual's meanderings. A chill settled over the room. When Pascual shifted to take a look at Katixa's face, her eyes were closed, her hair tousled, her lips slightly parted. He caressed her cheek.

"Fuck me," said Katixa.

"Katixa," Pascual breathed, brushing hair out of her face.

"I said fuck me." She writhed, seized him by the hair, pulled his face down to hers. Pascual cried out when she bit his lip and then she was pulling at his sex and pleading in a low urgent whisper. Amazed, Pascual did what she wanted, ramming her into the sheets. When he was finished she was crying beneath him.

Pascual wiped tears from her face, kissed the corners of her eyes. "Don't cry," he whispered. "We'll stay together. We'll heal you."

Katixa opened her eyes and put her hand over his mouth. "Don't talk," she said. In her eyes he could see through to her heart, full of rain.

They ventured out for a meal on the second day. The papers had nothing about terrorist outrages, foiled or unfoiled; the city was sodden, indifferent, ugly. They walked on eggshells but began to feel they might live to leave Brussels. Back in the room they talked about places. "Algiers," said Katixa, sprawled on the bed, gaze far away. "You can feel the ghosts in the streets. Tears and blood. The Casbah is pure witchery. Stairs, faces in doorways, glimpses of the sea. Algiers in the moonlight is the most beautiful place on earth. But sad, my God, it's sad."

Pascual told her about Damascus. "Hidden gardens, fountains in shaded courtyards. Tea and backgammon on the balcony at night. In desert cities nighttime is exquisite. I could live in Damascus. Maybe Aleppo, too. Beirut if they ever put it back together. Lovely cities at that end of the Mediterranean. Politics is always a problem but if you're careful you can live well. Even a woman; in the Christian quarters it's not too bad." He fell silent, startled by the trend of the conversation. For four years he had never given any thought to the future beyond the next operation, the next period of penury and dependence, the next hotel room.

"Donostia," said Katixa after a long silence. "Pity we can't dream of a house overlooking the bay."

"Someday." Memory stirred. "Barcelona. I'll take you down the Ramblas." He told her about being a schoolboy in Barcelona, waiting for Franco to die. Sensing a new world coming, exploring a city. Growing up, stretching his legs, cutting school, learning to drink, smoke, steal kisses. The happiest time of his life.

Silence. Bilbao for Katixa was rain, smoke, misery. A crowded flat in a dark riverside quarter across from the shipyards, a mother who prayed and a father who drank. "I stayed for my little sister," said Katixa. "If he had touched her, I would have killed him. I had the knife hidden under my mattress. A man he insulted in a bar saved me the trouble. Two weeks after the funeral, I left."

Pascual cannot remember how many times they coupled in the dim curtained room. With Katixa he had entered a new realm of loving. She was supremely carnal but fathomlessly tender. There was a touch of the whore about her but more than a little of the sublime. Pascual had loved women before but this was seeing new colors, taking off dark glasses. This was something Pascual had given up on: devotion.

The following day the hotel room had begun to take on oppressive tones. They went out again but spoke only rarely. The papers spoke of police triumphs, arrests, without too many details. The afternoon passed slowly, Pascual failing to concentrate on something he had found at a secondhand bookstall, Katixa dozing. Pascual waited for more talk about conceivable fixtures but it never came.

Pascual remembers the third night, awakening in darkness to find Katixa's side of the bed vacant; he thrashed upright in alarm and then made out her shape at the window, holding a curtain just open. "What are you doing?" he said, breathless.

"Planning."

Pascual came to stand beside her. Through the gap in the curtains he could see empty streets, mournfully lit. It was still raining. Pascual put his arms around her waist, pulling her naked flanks close, burying his face in her hair, his heartbeat subsiding. "And what's the plan?"

"Yours? That's for you to decide. I'm thinking of ways of getting back to Spain."

Pascual stood frozen. Katixa squeezed his wrist gently. "We never had a future, did we?" She turned to face him, her arms going around his neck. In the light from the street he could see her face, grave and composed.

"Te quiero," said Pascual. In Castilian you can want and love with the same word.

"No. You don't want me. You want something else. You can't love me. It's a waste of time."

"No."

"Pascual. We have no future."

Her forehead was resting against his cheek; he could smell her hair. "We can make a future."

"In this business?"

"We won't be in it forever."

"No. We'll die before too long."

"Then let's get out."

She pulled away, and her look was serene, melancholy; Pascual could see none of the desolation he felt. "Don't be foolish," she said.

Pascual looked at Katixa, thinking it was happening again. Desperate, he said, "You never doubt?"

"Doubt?" Katixa smiled in the darkness. "I was standing next to a boy called Zugarramundi in Pau when two Spanish triggermen blew his brains all over the bar. They're all pretending to be shocked now in Spain but they've been running the death squads for years. The GAL, they call them. I suppose I have as many doubts as they do. Do you suppose they doubt when they cluster-bomb your Palestinian children in Tyre and Sidon?"

Pascual found nothing to say. Katixa was stronger than he was. She sensed his shame and kissed him, tenderly. Katixa's tenderness appeared and disappeared like a moon behind ragged clouds. Pascual held her, trying to retain it by force.

In the morning he was a realist again, and there was no more sentimentality. They checked out, a bit of a joke to the hotel staff, who grinned at them as they went, the couple who chose Brussels for a honeymoon. The rain had finally let up but the sky was still gray. They had decided they must avoid the Action Directe infrastructure in the French-Belgian corridor, not knowing how much of it was compromised. Katixa would go overland; she knew where to catch a coach to Paris. Pascual still had confidence in his Spanish passport and would try the airport; his cash would just get him out to Frankfurt, where he had contacts. Katixa flagged a taxi for him on the Chaussée d'Ixelles. Taken by surprise, Pascual had time only to say, "Till next time, then."

Katixa kissed him. "An optimist, you are."

As the taxi pulled away she was a slim dark girl on the pavement, and Pascual was a man who had been shot through the heart.

Pascual descends the Ramblas in the hour just after dawn. There are vagabonds washing at the Font de Canaletes, women in blue smocks unveiling birdcages, waiters setting out café tables. The Boqueria is open, exhaling smells of fish and crushed vegetables. The air is not yet fouled by the exhaust of a million cars. The light, coming through the plane trees, seems crystalline and fragile. Pascual moves in a daze.

He has coffee in a bar in Carrer Ample. Someone has abandoned a copy of *Avui* and Pascual stares at it, trying to read but seeing nothing on the page. He smokes, watching sunlight climb stone and feeling like a man about to jump off a high cliff. The bar is filled with working men, snatching five minutes' ease before the workday descends on them. Beside Pascual at the bar stands a Moroccan with the face of a cinema villain and the haunted look of a man who lives on day-labor wages, counting out his pesetas with calloused hands. Pascual has been thinking of Katixa; now in his dazed way he begins to think of five million French francs. One million dollars, one hundred million pesetas and change.

Pascual makes his way through the dark lanes of the lower Gothic Quarter, shielded from the sun. In Avinyó he turns into the doorway where Katixa reappeared last night, and climbs the four flights of stairs to the Pensión Alameda, beginning to feel the effects of a night spent in delirium rather than sleep. Sounds echo through the stairwell from open doors: the clank of a pail on the floor, a snatch of song, mellifluous Catalan chatter.

In the foyer of the pension, Pilar is already stationed in front of the TV and favors him with her radiant smile. Pilar is a middle-aged waif living on the charity of relatives who visit her once a month; she is mute and destitute and unkempt and unfailingly sweet-tempered. Opposite her, Baltasar is draped over a chair. He has sandals on his long feet and a limp khaki shirt long retired from somebody's army. "You're out and about early," he says, a smile showing white teeth.

"La Puig has made you *conserje,* has she?" Pascual steps over Baltasar's feet.

"In bed there are nightmares." Baltasar cocks his head to one side. "The redhead, was it?"

Pascual smiles. "A gentleman does not tell tales."

Baltasar has the saddest eyes in the world when he wants to. "A poor black man can only envy you. What's her name?"

For a moment Pascual has a supernatural conviction that Baltasar knows. "I forgot to ask." He pauses. Come out with me for coffee, he almost says, there's a matter I'd like to discuss. Baltasar is waiting for him to speak but Pascual lets it go and turns down the hall; he is tired and there will be time. Over his shoulder he says, "If my Arab comes, just tell him to slip the money under the door."

Pascual's room is around the bend in the corridor, fronting on the street. It is small and squalid, cold and damp in the winter, stifling in the summer, and besieged by noise the year round. A tall narrow window gives on to the street, admitting light and tumult. There is just enough room for the narrow bed, a sink, a flimsy wardrobe and a chair. There are books and cassette tapes everywhere: on top of the wardrobe, on the chair, under the bed. Pascual sweeps clothing from the bed and collapses. The last time he lay on this bed he was a different person.

He drifts into sleep and awakens in the early afternoon. It takes him a moment to remember everything and he realizes with a start that there is a horizon now; he will not live in this room forever. There is work to do. He is meeting Katixa this evening and he must have something for her. His watch says two thirty and he is hungry. He has just over two hundred pesetas in his pocket.

Five million francs or no five million, in the short term there is the problem of lunch. On the Ramblas there is the midday bustle of traffic and people; it is cool and sunny. Larbi's shop is in a narrow alley across the Ramblas in the Barrio Chino. There is a carefully hand-lettered sign in Arabic above the door that advertises a good rate on Algerian dinars. Inside the long narrow shop is a display case and shelves laden with vaguely oriental bric-a-brac: water pipes, beaten brass trays, burnooses, wooden clogs. Larbi is a morose bird of prey: long sharp nose, graying hair, deep-set black-rimmed eyes. He shakes hands with Pascual. They speak French because Pascual has never been able to make much of Larbi's Maghrebian Arabic. "They tell me you were looking for me," says Pascual.

"Me? When?"

"Last night?"

"I don't even know where you live." Larbi looks at him suspiciously.

Pascual shrugs. "Somebody told me an Arab came looking for me."

"Ah, well. For your compatriots, an Arab is anybody they can't quite place and don't like the look of."

Pascual hesitates, delicacy vying with need. "I thought perhaps it was about the money."

"Ah." Larbi is desolated, crushed by regret. He waves a hand at the cash register. "Take a look. I have barely enough to eat. I can give you a thousand today, maximum. But business will pick up and you're at the top of the list."

Pascual would be irritated but for the thought of Katixa and five million francs. "Fine. I'll take the thousand." Larbi hands them over with bad grace. "Did your shoes clear customs?"

"Finally. And the lawyer ate up all the profit." The five thousand pesetas are owed Pascual for his translation of some documents marginal to a tangled dispute over a shipment of Algerian footwear Larbi hoped to import from a workshop in Annaba.

"Lawyers will do that."

"There's no profit on a small scale. But I have no capital to expand."

"I'd lend you my five thousand at interest, but I need it to eat."

"Four thousand." Larbi raises a finger, reminding.

Pascual is already writing the money off as he ascends the Ramblas. He hears his name called, a woman again, and his heart leaps. When he sees Montse waving at him, coming across the tiles, the letdown is severe. He manages a smile and goes to meet her, but one mark of his radically new status is that Montse suddenly counts as a problem.

Montse is walking briskly in jeans and a dark brown sweater, bag slung over her shoulder; she will be on her lunch hour now, released from the travel agency near the head of the Ramblas until four. She has classic Catalan features and color: clear brown eyes and perfect olive skin under a mane of wavy auburn hair. Montse is thirty-five and was a beautiful girl; now she is a handsome woman somewhat worn by a childless marriage and bitter divorce, with a figure growing fuller and a heart growing desperate.

That, in any event, is how Pascual explains her interest in him, a penurious relic of her distant childhood. "You don't return your phone calls, eh?" she says, offering her face for a kiss.

Pascual pecks her lightly on the lips. "I just got up."

"Another night on the tiles? Who was it this time—the disreputable Irish or the tragic Andaluces?"

Pascual gropes for a lie. "This time it was the alcoholic Germans. I left them passed out on the Moll de la Fusta as the sun came up."

"You're a disgrace."

Pascual shrugs. "I only have disgraceful friends."

Montse slips an arm through his. "Have you eaten?"

"I was just thinking about it."

"May I join you?"

"Of course. I'm afraid I can't treat you today."

Montse smiles. "My treat."

"You shouldn't." Pascual allows her to steer him toward the opening of Carrer de Ferran, hunger pangs mounting.

"Don't worry, I know how it goes. The publishers don't pay and you spend your money on drink."

"Publishers? I haven't had any translation work in months. I'm relying on students these days."

"And are there any?"

"One right now."

"The Swiss girl."

"That's right. Thank God she's persistent. There was a fellow in a school who offered to send clients my way if I would split the fees fifty-fifty. I told him to go to hell."

"What about that *colegio* up in Gràcia?"

"They hired a Brit, of course. It was starvation wages anyway."

They dash across the street and into Ferran. There is a restaurant a hundred meters up that Pascual favors when he has money; it offers a decent *menú* for 950 pesetas, wine included. *Tête-à-tête* over a square of white paper with a basket of bread and a half-full bottle of *tinto* on it, lunchtime din at its peak, he and Montse fall silent. "It's no life for you," she says finally. When Montse is serious she looks five years older; she is at her best when laughing.

"I'm suited for nothing else."

"That may be. With your languages you could make a perfectly decent living as a translator. Or a teacher. What you need is more energy. And better presentation."

"Clean myself up a bit?"

"You could stand a few new clothes, but that's not it. What you need is ambition."

Pascual looks into Montse's face and wants to shout at her about Katixa and five million francs. For years he has kept life-and-death secrets; Montse thinks he spent the eighties working in a bookshop in Paris. She has not even questioned the curious fact that the last name he gives now is not the one she knew him by as a boy. Pascual swallows wine and the secrets along with it. "Perhaps."

"Forget what I said about the clothes." Montse smiles. "The bohemian look suits you." Pascual knows that for Montse he is adventure, the slightly disreputable boyfriend to spice a bleak and conventional life. "Listen," she says, voice a shade lower. "Mama goes off to visit her sister in Girona tomorrow. We'll have the flat to ourselves. You could spend the night."

Pascual toys with his glass, wanting to laugh. Katixa is offering him the world and Montse is proposing furtive adolescent sex in the family apartment. He forces a smile. "Sounds nice. Only."

"Only what?"

"Only I might be leaving town soon."

Montse holds the shocked look while the waiter sets bowls of *caldo gallego* in front of them. "For how long?"

"I don't know. Indefinitely." The silence lasts through the soup. Pascual has not eaten a full hot meal for two days and the steaming broth of cabbage, potatoes, beans and ham induces a reverent concentration.

"Where are you going?" asks Montse, in control of her face.

"France again," says Pascual.

"Work?"

"Possibilities. Old contacts in Paris."

Montse smiles gamely. "I'll be sorry to see you go."

Pascual drinks and looks at her. The lying is getting easier again, and it brings other ignoble thoughts with it; it occurs to Pascual that Montse has a car. "I'll be back. Paris isn't far."

"Don't wait another twenty years this time," says Montse.

"I'll stay in touch. In any event, I don't suppose there's any hurry." Pascual makes quick and sordid calculations. "This weekend sounds good."

Montse's smile is less than wholehearted this time. "Don't do me any favors," she says.

Pascual does his best to look injured. "We could say goodbye now."

Montse softens and says, "No. Let's make it a farewell party."

Pascual runs Benigno to earth in a grimy *tasca* in the Carrer de la Mercè, with a crapulous demimonde clientele. Benigno is a foundered merchant sailor who frequents the waterfront bars and if allowed will speak with prolixity on the decline of maritime Barcelona and his own personal tragedy. Hand on Pascual's shoulder and rum breath in his face, he will pour out a murky tale worthy of Conrad, the gist of which is the loss of Benigno's certificate and his reduction to water-front odd-job man and other expedients only hinted at. Pascual's impression is that Benigno may just possibly possess the required combination of special expertise and ethical vagueness.

Today he is hunched at the long zinc bar, nursing a beer and gnaw-ing a toothpick without enthusiasm, apparently disgusted by his com-panions and his surroundings. Benigno is the result when the dark, hirsute Iberian type simultaneously ages and slips into dissolution: permanent white stubble on a leathery face enlivened only by recon-dite black eyes, yellow twisted teeth. His eyebrows rise at the sight of Pascual, who slaps him on the back and orders two beers, sliding onto the stool next to him. *"Joven.* What a surprise." Benigno is clearly baf-fled by Pascual's rare diurnal appearance.

The small talk dies a mercifully quick death. A violent argu-ment has erupted at the other end of the bar and Benigno casts a malevolent glance over his shoulder. Quietly, Pascual says, "You told me once that around the harbor you could get anything a man could want, for a price."

Benigno clearly does not remember saying anything of the sort, but he nods. "Thirty years I was a sailor," he says. "Until they stabbed me in the back. A matter of some bills of lading. I told you once, I think. It was the master's fault."

"Yes. Let me ask you a question." Benigno grunts, hunkered down on the stool. "Suppose," says Pascual, "I needed to leave Barcelona, leave Spain entirely, let's say, and I didn't want to leave any traces. No passenger manifests, no computer entries, no passport difficulties, no customs. Just a quiet exit with a little personal luggage and a landfall somewhere not too far away but fairly tolerant. How would I do it? Just supposing."

Benigno grunts again. He stares at Pascual and his eyes narrow. "Just, what is it they say, hypothetical?"

"Exactly. Just as an exercise. What would I do?"

Benigno rubs the stubble on his jaw with a faint scratching sound. He is smiling faintly. "Would someone be looking for you?"

"They might be. That's usually the reason people need a quiet exit."

Benigno's eyebrows rise and fall rapidly. *"Joven,"* he says. "You surprise me."

"It's just a hypothetical question."

"Of course. Look, there are a thousand ways. It's a matter of knowing the right people."

"Suppose there were two people, traveling together. Suppose they wanted to go to Morocco."

"Morocco? What do you want to go there for? A lot of filthy *moros* and nothing decent to eat. Believe me, I've been there."

"Call it curiosity. How would you get a couple of tourists to Morocco without leaving a trace?"

"Morocco? Go south. From there it's easy. Hell, you can practically swim from Algeciras. Stand on the beach waving a flashlight and wait for one of those tubs they bring the illegals over in, twenty *moros* in a rowing boat held together with chewing gum. Flash a little money and get them to take you on the return trip. They'll be delighted somebody wants to go the other way for a change. Of course, like as not they'll stab you in the back for the rest of your cash, or the thing will sink and you'll wind up swimming anyway."

"And if we wanted something a bit . . . less adventurous? I mean, I've heard cargo ships will take the occasional passenger. We don't need luxury, but a dry place to sit would be nice."

"You'd still have to clear customs. The master's not going to jeopardize his livelihood by trying to smuggle you ashore. Unless . . ." Benigno wags a hand. "You pay him well enough."

"Of course." Pascual drinks. "Just supposing I had the money, would you know the right sort of master for me to talk to?"

Benigno muses, working on the toothpick. "Still just supposing, eh?"

"Purely hypothetical. However, were it ever to be realized, the deal would certainly include what you might call a finder's fee."

The argument at the end of the bar has ended and a sullen silence reigns again. Benigno takes a drink of his beer and vents a sigh. "Now that's an interesting hypothesis." He shrugs elaborately. "I can always ask a question or two. Look for me here tomorrow."

6

Heike insists on holding lessons at the frowsy Cafè de l'Òpera, a catch basin for foreigners and other deviants on the Ramblas. The Cafè de l'Òpera is a superannuated diva under layers of makeup. Pascual would prefer a more sober venue but has chosen not to argue; the customer is always right. Heike is a robust apple-cheeked blonde of the honey-tinted variety, and for a month Pascual has been certain that he could sleep with her if he wanted to. What has stopped him is the stark reality that she is currently his sole source of income. What she pays him each week for her hour of instruction in the Castilian language keeps him fed, if barely; rent and incidentals have begun to loom as a problem. Pascual knows that if he becomes Heike's lover the lessons will stop, and she will be converted from a source of financial independence to an enormous temptation to dependence. His standard of living would possibly improve but he cannot abide the thought of being kept. He has thus maintained at each lesson a severe professional distance, the better to ward off her considerable charms. Heike is twenty-four, Swiss, and ashamed of it as certain types of Swiss are, possessed of a disconcertingly level blue-eyed gaze, and given to sudden bursts of charming musical laughter.

Today Pascual is impervious; since Katixa's appearance no other woman on earth can tempt him. His consequent relaxation is mixed with impatience; Pascual has lost all interest in whether Heike learns Castilian. All in all the lesson has sailed along rather jauntily. As always Heike's fluency kicks in halfway through the second beer, and Pascual has set aside the text rather than belabor the *pluscuamperfecto.* "They suggested we sleep in the barn," says Heike, botching the past subjunctive. "But we couldn't sleep because there was a cat outside that pissed all night long."

Puzzled, Pascual realizes she has confused *miar* and *mear.* "Poor creature," he says. "What an affliction." Heike frowns suspiciously. Pascual checks his watch and reaches for a book. "Why don't we take a look at this passage now, read and write me a precis?" But Heike has understood and hoots with laughter, drawing a wondering look from two fastidious transvestites at the next table. Pascual shoves the book across. "Here. Read this. I'll give you ten minutes."

"I have a better idea," says Heike.

"What's that?"

"Why don't we go back to my flat and go to bed?"

Pascual stares. Heike is looking at him with that devastating gaze, twisting a strand of honey-blond hair around a finger, the laughter having faded to the merest hint of a smile. Pascual's hand falls away from the book; he opens his mouth and says nothing. Yesterday, he thinks. Yesterday I would have followed her home, in spite of everything. Today, there is Katixa. "I can't," he says.

The smile goes but Heike's eyes never waver. "Ah. All right."

Pascual cannot take his eyes off Heike's face; now that he has no trouble resisting her charms he sees how considerable they are but also how vulnerable she suddenly is, the price she is paying for an impulse heightened by alcohol. "I'm sorry," he says.

"Why?" Heike slips into German. "It's me who should apologize." For the first time her eyes fall; she picks up her glass and drains it.

"Not at all." Pascual hesitates for a second and rather to his surprise says, "I love somebody else." He can sense the transvestites' frustration at their change of language.

"Ah." This is a look Heike has never shown; until now she has maintained complete Teutonic imperviousness.

"Besides," Pascual begins to shuffle books and pencils on the tabletop, "I was going to tell you. I'm leaving Barcelona soon."

"I see. Where are you going?"

"France."

Seconds pass. "With her?"

Pascual nods. "Maybe very soon. I should have told you before. This is probably our last lesson." He can see Heike trying to decide whether to believe him.

"Well, then." Heike loses a brief interior struggle and a single tear tracks down one rosy cheek, whether from humiliation or genuine regret an appalled Pascual cannot say. She rummages in her bag and comes out with a handful of bills, which she offers him across the table. Pascual looks at them distastefully but finally takes them. He stows them away and looks up at Heike, who has wiped away the tear and is looking a bit sullen.

"Life is a roll of the dice," says Pascual. "If a couple of throws had come up differently, you'd have had me in bed a month ago."

After a moment Heike smiles, and Pascual feels a small but

distinct pang of regret. "One of those things that wasn't meant to be," says Heike.

"Not in this life."

Walking down the Ramblas, Pascual is beginning to smell bridges burning behind him; ahead there is the road, fraught with peril and exaltation.

La Estació de França is rife with symbolism for Pascual; he remembers clutching his mother's hand, being led along the platform to the car that would take them away to Paris, Eden of the North. Pascual has visited enough Edens by now so that the Estació de França has come to stand powerfully for disillusion. Even cleaned and tarted up, with its elegant curving vault overhead, it depresses Pascual. He drifts along the concourse, stares up at the arrival board for a moment, then gravitates to a bench where he unfurls the copy of *La Vanguardia* he picked out of a litter bin outside.

When Katixa dumps her bag at the end of the bench a meter away Pascual has no trouble playing the role of a man whose eye is drawn by female beauty; given free rein he would sweep her into his arms. He manages to feign continuing interest in the paper until she wanders over to ask him for a light. Today she is fortified against the cool in a white turtleneck sweater beneath the leather jacket and her hair is confined under a copious purple beret, revealing the shape of her round head on its slender neck. She is vivid and distinct and intoxicating, and Pascual fumbles like a flustered adolescent in fishing out his lighter.

Katixa's smile is full of secret amusement as she hands it back and thanks him. Pascual has chatted up dozens of pretty girls in train stations and airports in his life but is struck dumb here. "Going far?" he says finally.

"To the end of the earth," says Katixa. She wanders off to look at the posted departure time at the head of the quay as he gets his own cigarette going, regaining his footing. Katixa returns to the bench and in passing says, "Anyone watching would think you'd never talked to a woman."

"I never had, until I met you." Katixa raises one eyebrow and sits at her end of the bench. Pascual says, "All clear?"

"As far as I can tell. What news?"

"I talked to a man who knows how things work in the port. He's going to look for our way out."

"What kind of man?"

"An old sailor. And a bit of a crook."

"Not political?"

"That would surprise me greatly. Why?"

Katixa smokes. "Years ago, under the dictatorship, ETA used to get a lot of people out through the port of Barcelona. There was a whole network of sympathizers, not just Basques but politicals, leftists who were glad to help people get away from Franco's police. Stevedores, port officials, captains. I'd be surprised if part of the network wasn't still there."

"So?"

"So if you're looking for someone who's run off with a lot of your money and you know she's going to have to leave the country, you put out the word to watch for her. Anywhere she might try to slip through."

"But they don't know you're here."

"They don't have to. They'd cover all the ports. Look, I'm just saying it's a risk we should be aware of."

Pascual considers. "I'd say this fellow's a lot more likely to land us in the middle of a smuggling ring than an ETA cell."

"You're probably right. But we still have to be careful."

"So we'll be careful. Where are you staying now?"

"A hostel in Bellvitge. I'm a nice Basque girl new in the big city, looking for work."

"Any chance of sneaking me in?"

"Forget it. Nice Basque girls don't stay in the type of place where you can sneak a man in."

"I could get you into mine."

"You're forgetting all about security."

"I want to steal into your room tonight and thrash till the sheets are damp."

"We have to be chaste for a while, I'm afraid. I'm dangerous and I'm contagious. You don't want to catch what I have."

"But I do," says Pascual. "Whatever you have, I want it."

"No, you don't. Believe me, you don't." There is a fervor in Katixa's voice that Pascual has not heard before. "You're not scared enough. Let me tell you something about Goikoetxea and Arrieta."

"All right, I'm listening."

"A couple of years back we had an informer in the group, a kid named Echeverría. Whether he had been infiltrated from the start or somebody got to him with money, we never figured out. But Goikoetxea sniffed him out."

"And?"

"He and Arrieta bundled Echeverría into a car one night and took him to a tidal pool on the coast. They wired his hands together behind him and tied a thin piece of copper wire to his penis. The other end they wound around a cinder block. Then they sat him down in the pool up to his chin and waited for the tide to come in. If he'd stood up he could have kept his head above water but the wire was only a few centimeters long. That presented him with what you might call an intolerable choice."

Pascual looks for signs of amusement or irony and finds none. "And what choice did he make?"

"He made the choice I think any man would make. He drowned."

There is a silence while the noises of a large train terminus echo around them. "All right, I'm getting scared," says Pascual.

"That's better. What about tomorrow?"

They settle on a meeting place and Katixa picks up the bag and drifts away. Pascual longs to follow her but knows she would spot him. He stares at the *Vanguardia* for a while and then rises. Katixa is nowhere to be seen. He leaves the station and wanders across the road into the park. It is littered with fallen leaves. Pascual shivers in the chill.

In a bar in the sheltering narrow streets behind Santa Maria del Mar he has a *carajillo,* cognac stiffening a shot of jet-black coffee, and tries to work it out. Pascual lives on the Ramblas and he remembers the Chilean buskers, but he is certain he has not seen them since the rain, the daylong drizzle that swept the Ramblas clean a week ago.

The same day, he believes, that he read about the abandoned car in Bilbao and the rumor that a notorious *etarra* might be dead; a Sunday, he remembers. Pascual is an avid reader of the press and has a good head for dates. There is an explanation, he is sure, most likely a fault of his memory; a much more likely explanation than to suppose Katixa is lying.

There is an evening to fill. Pascual is dazed and restless; Katixa a hallucination, he fears. He takes the Metro up into the Eixample and emerges on Urgell outside the high wall of the Industrial School. At the rear of the complex is a ghastly hulk that falls somewhere between a prison and a hospital on the scale of visual appeal. It is in fact a student residence where aspiring architects, engineers and other ambitious types from the provinces live while pursuing their studies. It was a state-of-the-art building when Spain lost Cuba and successive renovations have had mixed success. The place terrifies Pascual, whose mistrust of institutions is deep enough to be genetic. Inside the massive double door is a security desk manned around the clock. Here Pascual is known and he is buzzed through an inner glass door into a tenebrous high-ceilinged hall. A broad staircase sweeps up into shadowy regions.

Father Costa is a Jesuit, a former teacher of Pascual's, a friend of long standing to the family that has disappeared, and aside from Montse the only figure from his Barcelona childhood who has ever shown the least concern for him. Father Costa teaches history at the *colegio* on Urgell, where Pascual was broken on the wheel of academic discipline, and has occupied the post of chaplain here at the residence for thirty years. He lives at the end of a long echoing corridor with closed doors along either side. Pascual knocks at the door of the suite and enters at the sound of a voice.

"Ah, Pascual. Come in, come in." The man whose head appears around the frame of the door to the inner room has a square strong-jawed face that has retained its pugnacious cast despite the softening effect of advanced age, white hair combed straight back with ruthless discipline, and black-rimmed reading glasses on the bridge of his nose. He wears a brown turtleneck sweater and slippers on white-stockinged feet. His eyes are severe under black brows; as a child Pascual was frightened of them.

"I was passing by and thought perhaps I could buy you a coffee." The ritual: Pascual offers and Father Costa trumps.

"How kind, my boy. But look, have a seat and I'll make you one here. I've got all the paraphernalia. And I'll treat you to a very nice little cognac." The priest is speaking from the back room, shuffling papers on his desk to judge by the sound. "Have you eaten?" he asks, emerging.

"Yes, yes."

"With you one never knows. Though you're looking less haggard today. Things looking up?"

Pascual shrugs. Katixa and her millions have taken on the fevered tint of a dream. "Much the same. I'm thinking of leaving."

"Leaving. Where to now?"

"I'm not sure. France again perhaps." Pascual lies by reflex, though in this room over the past months he has told Father Costa more of the truth than anybody else, all but the details. They chat while the priest prepares the coffee. The room is dominated by books, shelves reaching to the three-meter-high ceiling, neatly aligned spines with more volumes stuffed at random into the spaces above them or standing in stacks on the floor. Amid the books there is a long couch, an armchair, a small black-and-white television set on a high shelf. At the end of the couch on a small wooden stand is the cask from which Father Costa draws the cognac. Pascual tosses off the coffee and nurses the cognac. Tell me I can run off with five million francs without making a total mockery of everything I have said to you in this room, he wants to say.

Instead, after a pause, he says, "Someday I may be able to take you out for a meal, for a change. There is a chance I may come into an inheritance." This is not total fabrication; Pascual's dying father once mentioned money in family channels that might someday trickle down as far as the mongrel offspring of the black sheep of a Lower East Side merchant family. Pascual never quite believed it and, in any event, trusts there is no hope of a New York lawyer finding him in his new CIA-guaranteed identity.

Father Costa raises his snifter. "I congratulate you."

"I wouldn't know what to do with money. Real money, I mean, beyond subsistence. I've spent my whole life sneering at wealth."

"My boy, you even sneer at modest comfort."

"Yes. I'm not sure I'm temperamentally suited to wealth."

Father Costa smiles and shrugs. "Then how wonderful that nobody can force you to be wealthy."

Pascual sips and breaks into a cold sweat; the truth is that in the past day he has realized that he would love nothing more than to be wealthy. "I'm asking you for practical guidance," he says, looking into his cognac. "If someone were to give me a lot of money, what should I do with it?"

"Live modestly for the glory of God, be generous."

"Live modestly, be generous." Pascual's mood lightens instantly. "I think I can do that."

"For the glory of God, I said."

Pascual raises his glass. "For the glory of whomever you wish, Father."

Father Costa fails to respond to the toast. He smiles at Pascual and says, "We may have taken you apart, but I don't think we've quite managed to put you back together again."

"Don't worry, Father." Pascual tosses off the last of the cognac. "Other people are working on that."

The light is going and Gaudi's lamps are on in the Plaça Reial with its impossibly tall palms. The plaza echoes with the shouts of children. There is the usual quotient of derelicts, but also a sizeable contingent of the respectable householders of the lower Gothic Quarter taking the air, maintaining an uneasy equilibrium. Pascual is making for the Glaciar when Baltasar intercepts him, drifting to leeward with cigarette in hand, a black marble totem in a tattered Bundeswehr field jacket. "Your Arab was back," he says.

"Can I have a cigarette?" Pascual accepts a light as well and asks, "When was that?"

"This morning, while you slept."

"I never heard a knock."

"He never got to your door."

"Why not?"

"I came out of the shower and found him trying doors in the passage. I told him you had gone out early. He looked past me at the doors he hadn't reached, but he left."

They walk toward the bar, smoking. "Trying doors, eh?"

"Like a thief. I told the widow Puig about him. And I'm telling you. I don't think he has money for you."

"What does he look like?"

Baltasar laughs. "Like an Arab."

"North African or Levantine?"

"Not a Moroccan, I think. He wore a gray jacket, something that was once part of a nice suit."

"Doesn't ring a bell."

In the bar Baltasar insists on paying for two beers. Leaning on the counter, Pascual drinks deeply. Baltasar says, "You're afraid of them, aren't you?"

"Who?"

"The Arabs."

"Afraid of them? No more than anybody else who lives near the port."

Baltasar drinks without taking his eyes off Pascual. "I don't mean these Moroccan punks. I mean, you speak French with the French, German with the Germans, English with the yanquis. But you steer clear of the Arabs. The Palestinians, the Syrians, that crowd. Even though I know you speak the language. Read it at least; I've seen the books in your room. And you wanted to know which end of the Mediterranean your visitor was from." Baltasar's expression is knowing but cautious.

Pascual stares into his glass. "I read it a little. Don't speak it much."

Baltasar smiles. "Forgive me. But I know if certain persons of obvious African provenance were to come round asking for Baltasar Mba Ondo, I should be very glad if I were informed."

Pascual drinks and says, "You have sound instincts."

"Developed at a high price. Watch out for my old friends and I'll watch out for yours."

"Agreed," says Pascual. They drink for a while, shoulder to shoulder, watching the crowd under a blue haze of smoke. Pascual finds he is glad not to involve Baltasar in his affairs. In his experience a relationship involving illegality is a prickly thing, and he values the simplicity of their shared poverty. He raises his glass. "Someday when I'm rich I'll buy you a beer," he says. This is a ritual and the African makes the ritual response.

"By that time, my friend, I'll probably be dead."

T

Benigno glances over his shoulder and says, "Let's take a walk." It is a brisk, lightly overcast day with a wind, hints of a damp Mediterranean winter coming. Benigno walks with his hands stuffed in the pockets of the dark-blue suit jacket he wears over a sweater. They walk in silence. Traffic tears along the Passeig de Colom; beyond it is the harbor. When they reach the Via Laietana, Benigno points up the broad straight street and they turn and walk away from the sea. For a hundred years the Via Laietana has housed offices of shipping companies. Benigno leads him past imposing entrances of buildings that recall a faded maritime prominence. A hundred meters up, a narrow street meanders off into the old city. Benigno leads Pascual to a small plaza a short distance off Laietana, a mere widening of the street. On the left there is a bar. Benigno stops. He scratches his nose with an index finger, not meeting Pascual's eyes. "Wait for me here."

Pascual smokes a cigarette, paces. He passes the entrance to the bar several times, can see only a long narrow interior, figures around a table far back from the door. He finishes the cigarette and tosses it in the gutter, leans against the wall. Dire possibilities sketch themselves;

Pascual hopes he has not misjudged his man. In ten minutes Benigno comes out of the bar with another man in tow.

This one has all the nautical bearing of a post box. He is a short round man in a brown suit with a cigar in his mouth. His hair is gone on top and his waistline is gone in the middle. He has tried to hide the first by combing a few strands over from the side but there is no disguising the second. Presented with a choice of up or down, the beltline has opted to climb upward over the belly and has wound up at the bottom of the chest. The man walks with great dignity.

Benigno introduces him as Prieto and leaves matters there; he has apparently forgotten Pascual's name. The three of them walk back to Laietana and then turn seaward. "It's going to rain," mutters Benigno, and that sets the tone for the conversation until they reach the port, at which point Benigno leaves them abruptly, turning back toward his hostel.

Prieto points with the cigar at the harbor opening out in front of them and Pascual follows him across the broad Passeig de Colom onto the Moll de la Fusta. When Pascual was a boy this was open dock space, but now it is a tarted-up seaside promenade with palms and cafés. Prieto walks at the water's edge, trailing smoke. Pascual waits for an opening. "Nice," says Prieto. "What they've done with this, no?" Across the water on a wharf jutting out into the harbor they have thrown up a huge entertainment complex: bars, theaters, an aquarium. Moored close at hand are yachts, harbor cruise boats, tourist claptrap.

Pascual scowls. "So they say."

"You can't even see the working part of the port anymore."

"They tell me it's declined," says Pascual with a false air of sagacity.

Prieto shrugs, waves the cigar. He has a toothbrush mustache, a wet lower lip, and brown eyes that do not linger. "Ah, declined, well, depends on who you talk to. It's not like it was, that's for sure. It's changed, is what has happened. It's all containers now. Everything moves in containers. Get yourself a ship five hundred meters long, a floating parking lot, really. Stack the containers up on the deck like shoeboxes, clear out of the way because it takes a day and a half to stop the thing. That's not sailing. But that's the way it works now. No room left for the old-time *armadores* like me. I'm hanging on by my fingernails."

"How many ships do you have?"

"Three. But only one is actually making money. One of them is in a Turkish port waiting for Turkish courts to sort out the aftermath of a fire. One is idle in the harbor down in Valencia waiting for my engineer to find parts for a diesel they stopped making in 1947. And one is somewhere between the Black Sea and Alicante with a load of timber that just may pay for the costs of the voyage. Most of the small-boat owners have been smart enough to get out. Not me. I'm a fool, I suppose. It's the only thing I know how to do. More of a pastime than a living."

"Pity."

"Yes." Prieto sucks at the cigar. "What's a man supposed to do?"

Pascual feels this is his opening. He also feels suddenly that he is out of place with his motorcycle jacket and long hair in a bad noir film from the forties. Self-consciously, he says, "I suppose he has to take on whatever cargoes there are." Prieto shrugs, makes a vague noise. "Do you ever carry passengers?" asks Pascual.

"She's not a cruise ship. She's a three-hundred-ton coaster, built to carry just enough men to do the work in just enough comfort to keep them from mutinying. Where would they want to go?"

"Say, Morocco, for example."

"Morocco. And why wouldn't they just fly, or cross from Algeciras or Málaga, like everyone else?"

"They might not wish to go through customs."

Prieto says, "ah," like a man disappointed to find evidence of turpitude in someone he previously respected. "That we'd all like to avoid, wouldn't we?"

"They'd pay for the trouble," says Pascual.

Prieto stops, his back to the palms on the Moll de la Fusta, facing out across the blackish sheen of the water. "How many people?"

"Two. A suitcase or two apiece. And willing to rough it."

Pascual can hear Prieto working at the cigar, a faint sucking sound. "Passengers, I don't know. We don't ever carry passengers. There's room for the crew and that's about it. Of course, if they're really willing to rough it, we might find a place for them on the crew roster."

"Ah."

"That offers certain advantages. Properly enrolled as crew members, they could go ashore without any difficulty, and if there's a dispute of some sort and they choose not to continue on with the ship, well, these things happen."

"Ah. I see. There is one thing. Suppose one of them was a woman."

Prieto shrugs. "No matter. These days, it's not unheard of for a ship to have a female cook. Or . . ." He chuckles, a deep rasping sound. "On longer cruises, a woman may provide a variety of services. One hears rumors." Perhaps sensing Pascual stiffening beside him, he adds, "What I'm saying is merely that female crew members are not unheard of. It's perfectly conceivable."

Pascual nods. "And what would it take to get them properly enrolled as part of the crew?"

"Well, normally it would take a *cartilla de navegación* and an opening in the roll. But I'm assuming these people are not really sailors and not really willing to wait for two places to open up."

"That's right."

"In that case it would take some money and the right sort of captain. The right sort of captain would simply put you on the roll without worrying too much about your *cartilla de navegación.*"

"Ah. And would you happen to know any of the right sort of captains?"

They walk a few steps, Prieto producing puffs of smoke. "The question would be, do I employ any of the right sort of captain? And there we run into the problem of how long you're willing to wait. My only working captain right now is still several days out of Alicante."

"I see."

"But," Prieto stabs at him with the cigar, "I believe I can help you anyway. I know quite a number of shipping agents, and they know quite a number of captains. With a little effort and, of course, enough money, I'm sure I could get two people onto a ship out of Barcelona. Let's say I'm willing to act as your agent in this matter."

"Er . . . fine. And what would you expect in return?"

"Well, not a percentage obviously, as that would give me the wrong incentive. You want me bargaining the price down, not up. Let's say a flat fee of one hundred thousand pesetas."

Pascual wishes Katixa was here. "Mm. That sounds reasonable. How long is all this likely to take?"

"Who knows? I'd have to make some phone calls, spend a little money on beer. God knows there are plenty of the right sort of people around. You'd probably need a Cypriot, maybe a Russian, any of these former Soviet types. Those people will do anything. I'll have to do some asking around."

"I see. What about the other end? How easy would it be to get ashore in Morocco?"

"As easy as walking down the gangway."

"I mean, without opening our suitcases. You see, there would be some things we'd rather not declare."

Prieto stops in his tracks. In a low voice he says, "One thing I'll tell you right now. No drugs. Nobody will risk it. That's absolutely out."

"No, no. You misunderstand me. What's in this suitcase wouldn't interest anybody but . . . Look, it's the revenue authorities we're trying to avoid. You understand me?"

Prieto raises his eyebrows, walks on. "Well, sailors don't go through customs. Once the captain has gone over the roll with the port authorities, you could come and go as you please. Now, obviously, if a Moroccan customs official happens to see you lugging a great bulging suitcase across the cobbles you can't be sure he won't say, 'Look here, what have you got in the bag?' But a little ingenuity, a long coat, some deep pockets, a little tape are usually enough to get a few trinkets ashore. You're in port a few days, you make six or eight trips down the gangway, there you are."

"There we are." Pascual is beginning to believe it.

"Of course," says Prieto, "everything depends on how much you are willing to pay."

"Mm, yes. Well, quote me a price and we'll talk about it."

"Ah, I'm not the one to quote you a price. I'll have to talk to the people who have the ships."

"You wouldn't have any idea of an approximate figure?"

Prieto walks to the very edge of the quay and knocks cigar ash into the water. "For this sort of thing? I wouldn't imagine it could be done for under a million pesetas."

Pascual is shocked, rapidly converting a million pesetas to something under fifty thousand francs. "I see. Well. Why don't you start asking around, and I'll confer with my partner."

Prieto is already turning back toward the Via Laietana. *"Muy bien.* Come and see me at my office tomorrow between ten and two. Don't look for me in the bar. I'd just as soon nobody has any recollection of us together. Laietana twenty-eight, fifth floor. You'll forgive me if I don't leave you my card."

The Eixample has always been a refuge for Pascual when he tires of the squalor and exoticism of the old city. Pascual's Barcelona childhood was spent here, where the streets are laid out in regular blocks, where bourgeois solidity reigns. The Bar Manhattan is between the Clinical Hospital and the Industrial School, old stomping grounds from Pascual's early adolescence, when he did his time in the dreary *colegio* just up Urgell. When Franco was still alive Pascual smoked his first cigarette here and learned to work a pinball machine. The lurid rendition of the Manhattan skyline behind the bar has gained dignity over the years; the same cannot be said of Manolo the waiter, who has grayed into a sour old man but remembers Pascual and treats him with indulgence.

"Alone today, sir? What can I offer you by way of consolation?" Manolo flicks a towel at the table, scowling out at the traffic on Urgell.

"I'm waiting for a friend. Bring me a beer and step lively."

"Very good, sir. Not that little blonde you used to nuzzle on the stairs to the toilet?"

"Nobody you know and damn your impertinence."

"Very good, sir."

Katixa arrives shortly after the beer. She is wearing a long skirt and her hair is unbound. As she sits down Pascual says, "You look like that hippie girl again. What happened to the Chileans?"

"I believe they were heading for Valencia." She is shaking out a cigarette.

Pascual watches her. "What day was it that you saw me? I'm sure I looked at the women, I usually do, but I'm damned if I recognized you."

Katixa gives him a puzzled look and then shakes her head in annoyance. "I don't know. The middle of last week. On my first trip."

"Your first trip?"

"Of course. I came to scout you out first. Then I went back for the money and had my little dispute with Mr. Bordagorri."

Inside Pascual, knots loosen; he is a fool. He leans back on his chair, nodding slowly. Manolo appears, furtively raising an eyebrow at Pascual, and agrees to bring Katixa a tonic water.

"I've found our way out," Pascual says. "A tramp steamer to Morocco."

"Fast work."

"Contacts, like you said. A shipowner who knows agents who know the right type of captain. We go aboard as crew members. They put us down on the other shore. It will cost us some money."

"How much?

"A hundred thousand pesetas for the man who sets it up, maybe fifty thousand francs to the agent and the captain."

"Good God. You didn't sign anything, I hope."

"Nothing's settled. We meet him tomorrow and see what he's come up with."

"All right, we'll talk to him." Katixa wears the look of calm concentration that he remembers from Brussels and Aden. Pascual has always envied people who are resistant to doubt. "What about the car? No car, no money."

"I've got a possibility. I'll see the owner tonight." Pascual has no desire to tell Katixa about Montse, from what motive he is not sure. Shame, most likely. The idea of spending the night with Montse and wangling the car on a pretext appears less feasible and less appetizing with Katixa in front of him. Still, it seems the fastest route to a clean car with no paper trail and Pascual is an accomplished liar. "When do we need it?"

"As soon as we know where we're going. It depends on how fast we can line up a way out of the country. I don't know. Your cut-rate Onassis bothers me. I'm not sure a ship is the way to go. We might be better off with one of those cigarette boats."

"They get caught fairly often, I understand."

"True. And God knows a lot of dodgy stuff moves on freighters. I'm just thinking aloud. We'll go and talk to your man and see what's what."

Pascual sips his beer, disappointed at her reaction. Still, if anyone's instincts are to be trusted, it is Katixa's. "What next?"

"We need to pick up the money. That's where the car comes in."

"Tonight," says Pascual. "Tonight I'll work on the car."

■ ■ ■ ■

Montse lives with her mother in a flat on Aribau, unchanged since Pascual first visited it in 1974, when it was home to a family of six children. The children are grown and the father is dead, but the heavy dark furniture is still there: glass-fronted cabinets full of china, brocaded sofas and armchairs, a dining-room table that could support an automobile. There are dried rushes in tall vases. The only rooms with any signs of life are the kitchen, where plainly the eating as well as the cooking gets done, and Montse's bedroom. Returning to the nest as an adult, Montse has made it into a light, pleasant woman's retreat, with air and sea shining from prints on the walls and bedclothes and carpet in counterpoint of blues and grays. Pascual has visited the bedroom once before; their other encounters have taken place furtively and in some discomfort at his pension or, most enjoyably, in a cheap hotel in Sitges.

They have eaten in a smart bistro on the Diagonal and it is late; Pascual has been exerting himself all evening to be a good companion. He stands now at a window in the salon, looking down through the branches of plane trees at intermittent traffic laboring up Aribau, steeling himself. Montse is hanging up their coats. Pascual turns as she approaches, forcing a smile and watching her with great and depressing detachment. Guilt rises to the surface and suddenly he sees not the thirty-five-year-old divorcée but the thirteen-year-old girl. He remembers a more somber but cleaner Barcelona, a hopelessly isolated boy bragging about adventures in Paris and New York to impress the first girlfriend he has ever had. They embrace; she kisses, probing, and Pascual has to fight down a tremor of repulsion as her cool tongue slips into his mouth.

What a difference a week makes, he thinks, drawing back far enough to look into her eyes. Before Katixa this was enough: just enough sex, just enough companionship, with a woman just young enough and just pretty enough. Katixa has rocketed him into a different layer of the atmosphere.

Montse looks grave for a moment and then puts a finger on his lips. "Wait for me," she says. "There's cognac in the sideboard." She disappears down a dark hallway. Pascual hunts out the cognac and takes a glass from the china cabinet. He goes back to the window and drinks. He hears a distant toilet flush.

When Montse returns she is swathed in a silk gown, bare feet padding the tiles. She comes to Pascual at the window, takes the glass from his hand and sets it down on a table. Again she kisses him; Pascual kisses back. She leads him to the long sofa against the near wall, pulls him down on top of her. Her hands are busy, her lips are busy. Pascual responds, working at it a little. He contrives to lose his shirt. Beneath her gown she has put on red silk underwear, her hips straining at the suspender belt.

Three minutes or so later Montse becomes still. Pascual raises his head and looks at her. Montse is a stranger. She puts both hands on his chest and pushes. Sitting up, he tries to look surprised, not quite pulling it off. "You don't want to," says Montse.

Pascual can only stare; once again he has shinnied far out along a branch only to hear it cracking behind him. He opens his mouth, groping for words. Montse closes it with her hand. "Don't lie to me."

Pascual takes her hand away gently. "I don't know what's wrong with me."

Montse shakes her head slowly, something dying out in her face, the last vestiges of hope maybe. "I do," she says. Pascual gives her a sharp look and she says, "You're going to Paris because of a woman, aren't you?"

Pascual resists the initial impulse to deny it. He stares for another few seconds; female reproach has always paralyzed him. "Yes," he says.

Montse is up off the couch, propelled by a spring, whisking the gown with her, tugging it on. "Bastard," she says. "You could have told me." She stands near the window, concentrating on knotting the sash, hair shielding her profile, and then turns toward him. "I told you not to do me any favors. You could have saved me the dinner. You could have saved me this. All you had to do was tell me. You think that would have been worse than this? You think I'm that desperate, I can't do without you? You think I need your pity?" Her arms are crossed, clutching herself; she is trembling.

Pascual can only stare, for he knows it is worse than she thinks; even now the main thought that occurs to him is that he will have to look elsewhere for a car. "I'm sorry," he says.

Montse turns to the window and begins to sniffle, head bowed. Pascual rises and goes to her, puts his hands tentatively on her shoulders. "Bastard," she manages.

Fleetingly Pascual casts about for ways, even now, to save the situation. He takes his hands away, irritation starting to assert itself. The car is a losing proposition but she was the one who wanted a farewell party. "All right, I'm a bastard," he says.

Montse's shoulders stop shaking; she sniffs. She turns to him, arms still crossed over her breast, cheeks glistening in the light from the street, looking sullen and formidable. "What you are is a coward.

So was Lluís. Too scared to tell me the truth. A lot of misery could have been saved."

Pascual glares, stung but once again conceding the high moral ground. He straightens up, takes a deep breath. "So let me tell the truth now. We've had some good times, I met somebody else. That's all. I'm glad we found each other again. But it was always just nostalgia, wasn't it?"

Montse's expression goes slowly from skepticism to something dangerously close to derision and then stabilizes. "Who is she?" she asks.

Pascual hesitates only a couple of seconds before saying, "She's French. Went back to Paris last week, invited me to follow."

Montse heaves a great sigh and shakes her head, arms dropping to her sides. "I'm going to make this a lot easier for both of us," she says. Pascual frowns a little, wondering, and Montse winds up too fast for him to react and staggers him with a slap that rings clear through his head. When he has finished seeing lights he is angry, but it passes quickly. Montse is watching him with a grave expression.

"You're right," he says. "That helps a lot."

Pascual enters a high arched doorway off Via Laietana and passes a grizzled *conserje* who looks at him with disapproval as he moves down the hall toward a lift in an ornate cage. On the first floor, he gets off and sees Katixa lurking outside the office of a travel agency, smoking a cigarette. He heads for the stairs and she follows. Katixa insists that they never be seen entering or leaving the building together; Pascual finds the precaution excessive but defers to her sharper instincts.

Prieto's office is not easy to find. It is hidden around the corner at the end of the hall, past marine insurers and shipping agents and offices of companies whose business is not clear. The building is typical of the grand and faded style of Spain on the verge of imperial collapse, with high ceilings and scrollwork and gilt. The door of Prieto's office has a window of frosted glass with the name *TRANSPORTES MARÍTIMOS DE LEVANTE, S.A.* painted in black. Pascual knocks, there is an answer, and he and Katixa go in.

A single high window dominates the tiny office, throwing light from an interior shaft onto Prieto's desk. Prieto sits behind it in a dark-blue suit, hair carefully smoothed over his shining pate. He rises and comes around the desk to shake hands with Pascual, giving

Katixa a very cool assessment. She is in jeans and leather again today, hair flowing free. Prieto gives her a little bow and offers her his hand. He looks like a man who is unaccustomed to female company. There are the usual greetings but no names are exchanged. Katixa sits on a heavy wooden chair in front of the desk and Pascual drags a second one out of a corner. Besides the desk, the office contains a rank of mismatched ancient wooden filing cabinets, a square table bearing a fan, a fax machine and an enormous electric typewriter, and a coatrack with a single overcoat hanging on it. There is a calendar on the wall with a picture of a long container ship on the high seas.

"I have good news for you," says Prieto, resuming his seat. "I believe I've found a ship for you."

"How much?" Katixa asks.

Prieto blinks at her. "Twenty thousand dollars."

"That's ridiculous. We'll pay no more than ten. And we'll pay in French francs."

"I'm merely passing on the terms I was given. There's a Liberian freighter with a Greek master and a crew of twelve, headed for Brazil via Casablanca, that's willing to take you on, no questions asked. But that's the price."

"It's way too high. You're getting a cut from them, too, aren't you?"

There is a stare-down, an old dog facing a young cat with sharp claws. *"Señorita,"* says Prieto. "I made an agreement with your companion here. I think if you inquire around the port you'll find my word to be highly regarded. I agreed to a flat fee precisely to avoid any conflict of interest. The agent and the captain involved will split the money you pay them."

Katixa inclines her head slightly. "My apologies. It's still too high. Bring them down."

Prieto shrugs. "I can try. But there's a limit to our leverage and there's a time limit, too. The ship sails in three days. Drag out the negotiations and they're likely to toss the whole thing over."

"Tell them we'll pay fifty thousand French francs. Does this agent have a phone?"

Prieto looks from Katixa to Pascual and back again. Pascual imagines he sees amusement under the scowl. Or perhaps merely disdain, as Prieto has now realized who the boss is. "Certainly," he says. "With luck, we may even find him in his office. But before we try, who's for a glass of sherry? I've got a nice little *fino* here." He opens a drawer and produces a bottle and three glasses. "Just the thing to lubricate some cordial conversation."

"We're not here to tipple and gossip."

Prieto gives Pascual a despairing look and uncorks the bottle. "That's another thing that's declined. The social graces." To Katixa he says, "*Señorita,* I implore you. Have a glass of sherry and sheathe your dagger. I'm going to call the gentleman who can deliver what you want and we're going to discuss the price. The way gentlemen have always discussed business. Calmly, at our leisure, with a glass and perhaps something to smoke. I imagine that particular vice does not interest you, but surely you'll accept a *fino* of the very best?" He holds the glass before her and she takes it, coolly. Pascual accepts a sherry but declines a cigar. "Very well," says Prieto. "I'm going to call this gentleman now and we're going to bargain." He sits and pulls the telephone toward him. He dials and leans back in his chair, drawing on the cigar. "Antonio? Prieto here. I've got our tourists here in my office. Yes, yes, I did. I'm afraid they think it's a little high." Prieto gives them a dubious look, listening. "Yes. Yes, yes. Fine, I'll tell them." Prieto holds the phone away from his mouth and says, "He'll come down to ninety thousand francs."

Pascual looks at Katixa. She has not moved, staring at Prieto. "Sixty."

Into the phone Prieto says, "The lady says sixty." He listens. He grunts a couple of times. He lays down the cigar and covers the receiver with his hand. "The gentleman says seventy-five thousand is as low as he will go. If that's not acceptable, he reminds you that Iberia has a regular service to Rabat. He points out that he and the captain are taking a considerable risk and that you would be extremely fortunate to find another ship within a month. He asks me to tell you that he is a very busy man."

Finally Katixa looks at Pascual. He tries to look wise and produces the barest shrug. Katixa turns back to Prieto. "Very well. Tell him we'll pay seventy-five."

Prieto speaks into the phone without expression. "I think we have an agreement. They'll go for seventy-five." He listens, grunts again, says, "Agreed, agreed," and hangs up. "Very well. There's your deal." He raises his glass of sherry and drains it. Pascual follows; Katixa is staring into hers.

"How do we do this, then?" she says.

"I'll take you to his office and we can handle the payment there. He suggested first thing tomorrow morning, as he's anticipating a long afternoon at the docks with a damaged shipment and a difficult insurance adjuster."

Katixa shoots a look at Pascual. "That might be a bit of a scramble. We'll need some time to put our assets in liquid form."

Pascual, having failed miserably to produce a car, is stung. "We'll manage."

She says, "How about tomorrow evening?"

Prieto shrugs. "We might have a day to play with, but not much more."

"Tomorrow ought to do it. We'll call you."

"Fine. You'll need to meet the captain, of course. I'm not sure how he'll want to handle that. As for myself, I'd be happy to take my fee in either pesetas or francs, whichever you find more convenient. I believe we agreed on a hundred thousand pesetas?" Katixa nods. "And of course the ten thousand for Domínguez."

"Who?"

Prieto looks at Pascual in surprise. "Your friend Domínguez. Benigno. He asked me to collect his fee." Pascual nods to Katixa, who shoots Prieto an irritated look but says nothing. Prieto says, "Well then. Who's ready for more sherry?"

"What happens in Morocco?" says Katixa.

Prieto fills Pascual's glass, then his own. "You act like any other crew member. In my experience departures are much more closely controlled than arrivals. We get you on board here, and the hard part's over. Once you're on the roll, at the other end you'll just be two more Spanish sailors coming down the gangway. They're used to us. Now, once on the ground in Morocco, I make no guarantees. I assume you'll do a bunk and then move on? I'm not sure what those people will want in terms of visas and whatnot when you go to buy a ticket out. But if you have money I doubt there will be much trouble. They'd mainly worry if you were indigent." Prieto drinks, vents a little sigh of pleasure. "I don't suppose either of you has ever worked on a ship before?"

Katixa drains her glass, sets it on the desk. "I can cook," she says.

Prieto looks at Pascual, who can think of no useful skills whatever he possesses. He smiles and says, "Me, I'm a quick learner."

"That may come in handy," says Prieto.

The Boqueria is not for the hungry. Pascual has been known to buy the occasional bag of oranges or hunk of cheese here, but in his penury he tries to avoid it; it is too painful to pass the makings of feasts he will never eat. Under the gloom of the vast vaulted roof lie endless rows of brightly lit stalls offering mounds of geometrically stacked fruits, slabs of red meat lately hacked from cattle, spices in lurid green and orange, heaps of gasping fish. The arched entranceway frames a busy slice of the Ramblas. There is a strong smell of fish, fresh and invigorating.

"What are you afraid of?" says Pascual.

"I don't know. Can we trust him?"

They stand in front of a fishmonger's stall, jostled by the crowd. Pascual runs his eye over glistening ranks of cod. An enormous severed head, a tuna perhaps, surveys him in mute horror from the back of the booth. "Can we trust anyone?"

In response Katixa moves away, turns up the aisle. Pascual trails after her; when she is held up by the crowd around a stall heaped with cheeses he stops beside her. Over the clamor of women's voices she says, "I'm just thinking about being on a ship with twelve able seamen who know we have money." The crowd shifts and she moves on, Pascual at her shoulder.

"What's the alternative? You have to trust somebody at some point. You get the terms spelled out and watch your back."

"I'd prefer a smaller boat. Fewer people to watch."

"And more likelihood of being pinched. I think our chances are better with Prieto's Greek." Katixa says nothing. They gain a clear stretch of aisle and he draws abreast. "Or else we think about something different altogether. There are tour groups and things. Cruise ships dock at Tangier. You can work fiddles with that kind of thing. Go on an adventure tour, sneak through with sixteen hippies on their way to India or something like that."

"God, no. That's just inviting a search."

"All right. So maybe we clean up a bit, cut my hair and buy new clothes, bribe somebody at Globus and go with a group of accountants on a package tour. I don't know. I thought it was a good idea."

"I never said it was a bad idea. It's just a risk."

"Well," says Pascual. "What's life without a little risk?"

"I couldn't tell you," says Katixa. She has halted in front of a poultry stall; an angel-faced girl is hacking a chicken apart with a cleaver, with utter ruthlessness. "You have to get us a car somehow. Can you do that?"

"Beg, borrow or steal, maybe. I can't afford lunch, much less a car."

"Forget stealing. It has to be clean. And it has to be available fast."

Pascual nods. "I can do that."

An imposing matron in a blue smock greets them in Catalan; Katixa smiles and moves away. "I'll work on it too, see what I can turn up. We'll need a place to meet. Preferably with a phone."

Pascual remembers trysts of twenty-odd years ago. "They took phone calls for me at the Manhattan when I was a kid. They'll probably do it again."

"All right, let's give ourselves until three o'clock. Who shall I be if I have to call?"

"Montse. For realism."

"Not Montse. They'll come back at me in Catalan and the game will be up."

"All right. Say, I don't know, anything. Say María."

"María it is." An eyebrow rises. "And who's Montse? Somebody who will miss you?"

"Not anymore."

Something passes briefly across Katixa's face: curiosity, jealousy, relief? She smiles. "Not anymore. I like the sound of that."

Things come to a boil inside Pascual. "Katixa, come back to the pension with me." He catches her arm, pulls her to him. "I need you," he says in a strangled whisper. They are blocking the aisle; people brush past them.

Katixa closes her eyes for perhaps two seconds. When she opens them there is no archness, no distance. She is the Katixa of Brussels, of rain and solace and sexual hunger. A thousand voices echo around them.

"Your pension?" she says at last. "You might as well give out tickets."

"A hotel. We'll rent a room for an hour." Pascual would pawn his soul for the pesetas.

Katixa gives her head a brief shake, like a woman recovering from a dizzy spell. "Soon. Soon we'll have time for everything. We'll go to bed and only come up for air."

Pascual stands paralyzed as she eases herself from his grip and makes for the exit. A man in a stall looks at Pascual over ghastly flayed heads of sheep and gives him a sympathetic cluck of the tongue.

Pascual does not doubt that Katixa could produce a usable vehicle, legal or illegal, with a snap of the fingers; he feels this assignment is a test. Katixa will not want to flee the continent with a man who cannot even wangle a car at short notice. Larbi's shop is closed but Pascual bangs on the door until the Algerian opens it a couple of centimeters, peering out through the gap. "I have nothing for you," he says.

"I propose a deal," says Pascual.

"I can give you maybe another thousand. Times are hard."

"I don't want your money. Let me in, for God's sake. All you have to do is listen."

Larbi lets him in and locks the door behind him. "What kind of deal?"

"Lend me your van for two days and I'll write off the debt. Five thousand pesetas for forty-eight hours' use of the van, not a bad deal."

"Four thousand, you mean." Larbi is scratching at his belly through a gap between buttons. Pascual follows him into the back room, where the Algerian plugs in a hot plate and sets a battered kettle full of water on it. Pascual takes this as an encouraging sign of preparation for negotiation. "What for?" Larbi says.

"I'm moving into a flat. There's a house full of furniture up in Girona that belongs to a deceased relation. I can have some of the furniture if I can move it. Maybe two loads."

"When do you need it?"

"Tomorrow."

"Not possible. I need it tomorrow myself."

"All day? If I could get my hands on it in the afternoon, I could probably do both loads, have it back to you tomorrow night."

Larbi rummages for tea on a crowded shelf. "Girona's a long way off."

"Not that far. A couple of hours drive, an hour or so of work at each end. And then you won't owe me a thing."

"You know how to drive?"

"Of course I know how to drive."

"And you'll have it back tomorrow night?"

"That's a promise." Pascual figures that out of five million francs he can afford a little remuneration in case of delays.

Larbi shifts the kettle on the hot plate, scowling. "Don't leave me with an empty tank."

"Of course not."

"All right. Come see me after lunch tomorrow."

Pascual makes for the pension, elated. Upstairs, Pilar is camped in front of the television. Pascual's nose leads him to the kitchen. Old Pep is making a tortilla. Rheumy-eyed, unshaven, swathed in layers of sweaters, capped with a *boina,* he is a caricature. The air sizzles with the sound and smell of frying oil. The old man waves the spatula at him, dripping hot oil on his sleeve. *"Com va això?"* Old Pep treats Pascual like a grandson, perhaps because his own have abandoned him to the poverty of the Pensión Alameda. "Hungry? There's plenty for two."

Pascual has exploited Pep's generosity many a time, but the thought of five million francs makes him suddenly ashamed. "No, no, please. Just popped in to say hello."

"I've got some cheese, too. And a bit of wine left."

Pascual sees Old Pep is desperate for company. "Perhaps a bite or two." Pep splits the tortilla and they eat at the rickety table, passing the wine back and forth while Old Pep talks soccer. Barça has a crucial match tonight and Old Pep is a Barça encyclopedia; he can tell you which foot Kubala used for each of his most famous goals and precisely how the tragic Ramallets blundered into his catastrophic own goal against Benfica in 1961. Out of one hundred million pesetas, Pascual thinks guiltily, he must set aside a few thousand for Old Pep.

The widow Puig appears and begins tidying and grumbling. The Africans, she says, have been washing clothes in the sink. "If the Ajuntament didn't pay so well, they'd be out on the street."

"At least they're washing," Pascual says with his mouth full.

Old Pep laughs. "Go ahead, toss them out. You can give their rooms to some of Teresa's friends, take a little commission." The mostly nocturnal Teresa is a favorite of the widow Puig, who seems oblivious to the fact that she is clearly a prostitute.

"Ah." La Puig throws up her hands. "If my husband were still alive." She trundles sadly away.

Pascual retires to his room and flops on the bed with the earphones of the little Walkman in place. He has a tape of Heifetz playing Bach's third Violin Partita and in the airy spaces of the Preludio there are no earthly cares. Pascual dozes with the violin in his head until a pounding noise fills the room, cutting through the music; he tears off the earphones. "Pascual," someone is calling.

He recognizes Baltasar's voice and sits up, not quite awake, saying, "One moment." He swings his feet to the floor. The handle of the door rattles. "Just a moment," he repeats, standing.

"Pascual," says Baltasar distinctly, very close to the thin wooden panels of the door. "Don't open. Get out through the window if you can. Your Arab is here."

There is a moment of suspension, then an ear-splitting detonation blows splinters and a fine red spray into the room through a hole that appears at eye level in the upper panel of the door. The door shakes as something falls against it and the handle rattles again, violently. Pascual is awake now, and he pitches backward across the bed and onto the floor as four more shots come through the door in quick succession, fragments of wood and plaster flying. There is silence and then the crash of a foot hitting the door, something splintering, and Pascual is at the window. He sees the door shake in its frame from another kick; absurdly, one of the holes in the door is bleeding. Pascual tears the window open. He is four stories up but vertigo cannot compete with firearms powerful enough to blow a man's brains through a door; as the third kick lands, Pascual is poised on the rail of the mock balcony, teetering above the street. Far, far below, a couple of meters to the right and across the street, there is a green awning that might break his fall, but Pascual can already feel the compound fractures.

As the door gives way behind him, his muscles make the decision for him; Pascual leans out past the point of no return and pushes off with his feet. The streets in the Gothic Quarter are narrow, and with death at his heels, it is the meanest of feats for Pascual to sail across four meters of space and down one story, to land on the genuine and blessedly spacious balcony across the street, his descent broken by lines of washing stretched out to dry, but not enough to prevent him from wreaking havoc, shattering panes of glass as he bursts the double doors inward, bringing tangled laundry, earth, flowers and shards of pottery with him into the parlor of a very respectable and very surprised Catalan ménage just tidying up their lunch table.

The narrow street is in an uproar, choked with people. There are police cars, an ambulance, a milling of the idle and curious and alarmed. Pascual is limping in his threadbare socks; his right leg is beginning to hurt from ankle to hip as adrenaline ebbs. He is bleeding from a cut in the meat of his right hand and his elbow complains when he flexes it. He has refused to go upstairs, but the policemen are insisting.

In the pension the widow Puig is moaning softly somewhere down a hallway, a soft male voice providing counterpoint. Pilar is sprawled in the foyer, next to the chair from which she must just have risen, eyes open in surprise. Nobody has turned off the television. Pilar did not bleed much, but a crimson Mississippi has snaked its way out of the kitchen where Old Pep lies. Baltasar is crumpled in the hall, legs bent at the knees and splayed, a huge black frog crouched at Pascual's door. There is a smear of blood and matter down the dull green paint of the door, which hangs half off the hinges, peppered with holes.

Pascual can see only the hole in the back of Baltasar's head and has no desire to see the front. His legs give way and, unaided by the policemen, who are having their own problems with the visual data, he manages to sag against the wall and slide gently to the floor.

In his clandestine years Pascual always managed to stay out of police stations; it is ironic that his first experience with interrogation should come here, in the building he was taught to fear as a youth because it housed Franco's police. Franco is long gone but the police are still here; noise from the busy Via Laietana does not reach this fluorescent-lit room with gray walls, deep inside the vast gray building. Men come and go with a quiet tread, shooting uneasy glances at Pascual; carnage like that in Carrer d'Avinyó is not everyday fare in Barcelona.

"Who was the black?" This is the third wave of policemen. Pascual has no idea whom he has talked to: every section of the Policía Nacional seems to want a piece of him. This detective has jet-black hair as stiff as wire, just starting to gray at the temples. In five years it will be as white as snow. His square jaw needs shaving twice a day to keep the beard at bay. He has glittering black eyes that did not like what they saw in the Pensión Alameda. He wears a black leather jacket that just fails to conceal the automatic on his belt and he smokes black tobacco, holding the cigarette between thumb and forefinger.

"His name was Baltasar." Pascual's injured leg throbs; they have bandaged his hand and found him some shoes. "We were casual friends. I don't even know what he did." Pascual's voice is steady but without breath behind it.

"Tell me again what he said at the door."

"He said, 'Don't open, your Arab is here.'"

"That's all?"

"That's all."

"And then the shot."

"Yes."

"So it seems he was trying to protect you."

"Yes."

"With a gun held to his head."

"So it seems."

"Remarkable devotion."

Pascual can say nothing. The detective waits; finally Pascual says quietly, "Yes."

"This black is the one who told you about the Arab in the gray coat?"

"Yes."

"Did anybody else see this Arab?"

"The landlady might have, today."

"You think she'd still be alive if she had? She was on the toilet; that's what saved her life. I have a feeling she'll be wanting a better class of resident after this." He smokes and says, "Why you?"

"I don't know." Pascual has recovered sufficiently from the trembles to have sorted out what he can and cannot say. "You want a guess?"

"Why not?"

Pascual swallows. "I would guess that it was a male relative of a young woman with whom I was involved in Paris several years ago. A brother, probably."

Whatever the cop expected, it was not this; through a cloud of smoke he says, "I see. Arab girl?"

"Syrian, daughter of a UNESCO functionary or something. We met at the university, faculty of letters. Things progressed. Then her family raised objections; she disappeared. Nobody bothered me and I forgot about it. If it's the right guess, they didn't start looking for me until after I left Paris. Possibly because they didn't discover she was no longer a virgin until it was time for her to marry. That would have set them off."

The policeman is looking at him with distaste. "Couldn't keep it zipped, eh? Any fool knows not to mess with those women."

"She was highly cooperative," says Pascual.

The story is fabricated. A week ago Pascual would have told the truth to see the Arab caught but now he will do nothing to jeopardize his getaway with Katixa. "How did this Baltasar earn his keep?" asks the detective.

"I told you. I don't know."

"Yes, you made a point of that. You were friendly enough with him so that he saved your life at the cost of his own, but you don't know what he did for a living?"

"He was a political refugee. I think he was an engineer of some sort."

"An engineer."

"That's what he told me."

"What about you? How do you support yourself?"

"I'm a teacher of languages. Occasionally I do some translation work."

"Where do you teach? What school?"

"I have private students."

"How many?"

"Right now, one."

"Good living, is it?"

"Not at the moment."

"What languages?"

"French, German, English."

"Not Arabic? There was a pile of magazines in funny writing in that rat's nest of yours."

"I read it a little."

The detective says nothing. He smokes and watches Pascual until the glowing end of the cigarette nearly singes his fingers. He grinds it out in an ashtray and says, "A black vagabond who sells hashish to schoolboys gets his brains shot out. A so-called teacher with no visible means of support jumps out of a fourth-floor window and manages to land without killing himself, worse luck. He tries to tell me it's all an affair of the heart gone wrong. Normally I enjoy it when the guttersnipes kill each other off. But here I've got two innocent people shot to hell along with them." The cop slides off the corner of the desk. "I'm going to take a piss. When I come back I want you to tell me the truth."

Pascual raises his eyes to the detective's. "I already have."

The detective leans close, a hard man who can remember the days when police work was less punctilious. "Shit. You've told me shit. You've sat there and as good as spat in my face. Pity the old days are gone. I'd love to take a sock full of ball bearings to that pretty face of yours. The things we've had to give up, just so they'd let us into Europe."

■ ■ ■ ■

Through the window in the door Pascual can see them, milling, smoking, checking their cameras. "Good luck," says the detective. He reaches for the door handle.

"Wait." Pascual understands now the sudden change of heart, the cheerful agreement to release him after six hours of interrogation.

"They're all there," says the detective. *"La Vanguardia, El Periódico, Avui,* I think even maybe that's the fellow from *El País* out there. We didn't let the TV people in. They'll be out in the street." He slaps Pascual on the shoulder. "You're going to be famous." Pascual refuses to look at him. He stands watching the reporters in the hall, starting to concede defeat, trying to stave off panic. At his shoulder the detective says, "Go on, you can complain about how we've mistreated you. Or you can just walk out there with your jacket over your head and try to run. They won't be able to keep up with you, weighted down with all those cameras and things."

Pascual turns and says, "All right, you win."

Eyebrows rise. "Don't tell me you're going to change your story now that we've done all this work." The detective moves closer, into Pascual's face, black eyes glittering with malice. "You mean to tell me you lied to me? Is that what you're trying to say?"

Pascual blinks. "I'm not who my papers say I am." Whatever they expected, it was not this; for once he has caught them short. "I'll tell you the story and then maybe you can tell me how to stay alive. A good start would be keeping me out of the papers."

The detective blinks, shakes his head, and takes Pascual by the arm to steer him back down the hall. "See if José can have somebody send us up some coffee and a couple of *bocadillos,*" he says to his colleague. "Fucked again. I'm going to miss the football tonight."

10

In the middle of the night they release him to two men who do not identify themselves. Pascual has been dozing at a table, jerking awake each time his consciousness strays into images of mayhem. He has had his nose rubbed in distasteful realities and he is full of new knowledge. In his years underground Pascual never once got this close to the business end of a gun, and he does not like this sour new taste life has taken on. Footsteps sound in the corridor and a door opens. "Let's go. Your minders are here."

One man is bald with hard blue eyes and the other could be a stevedore: the muscle. They take Pascual out into the cold air of an interior courtyard and into a black Mercedes, the stevedore driving and the bald man in the back with Pascual. The car eases out onto a deserted Via Laietana. "You've had an exciting day," says the bald man.

"The police were skeptical," says Pascual. "I wasn't sure they'd call you."

"They didn't want to, I don't think. But they couldn't just laugh off a story like yours without calling us."

"And just who are you?"

The man offers him a cigarette and lights it for him, then busies himself with another. "You've been kicked progressively upstairs. From Homicidios to Informaciones and then clean out of the Policía Nacional to us. After all, I don't think they were too unhappy to see you go. They couldn't charge you with anything. They'll put the killings down as a settlement of accounts among delinquents and try and sell it to the press. The press will try to find you for a couple of days and conclude you've wisely done a bunk."

Pascual is silent, feverishly speculating as to how he can do just that. "So you believe me, eh?"

"Provisionally. We had a talk with your yanqui friends. Quite a story they told us about you. Imagine, dumping their wastes on our doorstep."

"I'm glad they remember me."

"Oh yes, they remember. Turns out they did clear it with somebody in Madrid. But they didn't see fit to inform anybody here."

"It was supposed to be a secret. They decided I was harmless."

"Harmless? Ask your friends in Carrer d'Avinyó."

"You can catch the bastard. There's a good chance he's still here. They've waited a while to find me and I don't think they'll give up now. He'll be Palestinian, possibly with a Syrian passport. It could be somebody I worked with, so I'll give you all the names I can. I'll look at pictures if you've got them. If they've sent somebody who speaks Castilian that narrows it a bit more. I can think of two who spent time in Madrid."

Smoke fills the silence. They are heading up the Passeig de Gràcia, toward the hills. "How can you be so certain? You never saw the man. Nobody besides you said it was an Arab. There was a lady in a shop downstairs who saw a man leaving in a bit of a hurry, but she wouldn't swear it was an Arab. The landlady says the black told her about an intruder but never said it was an Arab."

"There aren't that many candidates. You cuckold a man and somebody takes a potshot at you in the dark, what's your first guess going to be?"

The man smokes and grunts gently. "So how did they find you?"

"Yes," says Pascual. "That's the question, isn't it?"

"Well, you'll have a chance to ask the right people."

"What do you mean?"

"They want to talk to you, too. Your yanqui friends."

"Wonderful."

"We'll try to arrange it. But first you have to talk to us."

"I've got all night," says Pascual.

The apartment is somewhere off Balmes in the upper reaches of the city, in a newish building on a sloping narrow street; Pascual could not quite keep track of their route in the night. Lying on the bed, he can hear the rush of water through pipes, footsteps in the apartment above, voices coming faintly through walls. They have allowed Pascual to lie down and he has finally got a little feverish sleep; now there is light coming in around the slats of the shutters and he has awakened to find that the world is still fouled. He has no idea what time it is.

There is a rattling of locks and the front door opens; a shuffling of feet on tile and muted voices. Pascual rises, grimacing from injuries and inadequate sleep, and limps out of the bedroom.

"Good morning. You look like hell." The bald man looks rested, fed and newly groomed. "Is there more of that?" he says to the stevedore, who has been nursing a cup of coffee at the round table in the corner. To Pascual he says, "You want a wash, take a shower, comb your hair, at least?" Pascual shakes his head, staring at the person who has just come in. The bald man grins. "I told you they wanted to talk to you." He gestures at the newcomer, who has taken a seat at the table, setting a shoulder bag on the floor.

Pascual cannot believe his eyes. The woman cannot be more than twenty-two or -three, and in her jeans and sweatshirt she could be the poster girl for "Spend a Semester in Europe." Women who look like this have accosted him on the Ramblas, asking the way to McDonald's in execrable Spanish. Her hair is brown and straight, cut short for practicality rather than appeal. She has a plump face with the open credulous features of the tourist and the *tenue* of the girl who makes the posters for the pep rally. Pascual has heard women who look like this ask for cornflakes in the Café Zurich. He looks at the bald man suspiciously. "This is who you deal with?"

"Who do you want, James Bond? This is the new model. Watch out or she'll shoot you with her cigarette lighter." He smiles at both of them and joins his partner in the kitchen.

The woman has remained silent, with an impassive look on her face. Pascual limps to the table, where somebody has left a pack of cigarettes and a lighter. He gets a smoke going and proceeds to the couch, where he collapses.

"What did you do to your leg?" says the woman in very creditable Castilian.

"I jumped out of a window," Pascual answers in English, sullenly. She will not beat him at the language game.

In English she says, "I understand you had a miraculous escape."

Texas, thinks Pascual, maybe Oklahoma; they've sent me a cracker. He wants to ask how old she is but instead says, "Who are you with? What agency are you from?"

"I work for the government. I don't carry credentials." There is a cool smile now, and Pascual begins to revise his estimate of her age upward. Twenty-five, possibly. "And what about you? Who are you with these days?"

"Nobody. If you're really CIA you should know that."

"Oh, I know who you are."

Pascual blows smoke toward the ceiling. "Who am I?"

"You're Pascual Rose, maybe the most productive source ever on international terrorism. And a defector of dubious background and motives."

"Dubious, huh?"

"Well, you're still a little bit controversial. And now you're making waves again."

"I'm not making waves. I was trying to keep my head down and a PFLP hit man found me."

She frowns a little at that, watching him smoke. "How do you know who it was? The police seem to consider you either a bad liar or a hysteric."

"I was told an Arab was looking for me. If you've got a better explanation than the people I sold out coming to get even, I'd like to hear it."

"I didn't say I had an explanation. I'm just trying to make sure we know what's happening to you."

"What's happening is someone's trying to kill me. With my background there's a very narrow range of people it could be. I could probably give you a list. If you and your colleagues in there move fast you can probably get them wrapped up in a hurry."

"Well, that's not actually what I'm here for."

"What the hell are you here for, then?"

"I'm not a cop. I'm in the information business. You allege you were the target of a PFLP hit. Your background gives you some credibility. We're interested in that bunch, so I was sent to see how reliable your information is. Now I find you don't really have much information to offer."

Pascual smokes, irritated. "OK, here's some information. In 1992 a man in Rome set me up with a new identity and gave me a plane ticket to Barcelona and the address of the pension where I lived until yesterday. He told me the only people who would know where I was were CIA. Now I find out they told the local spooks, but that's OK; I guess they had to. In any event I took all that to mean my old friends would have to get pretty lucky to find me. They didn't even know I was from Barcelona originally. To them I was always French. Now they show up at the door of my room, gun in hand. So take that information and work with it. If they could find me, something went wrong. Who told what to whom?"

The woman studies Pascual. Clattering noises come from the kitchen. "Until we have an ID on the shooter, that's just speculation."

Pascual closes his eyes. He is walking a fine line here; he must cooperate but he must not invite too much scrutiny. He smokes, scratches, softens his tone. "Look, am I under arrest?"

"Not that I know of."

"Then I can walk out that door anytime and, believe me, the first thing on my mind right now is to run as fast and as far as I can. Why am I up here?"

She considers that, gives a little shrug. "Well, you're up here because I need you and you need me."

"How so?"

"I need you to justify my existence this week. I'm supposed to bring back a report on this supposed PFLP sighting, and you'd probably appreciate whatever help I can give you in staying alive."

"Not if there are too many strings attached."

"There's always a quid pro quo. We're not a charitable organization."

"No. I'd say that's clear."

"But hey, you've got me interested. You tell me what you can about this Arab of yours, and I'll see what I can do to put you out of reach again. Fair enough?"

"Fair enough."

"So this may take a while. You got another place to stay? I don't know how long they're prepared to put you up here and I'm not authorized to offer you anything else. Not yet, anyway."

Pascual smokes, leans forward and grinds out the butt in an ashtray. "I'll find something."

She studies him for a while, and Pascual has the feeling she is not impressed with what she sees. "Can we set up a way to keep in touch?"

"Sure. There's a bar I go to sometimes. They'll take a message for me."

"I'll tell you right now, you're likely to be a fairly low priority. Frankly, I don't think anybody much cares what happens to you."

"That's the impression I get," says Pascual.

Pascual limps in through the gate of the Industrial School. He heads down an alley, ducks through a pair of glass doors, lights a cigarette and watches. Emerging, he tosses away the butt and makes for the residence. "What happened to you?" asks Father Costa, cocking an eyebrow at him around the edge of his door.

"Somebody tried to kill me." Without waiting for an invitation he sinks onto the sofa.

The priest closes the door and merely looks at him for a few seconds, frowning. "Not the business in Carrer d'Avinyó? I did wonder when I heard the address. The radio didn't mention any names."

"Can I hide here for a day or two?"

"Are you all right?"

"I could use some coffee."

"Certainly. What on earth happened?"

"I think an old friend caught up with me."

"Who?"

"Probably a representative of my former employers. The Popular Front for the Liberation of Palestine."

Father Costa goes about the business of making coffee in silence. Hands in his pockets, watching the pot simmer on the hot plate, he finally says, "That bunch, eh? Somehow you gave me the impression of something a bit more innocent."

"I was trying to be vague. Can I hide here, please? I'll be leaving town as soon as I can."

"Are the police looking for you?"

"They've already had me."

Father Costa shrugs. "We can probably find you a vacant room upstairs."

"I have no money for a room and the fewer people that know I'm here, the better. If you can possibly put me up right here, it will be one more thing I owe you. I'll sleep most of the time, probably."

Father Costa pours coffee for two. "I'll make one condition."

"What?"

"You tell me the uncensored version of your adventures."

Pascual rests his head on the back of the sofa, eyes closed. "Agreed," he says. He is already editing, carefully drawing lines around Katixa.

"All of it, from the start."

"Confession, you mean," says Pascual.

"I don't trifle with the sacraments. You insist you're an atheist, so I cannot confess you. But I should like to hear the truth about your past, and I suspect you may find it a relief to tell it."

Suddenly Pascual is shaken by the prospect. To tell it all, every-thing, to have the abscess of remorse lanced, to be blessed and for-given. For an instant he teeters on the brink of very deep waters.

"I wanted to be a killer," he says. "But all I was was a fool."

11

After six hours of sleep on Father Costa's sofa Pascual's leg is, if not healed, at least recovered enough to keep the limp within manageable bounds. He finds a shabby woolen coat in the depths of the priest's wardrobe and descends to the main entrance, where he stands smoking a cigarette, watching students come and go. Then he makes his way out of the school complex and across Urgell.

Through the glass front of the Manhattan, Pascual watches Katixa emerge from the Metro and approach the bar; the knot in his stomach eases. Today her hair is done up in a braid and her figure disguised in a baggy green sweater over black tights; she could be an art student, a stray Brazilian tourist looking for the Sagrada Família. She drops her bag onto a chair and sits opposite Pascual. There is no one else within earshot; at the bar an old man droops over his *copa*. "You're all over the papers today," she says.

"Christ, don't tell me. I was afraid to look."

"Questioned and released," they said. "But your name's there, in black and white."

"They had to give it out eventually."

"That may make things harder."

"I didn't do it on purpose."

Katixa gets a cigarette out of her bag and lights it. She searches his face. "Are you all right?"

Pascual wants to tell her about Baltasar's brains coming through the door. "I'll live," he says.

"Who was it?"

"My old comrades, I think."

Manolo looms, morose but ready to serve, and Katixa orders a coffee. "I told you you're not hiding very well."

Pascual considers. "You knew where to look because you knew I'd come back to Barcelona. How did they know?"

Katixa considers this, unblinking. "I don't know. Maybe somebody sold you."

"Sold me?"

"To an intelligence agency, you're a commodity. Don't ever forget that." This is an unpleasant thought and Pascual cannot begin to work out the implications. Katixa says, "How did it go with the police?"

"I had to tell them who I was. That brought in the spooks."

Katixa freezes. "What spooks? Whose?"

"Everybody's. Spaniards and yanquis. I answered a lot of questions. Not a word about you."

"And they let you go?"

"Nobody cares about me. There's no evidence I'm right about the killer and the police can't hold me. I'm a curiosity."

"That's what they'd tell you. Christ, we could be on camera right now."

"I don't think so. I'd swear I haven't been followed."

Katixa shakes her head. "This is bad."

"Not necessarily. I was advised in so many words to take to my heels. I don't see why we can't just carry on with Prieto."

"It may be too late. We haven't even got the money yet."

"I can get a van. I had it all arranged."

"Even so. I don't like the risks. The controls will be tighter now. They'll be looking for your Arab and they'll try to sew up the port. At best we're ripe for a good case of blackmail, somebody doubling the price on us. We're too vulnerable. I say it's time to head up the coast. There's always someone there willing to run a small boat across the water, for a fee."

Pascual blinks at her, tight-lipped. "So we'll ring Prieto, see what he says. He won't be any more willing to take bad risks than we are."

Katixa says nothing while Manolo brings her coffee and discreetly withdraws. "All right, ring him." Pascual makes for the phone. Prieto gave them the number of his office and also that of the bar; Pascual tries the bar first and scores. "What happened to you?" says Prieto.

"I've had a rough twenty-four hours."

"*Hombre*. I saw the papers. No wonder you're running."

"Are we still on?"

There is an exhalation at the other end of the line and Prieto's voice drops to a murmur. "That depends on two things. Whether the police are still interested in you, and whether the man who killed all those people in Carrer d'Avinyó is still interested in you."

"The cops are finished with me. The other guy's not, but he's lost me for the moment."

In the ensuing pause Pascual can almost hear Prieto calculating. "Then we'll have to be careful to keep it that way."

"So you're still willing to take us?"

"You've got the money?"

"Not yet. We'll have it tomorrow."

"Tomorrow. Always tomorrow. Look, the ship leaves tomorrow. The agent told me if we don't seal the deal tonight, it's off. In fact, he'd like to have you on board tonight."

"Tonight, Christ, I don't know. We still have to retrieve the money. We're having transportation problems."

There is a pause at the other end of the line. "Would it help if I drove?"

"Drove?"

"In my car. Would it help if I took you where you need to go?"

Pascual can hear the acid in Prieto's voice. "You'd do that?"

"To get this show on the road, I'd do it. Now where do you need to go?"

Pascual makes fast decisions. "A couple of hours drive north."

"Four hours there and back. I think we can just swing it. When can you leave?"

"Anytime, soon. I think. I'll have to talk to my partner."

"Consult her. I'll be in my office. I can leave at short notice. Call me with a decision."

Pascual returns to the table. "We're going," he says. "Prieto will drive us to pick up the money and then we go on board. Tonight."

Katixa watches him as he sits. "You're joking."

"We give him a call, he'll be ready to go."

Katixa blinks for a while, breathes deep and says, "Are you ready?"

"I can be. If you can lend me a couple of thousand I'll buy a toothbrush and a change of clothes."

Katixa nods once. "All right. I'll need to go and retrieve a few things. Where shall we meet?"

"The post office at the bottom of Laietana? Six o'clock?"

"Six o'clock." For the first time, as Katixa sits biting her lip and gazing at him, Pascual feels he has taken the lead in the partnership. Katixa shakes her head and says, "Shit, what are we doing?"

Pascual drains his drink. "Man the capstan, weigh the anchor. We're going to sea."

On the street, night has fallen and it is not quite raining. The wind is nasty and damp, intent on crawling down Pascual's shirt. He turns up the collar of Father Costa's old coat and slings the cheap flight bag containing his purchases over his shoulder. Tomorrow the open sea, he thinks. Katixa estimates it will take half the night to recover the money from its cache in the hills near Vic and get back to Barcelona.

The post office is a huge echoing vault with marble columns and floor. Pascual makes a circuit or two, as if to decide which queue to choose. Katixa appears out of nowhere, a bag slung over her shoulder. She has put on her beret and a pair of black boots. "Ring him," she says. "Unless you've changed your mind?"

Pascual shakes his head. He finds a vacant phone. Prieto answers on the first ring. "We're coming," says Pascual.

"Very well. You're nearby? Come up to my office. I need twenty minutes to make a couple of phone calls."

Pascual and Katixa descend the steps together. There is little to say. They cross Laietana. It is a busy time of evening and the pavement is crowded. Pascual can see the city rising on the far hills, lights in the dark. They turn into the high entranceway and Pascual nods at the *conserje,* who returns it coolly. The lift takes them up, creaking. Katixa has pressed the button for the floor above Prieto's, cautious by reflex. They get off and walk down the stairs. Katixa stops Pascual on the landing, a hand on his shoulder. The building is quiet; he can hear the traffic outside. Footsteps sound in the hall below. Pascual cannot see, but he hears somebody stop at the lift, punch impatiently at the button. The lift comes down from the floor above and takes him away. Pascual and Katixa wait; he can feel she is uneasy. They descend into the hall and make for Prieto's office. There is a light on beyond the frosted glass. Pascual knocks; there is no answer. He tries the knob; the door swings open. Pascual steps inside.

Prieto is resting, his head on the desk. Pascual can see six strands of hair plastered across the bald pate. Prieto's hands are on the desk, on either side of his head, relaxed, unclenched. Pascual crosses the office slowly, trying to understand how a man can rest comfortably facedown on his desk, nose to the blotter. He has laid his face down on a handful of slips of paper. Strangely, the top paper bears a small, glistening red stain, just beneath Prieto's left eye. The shock is unpleasant when Pascual realizes that the messages are impaled on a spike, and there is no place for the spike to be except in Prieto's brain.

When he finally looks at Katixa she is riveted, just inside the door, staring. Her eyes flick to his and Pascual can see that for all her sang-froid she is human, too. Then she is moving, pushing the door gently to, coming across the floor toward him, unslinging her shoulder bag.

"Touch nothing," she says. "Change your clothes. Put on a hat, switch to a different jacket."

Pascual understands, and for a minute the only noise is the frantic shuffling of clothing. Pascual cannot help stealing glances at Prieto, cooling on the desk. He has only the old woolen coat but Katixa gives him a scarf to drape around his neck and a beaded African cap. Katixa is stuffing the beret into her bag, hair falling free, having thrown a huge baggy sweater on over her leather jacket. "We go out separately. They'll be looking for a couple." There is a tremor in her voice. "Meet me in front of the post office in ten minutes."

Pascual sees her into the lift and waits on the stairs, watching the second hand of his watch creep around the dial. Emerging from the lift five minutes later he ignores the *conserje* and walks out into the bitter night.

"We almost walked into it," says Katixa on the Passeig de Colom, wind in their faces, coming hard across the harbor. "We heard him."

Pascual's mind has begun to work again. "Who?"

"Probably somebody I know. God, they're close."

"How? How, for Christ's sake, did they know?"

It takes Katixa five steps to come up with the answer. "Prieto wasn't careful enough. He ran into that old network. They'd just have time to send for the hard guys."

"Why didn't they stay and wait for us? If they knew we'd contacted him, they had to guess we'd be back."

"Who knows? Maybe Prieto tried something, forced their hand. The important thing is they've stopped us from leaving."

"We're fucked."

"If we stay here, that's for sure. When they find Prieto, the police are going to talk to the *conserje*. We may have confused him a bit, but he'll remember us. It's time to separate."

Pascual's heart sinks. "For how long?"

"For as long as it takes you to find a fucking car. I'll call you tomorrow. If you can get a car I'll tell you where to find me."

"Let's stay together."

"Forget it. I'm poison. You just find us a car."

"Where are you going?"

"Up the coast. You get off the street, get us a car tomorrow and be waiting for my call."

Pascual calls her name but she is running now, ducking up a narrow lane into the old city. Pascual follows but she turns a corner, and even though he breaks into a run, by the time he has reached the corner there is no sign of her; in the Gothic Quarter there are too many places to disappear.

Pascual's skin crawls as he crosses the Ramblas; he is a swimmer who knows there is a shark in the water, somewhere close. Night has fallen and there is bitter weather coming. On the promenade people are in a hurry and nobody looks at him.

He hurries to the mouth of the alley where Larbi's shop lies. The Algerian is in an armchair behind the long counter. Only his eyes move as Pascual approaches. He returns Pascual's greeting warily and finally rises, folds his newspaper and lays it down. "I need the van," says Pascual.

Larbi frowns at the newspaper as he squares it with the edge of the counter. "I thought you were still in custody."

"For what? For being shot at?"

Larbi shrugs. "There was a lot of speculation."

"And all of it foolish. Can I have the van tomorrow?"

Larbi shuffles, scratches, fails to meet Pascual's gaze. *"Pas question.* Sorry."

"We had a deal."

"I don't need any trouble with the police."

"What trouble? You lend me the van. There's nothing criminal about that."

"Can't do it. Wait for me here a minute." Larbi shuffles off and disappears into the back room, whence noises of jangling keys issue faintly. He returns in a few seconds with a roll of thousand peseta notes and counts out four of them. "There. I believe we're quits now. Sorry, my friend, but the van I can't do."

Pascual glowers. Finally he sweeps the money off the counter and stuffs it in his pocket, making for the door. He pauses at the mouth of the alley, scanning the Ramblas, then flees into the Metro. He has no credit left with Father Costa but he has remembered the priest's battered little Ibiza.

"I have a great favor to ask you," says Pascual, ducking inside the instant the priest opens the door.

"Another?" says Father Costa, with no apparent irony.

"I need to borrow a car. Can you let me have it tomorrow?"

"First the coat and now the car," says the priest.

"I'm sorry about the coat, I should have asked."

"Don't worry about it. Why do you need the car?"

"It's an imposition, I know. I'm willing to pay you for it." Pascual pulls Larbi's banknotes from his pocket. The priest gapes at him, astonished. "How much would you ask to rent the car for two days?"

"Put your money away, my son. Will you drink a glass of beer?"

Pascual shifts gears, exhales, stashes the money. He takes off the coat and tosses it on the couch. "Thank you, that's very kind."

Father Costa produces beer and glasses from a small refrigerator. "Now. Why do you need the car?"

"I need it to get some money. To finance my getaway. I'm leaving town."

"That doesn't surprise me. And where are you going to get this money?"

"From an uncle, up in the hills, somewhere near Vic."

"An uncle? Would that be Miquel? I thought he was here in Barcelona."

"No, no. Miquel will have nothing to do with me. This is, I don't know, perhaps uncle is the wrong term. Distant cousin perhaps. Some old favorite of my mother's I've kept in touch with. I went up there last year to see him. I got him on the phone today and told him what was what, and he's going to lend me a little cash to get to Paris."

"What is he, a farmer? I thought your mother's people were all good urban *burgueses*."

"We all came down from the hills at some point. I think he's the last remnant of the old landed branch of the family."

Handing him a glass, the priest says, "Isn't there a train that goes to Vic?"

"Of course. But he lives beyond Vic, I don't know how many kilometers outside of town."

"And he can't meet you in town? He's stranded up there in the hills?" Father Costa asks with a look of perfect innocence, devoid of suspicion.

Pascual raises his hands. "I don't know. He told me to come to the farm. I think it's hard for him to get away."

"And when will you return it?"

"The day after tomorrow," says Pascual with utterly unjustified assurance. "Perhaps tomorrow evening if I have no trouble finding the place. I can probably make it a day trip." He has given this part of it no thought; the crucial thing is to drive off in it.

The priest stands above him looking down at Pascual with absorption, a look Pascual could never weather as a child and from which he takes refuge in a swallow of beer. "Tell me the truth," the priest says finally. "Are you running from the police?"

Pascual stiffens, wounded. "Absolutely not. I'm the victim in this, for God's sake. What I told you was the absolute truth."

The priest wanders back across the room, stares for a moment out the tall window into the night. "You have a driver's license, I take it?"

"Certainly." Pascual has possessed a number of them in a variety of names and even earned a legitimate one in France long ago.

With his back turned Father Costa speaks. "I'll need it in the morning. You can have it by noon. Try and get it back tomorrow evening. In one piece, if you could."

12

The Manhattan offers a range of *tapas* that, if they will never draw gastronomic tourists, will feed a hungry man in a pinch. Pascual's appetite has returned with a vengeance after a day of shock and privation. He is an expert at economy; a dish of tripe with a plate of bread to soak up the gravy and a glass of *tinto* will fill him up for three hundred pesetas. He finishes the wine and waits; the appointed time has come and gone and Pascual has begun to fear that Katixa is lost. When the phone behind the bar rings, he tries not to look as the owner snarls into the phone. Manolo is his confidant but the boss has never approved of him. "Pascual!" the owner calls finally, holding the phone on high. Pascual answers and rushes to the bar. The look he gets as he takes the phone says, Don't make a habit of this.

"I thought you said they knew you there," says Katixa, coolly.

"Where are you?" As soon as he asks, Pascual knows she will never answer.

"At the North Pole. Where do you think I am?"

"All right, all right. Everything going well?"

"Fine. What about you?"

"I've got a car."

"Well done. Meet me in Vic tonight, then."

"Give me an address."

"There's a bar on the main square, called the Snack. Be there at six. Don't speak to me, just have a drink and then walk out when I come in to buy cigarettes. I'll follow you to the car. Got it?"

"Got it." Pascual will do anything to talk to her for a few seconds longer. "What if there's a problem?"

"Solve it." A second or two goes by and Katixa's voice softens. "If I don't turn up, hang about for at least a day. Then go back to Barcelona and wait. I'll contact you at the bar."

"Fine, understood."

"*Ciao,* then."

"Wait."

"What?"

Pascual is suddenly aware of men at his elbow, in his face. "Nothing. Take care of yourself."

"Always. You too."

Pascual hands back the phone. "I'm not running a telephone exchange here," says the owner.

Pascual shrugs. "What can I do? Women have ways of finding us."

"Ah." Appeased, the boss shakes his head. "There is that. There's no hiding from a woman who wants something."

It has been years since Pascual ventured into the Catalan hinterland and he has only the vaguest idea of the geography. He fights his way out of the city through a tangle of expressways, hoping to glimpse a helpful sign before he winds up in France or Andorra. He finally stops for a *carajillo* and directions at a roadside tavern in the vicinity, he thinks, of Granollers and then gratefully finds his way onto the N152 and climbs into the hills. By six he is rolling into Vic.

Vic is a cathedral town at the confluence of a couple of minor rivers in a moderately wide valley, a very old town and middling prosperous. Pascual shoots through the outlying developments on a long straight branch off the N152 and then finds himself channeled into a narrow street that winds around the old city on its perch above a rocky riverbed. He does a lap like Jackie Stewart at the Nürburgring and in desperation breaks off and follows signs to the train station, where he intelligently surmises he will be able to park the car. Then he limps back up a long uphill street, sweating on his injured leg, following signs to the Plaça Major.

Here an arcaded ensemble of old stone buildings encloses a broad empty space where there will no doubt be a market on Saturday, and Pascual senses immediately he is far from the cosmopolitan precincts of Barcelona. When speaking Catalan, Pascual feels he is masquerading; his roots, such as they are, are certainly not in the pure Catalan earth of towns such as this. He slinks guiltily around three sides of the square, hands in his pockets, before finding the Snack tucked under the arcade with a handful of tables on the pavement in front.

Inside he is reassured. A bar is a bar, and this is not so different from Barcelona: smoke and conversation. Pascual makes his way down a long narrow room, attracting little notice. He orders a beer and leans on the bar, facing the door. With a cigarette going he eavesdrops, monitoring the late-afternoon concerns of a comfortable provincial middle class. Sex, soccer, money, sex. As the beer goes down Pascual's tension eases, and then Katixa walks in.

He manages not to betray himself as they make eye contact; she is splendid again, today in tight black jeans and the leather jacket, hair flying free, a carryall over her shoulder. Pascual turns to his beer so as not to stare and listens as she pushes through the crowd and asks for cigarettes in unapologetic Castilian. The barman turns to the shelf; if Katixa is attracting notice it is for her looks. Pascual remembers with a start that the plan calls for him to leave first and he sets the beer down and shoves off.

Outside darkness has fallen but the population of the square has grown. Lights are on and children are milling and shouting. There is a nasty damp wind and Pascual turns up his collar and makes for the street that leads down to the station. He pauses to light another cigarette and let Katixa catch up, resisting the urge to look for her. The walk is much easier downhill. He gets into the car and waits.

He sees her in the mirror and leans to open the door for her. Pascual preempts any greetings by grasping the back of her neck and pulling her to him; he has been waiting for this kiss. It is long and healing. "My love. How are you?"

"Tired. I've covered a lot of ground in twenty-four hours."

"You like the car?"

"It's not exactly a Rolls, is it?" They watch commuters straggle out of the station. Pascual caresses her, runs fingers through her hair. "Are you sure you got out of the city clean?" she asks.

"I picked up the car inside a guarded complex and left by a side exit. They'd have had to read my mind to be prepared to follow. Anyway, nothing stayed in the mirror for very long."

Katixa nods and shifts on the seat, looking out of the windows.

A train is approaching and people are drifting through the car park. "Let's get going. I'll navigate for you."

Pascual leaves the car park and blunders only twice before Katixa steers him onto a road heading out of town. Lights are visible across the valley floor. A drive of a couple of kilometers through the countryside takes them into a village. Pascual sees a sign: Sant Julià. There is a grid of dark treelined streets, villas behind long walls. Katixa directs him, leaning forward on the seat, uncertain. "Here. Right and then the second house on the left."

The villa is two stories high and has a tile roof. There is a balcony with plants in urns and many shuttered windows. Katixa gets out of the car and unlocks the gate with a key she produces from her bag. Pascual drives through and parks at the side of the house, following her signals.

"Who lives here?" asks Pascual in a hushed voice, standing at the foot of the front steps, staring up at the dark facade through droplets of rain.

"Nobody. A textile maker from Barcelona built it and spent summers here until he died. His family sometimes rents it out in the summer. I don't know how Bordagorri did it, but he managed to get the keys. From a son whose politics veered left, I think. Bordagorri was good at that, finding people who would help him. When I was here two weeks ago the electricity and water were functional and there was gas for the stove."

"And nobody will be looking for you here? We're not walking into an etarra ambush?"

"It was Bordagorri's own private bolt-hole. It's never a bad idea to have one in this business."

"And how do you know about it, then?"

"I was here with him once." The answer hangs in the air for a moment and then she says, "Jealous?"

Pascual shakes his head. "One day you must tell me how it felt to kill him."

"I didn't have time to think about it."

Pascual looks at dark windows. "But you thought to take the keys?"

"I took every key he had and tried them all until one worked." She mounts the steps and fits a key to the door. The door swings open and she pushes into a dark hallway. Pascual follows. Katixa switches on a light to reveal a high ceiling, a stairway to the right. Their steps echo on a tile floor; the house is dank and cold. There is a living room furnished with massive modern sofas and armchairs, a dining room with a long table and china in a glass cabinet. There is no clutter, no signs of life. Katixa leads him to a kitchen resplendent with white tiles and devoid of food or utensils. She opens a cabinet. "I left a few supplies here. Hungry?"

"What's upstairs?"

"Bedrooms, bathrooms, the usual."

Pascual explores. In most of the bedrooms the beds are not made up. In one he finds a sheet and two blankets lying rumpled on a bare mattress, and a pillow with no pillowcase. He listens as Katixa comes up the stairs.

In the doorway she says, "There are some bedclothes in the closet there. We might be able to find another pillow and make the bed properly."

Pascual pins her against the wall. "No need." He kisses her again, an arm around her waist and a hand in her hair, crushing her. Pascual wants to fuse with Katixa, ingest her. Breath whistles through her nose and she whimpers once or twice, faintly, during the long kiss. Pascual disengages at last with a noise deep in the throat. *"Mi vida,"* he says.

Katixa's lips are at his ear. She says his name once, twice. *"Cariño."*

"We won't need blankets."

Katixa runs a finger down the ridge of his nose, lets him catch it with his lips. "We have work to do."

"Now?"

"Tonight. We go to bed now, we'll never get up."

Pascual locks his arms around her. "I need you."

Katixa closes her eyes. Pascual kisses her again and she responds. Her mouth is warm and moist. Her hand slides down between his legs and gently squeezes. "Perhaps we can make an arrangement," she says.

Katixa is a fellatrix *par excellence*. Coming in her mouth, Pascual gasps out her name.

13

Pascual wakes in the dark to the sound of the wind. He is lying across the bed, wrapped in blankets, trousers around his ankles, boots still on. The door to the hall is open and there is light from downstairs. Pascual is adrift. When he remembers, he untangles himself from the covers and pulls up his trousers.

Katixa is in the kitchen. She has lit the stove, and the kitchen is now passably warm. From the cupboard she has produced cheese, biscuits, half a *butifarra,* a mostly full bottle of wine. Pascual leans over her at the table and wraps his arms around her, face in her hair. This is what they mean, he thinks. Before this I was an animal, blundering in the dark. "Let me love you," he says.

Katixa squeezes his hand. "Later. When we come back."

"How long have I been asleep?" he says after a moment, releasing her and taking the other chair.

"Not long. Eat something." She produces a pocket knife and they make a meal of it at the table, passing the bottle back and forth. Outside, a filthy night is brewing. Rain splatters at the window. Pascual cannot take his eyes off Katixa, dark eyes and serene features, always focused on what she is doing.

"I've found our way out of the country," says Katixa, slicing sausage.

"What a woman you are. Tell me."

"There is a man in Palamós. A Frenchman. Filthy rich and useless. He has a boat."

"And he'll help us for a price."

"Maybe not even for a price. He'll take some cultivating, but he's the type who'll do it for the adventure. I've seen them before; used them."

"And he's competent to get us to Morocco?"

"That's not much of a run. It's a big seaworthy boat, a motor cruiser. He says he mostly slides along the coast from here to Italy and back, but he's taken it as far as Turkey. The man's completely idle and always in search of a party. So we'll give him one."

Pascual takes a pull on the bottle. "Just what kind of cultivation is it likely to take?"

One eyebrow raised, Katixa says, "Heavens, I believe the boy's jealous again. Look, so far it's only taken some concentrated flirtation. If it takes more than that, it's a small price to pay for a clean escape, isn't it?"

Pascual has no answer. He sets the bottle gently on the table. "So what's the plan?"

"The plan is we dig up the money tonight and hightail it to Palamós. I've got a date with the Frenchman tomorrow night. I'll make the proposal then."

"What if he says no?"

"If worse comes to worst we'll pull off a nice genteel hijacking."

Seconds pass. "I thought we were finished with that type of thing."

The look on Katixa's face is wary. "I'm not sure this is the time to be squeamish."

Pascual remembers a hole in a door, bleeding. "I won't hurt anybody. I'm finished with that." He reaches for Katixa's hand. "We're finished with it. Remember what it did to us."

Katixa blinks back at him. She disengages her hand. "Look, I don't anticipate any trouble. He'll do it for the fun of it. We'll be there in a week."

Pascual's stomach is suddenly lighter than air. A week. He rises and goes to the window. "We have to go out in that, eh?"

"Nobody else will be out in it."

"That's a point. Where's the cache?"

"About fifteen kilometers up in the hills. The hard part was finding the place with Bordagorri's wretched map. Tonight it should be easy."

"What is it, a cave?"

"Just a hole in the ground. Actually a watertight metal case set into the earth at the foot of some rocks, in a hollow. Easy to find, even in the dark, if you know the landmarks. And just a layer of earth to scrape off to get at it. I found an old spade out the back."

Pascual nods. The desire to get a sniff of five million francs is in close combat with the desire to remain warm and dry. "Well, let's get to work, then."

Katixa looks at Father Costa's old woolen coat with amusement. "Don't you have a hat? Here." She digs in her bag on the floor and comes out with a *boina* from her wardrobe of disguises. "It'll keep the rain off your head, at least."

Pascual starts the car while Katixa probes with the torch around a pile of junk at the back of the house and finds the spade where she discarded it two weeks ago. She throws it on the back seat and steers Pascual out of town. They go a few kilometers and she directs him off the highway onto a narrow road that climbs. They are quickly in the hills. Wind buffets the car and throws rain at the windscreen. Pascual is an urban creature and would call himself lost, but Katixa appears to know where she is going. The road rises and twists; the headlights wash over trunks of pine, falls of rock. Katixa is leaning forward on the seat, intent on the curving shoulder of the road unwinding under the lights. They pass an occasional farm, windows glowing in the dark. There are signs pointing up narrow tracks to apparently inhabited places. Pascual cannot believe people would choose to live in this isolation.

They pass another turnoff and Katixa says, "About three and a half kilometers now to a track you'll see just past a big bare rock face. Up the track until it levels off, then a hard slog until we find the hollow." They go slowly in the uncertain conditions, wipers working fast, rain whipping across the headlight beams. There is no talk until Katixa says, "There. Just past the slab of rock." Pascual leaves the paved road and climbs onto gravel.

This part of the journey is a trial to the nerves. The uphill track is soft at the best of times and is rapidly becoming mud. They go on endlessly, wheels spinning, crawling over humps of rock that threaten the underside of the little car. "How much further?" asks Pascual, when he has lost all sense of time and distance.

"I don't know. When we come to a level space we'll be there."

They press on and suddenly there is a rough amphitheater in the side of the mountain, ringed by trees. "Here," says Katixa. "Swing right, run the lights over the hillside." Pascual takes the car in a tight circle over rough ground until Katixa says, "Stop." Pascual would have missed it, but in the headlights he can see a cleft in the side of the bowl, a little gully running up into darkness. "Get as close as you can."

Pascual stops three meters from the mouth of the gully. He can see a trickle of water emerging onto the floor of the bowl. "We're going to climb up that?"

"Your shoes will dry. Bring the spade."

Pascual switches off. Outside, wind is sighing and rain is tapping on the car. "All right. I'm game." He reaches over the seat for the spade.

Shoes, trousers, coat. They all may dry, Pascual thinks, halfway up the gully, but I will never be warm again. There is footing on either side of the icy rivulet, but it is tenuous and their feet have a way of sliding into the water. Even Katixa is swearing, just ahead of him. The beam of the torch shows nothing but the gleam of cold trickling water in the dark. In a minute or two he feels the cleft opening out, and then the ground levels off; he bumps into Katixa from behind. Pneumonia, Pascual thinks. Hypothermia. Finding the Eiffel Tower in this weather would be a feat. "This way," says Katixa.

Pascual follows her silhouette against the feeble glow of the torch; the wind is sucking heat from his body. The torchlight slides over a sheer wall of rock and goes left. "Are you with me?" Katixa asks.

"Right behind you."

Pascual senses rock closing in. A lessening of the wind, a change in the darkness tell him they have reached the hollow. "Still with me?" says Katixa, close by. Pascual reaches out and finds her shoulder. "Give me the spade," she says, and hands him the light.

They are sheltered from the wind here and Pascual scans with the torch, finding rock ascending on three sides. "Put the light over here," says Katixa. Pascual watches as she plunges the spade into the earth, with a sharp chopping noise, again and again. He has begun to shiver. The spade strikes something solid and Katixa says, "Here."

"Let me dig." Pascual clutches at her sleeve, gropes for the spade, exchanges it for the light.

"You don't have to dig. Just clear the lid, make a bit of a trench around the edge so we can open it."

Pascual probes to find the dimensions of the box and then sets to feverishly. Under the sweep of the spade something reflective is emerging. Katixa kneels as Pascual clears mud and gravel from around the edges. "Enough," she says. She is feeling in the mud. She curses once and then with a grunt, she wrenches upward and the earth opens. Pascual kneels beside her. The light falls on a black canvas Pullman bag with leather handles and trim. The bag is lying in a sizeable tin trunk embedded in the earth, on top of a layer of tightly taped plastic bundles. The plastic is clear and through it he can make out a black metallic shine.

Pascual reaches into the trunk and grasps the handle of the bag and pulls. As it comes clear Katixa slams the trunk closed. "Here, hold the light." She takes the bag and fumbles for a moment at a zipper. She tears it open and raises the flap. Crouching, their heads together, Pascual and Katixa can see Pierre and Marie Curie gazing at them, row after row of banknotes, the figure 500 prominent. *"Hostia puta,"* says Pascual reverently.

Katixa closes the case and zips it. "There's our Caribbean villa," she says.

She holds the light while Pascual shovels earth back over the lid of the trunk and stamps on it. "Done," he says. "Let's move."

"Can you carry the case?"

"Got it. You take the spade." Pascual hefts the bag; it is heavy, but he will get it to the car if he has to roll down the hill with it. "Know where you're going?"

"I'll find the way. You just stay close behind." As they leave the hollow the wind hits them again; the rain cutting across the beam of the torch is horizontal. Pascual stays three steps behind Katixa as she veers away from the wall. The heavy case knocks against his leg, threatening his balance. His foot slips into cold water and he topples onto the ground.

Katixa shines the light on him. "All right?"

"Fine. I just took care of the last dry spot." He hauls himself up, rescues the case from the rivulet. The light sweeps away as Katixa resumes looking for the way down. Pascual moves toward higher ground, looking for firm footing. He stamps his benumbed feet, bends to run a hand over the bag, worried about soaking their five million francs. Ahead there is a scuffling noise and a sharp curse from Katixa. Pascual looks up but the light has disappeared.

Utterly. In Pascual's face are needle points of rain coming out of nothingness, pitch black. He calls Katixa's name. In reply he hears her, but indistinctly, from far away. "The light!" he shouts.

"I dropped it," he hears her call. She has fallen and slid partway down the gully, he realizes. In panic, Pascual starts forward, slips again, puts down a hand to steady himself and stops. Idiot, he thinks. Follow the stream. He turns and realizes he is no longer certain where it is. He kneels and begins to crawl, dragging the suitcase.

At a shout from Katixa he turns his head to see ghostly light sweeping through treetops, to his right. Katixa has found the torch. Pascual turns, rises, makes for the light. Just as he hears Katixa shout, "Follow the stream," his feet go out from under him. He hits the ground hard, clinging to the case for dear life, and begins to slide. In the dark he seems to slide for miles, for hours. He fetches up against a tree, one knee jammed against the trunk. The heavy case is tugging him downhill. He raises his eyes to the heavens and sees nothing, a black hole.

"Katixa!" Darkness and rain, nothing but the wind to hear. He struggles to disengage himself from the tree and find footing, cursing with every movement. Facing uphill again, he looks for light but there is none. Pascual has slid off the face of the earth. Straining, he hauls the case upward, gets both hands on it, pushes, digs for footing. He realizes there is no chance of climbing back up the slope.

He rests, face to the ground, and vents a long string of polyglot obscenity. There is no place to go but down. His limbs are intact, he believes, though all his previous injuries are suddenly reasserting themselves. Pascual rolls over, wrestles the case onto his chest, and begins a careful, controlled slide downhill. From tree to tree, rock to rock, digging in with his heels, vividly aware that if a precipice lies below he will find out only as he goes over the edge, he descends.

At the bottom he lies in the rain, grateful for the feel of solid earth under his rump. He can see nothing but his other senses tell him there are trees, perhaps an expanse of level ground before him. He struggles to his feet. "Katixa!" he launches into the wind, back up the slope. He listens in vain and sees no light in the trees. Pascual curses again. Idiot, clown, *boy scout de mierda*. He reviews his movements of the last half hour. They were on a road with the uphill slope to their right. They left the road and climbed, tending in the same direction. If he continues to work downhill, he must hit the road again. He can then turn left, walk till he finds the rock face marking the track, and climb up to find the car and, presumably, Katixa, who is too sensible to do anything other than wait for him there.

Pascual goes on the seat of his trousers, letting the heavy suitcase pull him downward, sensing trees as they loom out of the rain, fending them off with his feet. After several minutes he has begun to believe that he will go on sliding until he reaches the sea. Miraculously he has not lost the beret but rain is seeping down his collar.

Pascual has ceased to believe in the road when he finally tumbles onto it. The dark is more expansive here; there is a valley opening out before him. He gets what bearings he can, shifts the case from one hand to the other, and begins to trudge. Pain shoots from his knee to his hip with every step. The weight of the case quickly increases to several tons. There is a sort of visibility that allows him to distinguish hillside from sky, but nothing more. He realizes that recognizing the rock face where they turned off the road is much easier said than done. The rain has slackened but the wind cuts like a knife. When he stops to rest, the cold is intolerable; when he moves again it is as if he never rested.

It takes fifteen minutes for despair to set in. He can see just enough to stay on the road and he is exhausted, unable to drag the case another ten meters. His only hope is to keep marching until daylight or to find shelter. If he stops he will freeze.

The house appears as a lessening of the dark, just off the road and downhill. As he draws closer Pascual can make it out, low, formless, just perceptible. He staggers off the road toward it and slips, losing his footing. He slides again, down a short slope, and comes to rest perhaps ten meters from the wall of the house. He rises painfully, hefts the bag and approaches, things taking shape: white wall, small windows. He puts a hand on the wall and feels his way along to a corner. It is a large house, an old *masia* perhaps, the classic Catalan mountain farmhouse, thick and solid, built to withstand winter and banditry. Pascual rounds the corner and there is shelter: a gaping doorway in a structure tacked to the end of the house, a stable perhaps. Pascual ducks inside out of the wind.

He can see nothing, but he can smell decay. There have not been horses here for a long time, but smaller animals have left droppings. Pascual stumbles through the dark, scraping the rough fieldstone wall, thinking only of getting as far away from the wind as he can. The wall ends and there is a door that gives way at his touch; he pitches through into a deeper darkness.

Pascual drops the suitcase and stands listening. Outside, the wind sighs; here, in the dank still air he can almost believe he is warm. The house reeks of abandonment. He takes a careful step or two, arms stretched out in front, crunching debris under the soles of his boots. A match, he thinks. Pascual's hands are too frozen to get his coat unbuttoned. He rubs them, blows on them, curses, shivers. He tries again and manages to open the coat and get the box of matches out of his pocket. Striking a match is another trial but he succeeds; a tiny flame gives him his first glimpse of his shelter. He sees an uneven floor scattered with bits of wood, an overturned chair, a table, before the match sputters out. A second match takes him to the table. On the table is a candle in the neck of a wine bottle. Pascual stares at it until the match burns his finger. With a third match he lights the candle.

He is in a kitchen. Held aloft, the candle shows him the enormous hearth. The kitchen may once have sheltered generations of *pagesos,* but now there is only wreckage: another chair with a leg gone missing, broken glass, crumbling plaster. In the fireplace, litter lies on a bed of ashes. Nobody has cooked here in years but somebody has eaten things wrapped in plastic and paper. The flame of the candle wavers; cold drafts crisscross the kitchen. Pascual returns to the door and shoves it closed, but it creaks open again, the latch gone and the hinges awry. Pascual raises the candle and sees a door in the wall opposite the fireplace. He decides the suitcase will keep where it is until he explores a little. Shivering, he goes in search of a corner warm enough to lie down in.

He is transfixed the moment he goes through the doorway; the first thing that appears in the unsteady glow from the candle is the inverted crucifix on the opposite wall. Pascual peers at it, steps closer, holds the candle higher. Why the crucifix should be hung with Christ's head to the floor baffles him until he sees the goat's skull on the wall above it and makes out the words scrawled in red up near the ceiling: *Ave Satanás.*

Pascual is a realist, impervious to the supernatural, immune to the creepy-crawly. His breath whistles out in a noise of contempt. Village idiots need a place to play, he thinks. Nonetheless this is perhaps not the room in which he wants to wait out the night. He takes a few steps closer to identify what lies on the floor beneath the crucifix.

There is a low altar made of boards laid across bricks. On it are two objects, a bowl and a long, evil-looking knife with a wooden handle. The altar and the cracked tiles beneath it are stained black with irregular blotches.

Pascual does not believe in Satan, but he believes in derangement. He wheels, lifts the candle, sees shadows leap. The room behind him is strewn with scraps of wood, shards of pottery. There is more graffiti on the other walls but Pascual does not trouble to make it out. There is a wooden stairway with steps missing, two other doors. Pascual has lost his desire to explore. He steadies and tells himself that anything that needs a candle to see by will bleed. He takes the knife from the altar and retreats to the kitchen, watching shadows.

In the kitchen he drags the table across the tiles and shoves it against the outside door to keep it shut. Now, he hopes, neither drafts nor demented peasants can get in. He scrapes debris into the fireplace with his foot. There are enough scraps of cardboard and paper to light kindling. He sets the candle on the floor and kneels to sort combustible from noncombustible. Mixed with the paper and cardboard are scraps of plastic with black electrical tape attached, cut through in places. Pascual sorts clumsily with stiff hands. When he has a pile that will burn he musters his courage and returns to the other room. Striking a blow against superstition, he dismantles the altar and gathers a few other scraps of wood. Back in the kitchen he sets the candle on the table and pokes rubbish and kindling together. In two minutes he has a tenuous fire going. He lays the larger pieces of wood carefully on the flames.

When Pascual is certain the fire will sustain itself he drags the black canvas suitcase into the corner by the fireplace, away from the door. He blows out the candle and sets it down along with the knife.

Then, in utter exhaustion, he sinks to the floor, back to the wall. The glow of the fire lights the kitchen fitfully; the doorway to the devil's room looms black in the far wall. Pascual keels over gently and rests his head on the bag with five million francs in it. For the first time he believes he may live until morning. He dozes but does not sleep; fitful dreams probe at the edges of consciousness, the room growing darker as the fire dies.

He wakes suddenly, in blackness and cold, with the conviction that he is not alone. The fire is dead, he has slept after all, and something close at hand has moved. Pascual lies rigid. He can make out the faintest orange glow in the fireplace. Outside the wind sighs. Incredulous, appalled, Pascual hears soft footsteps coming distinctly across the tiles from the direction of the inner room. He reaches for the knife and knocks over the bottle with an atrocious noise. The footsteps cease for a second but resume, coming toward him, slow and measured. Pascual finds the handle of the knife and scrambles to his feet. He can see nothing at all but he can hear the devil, almost upon him now. There are too many footsteps; the room is full of demons.

There is a tremendous braying reverberation, hell itself opening up. By the time Pascual has realized that it is the sound of the table being dragged away from the door, something is flying out of the darkness into his face and he is stunned and thrown back into the corner by a blow on the head, lights flashing. He staggers but he will not die on the floor; with a spasm of terror he launches himself out into the room in a blind charge. He stumbles over whatever hit him and goes down again. There is somebody above him sensed more than seen. He strikes out with the knife in a vicious upward swipe meant to eviscerate. There is a hiss of indrawn breath as the blade catches something, just a snick, and Pascual is scrambling away. Others are scrambling too: the door slams open against the wall, and the scuffle of feet on earth is outside now. Pascual has found a wall to put his back against and he sits with the knife held in front of him, listening to the sound of automobile doors opening and closing. When the engine starts with a roar, seemingly just outside the door, he wonders if he has lost his reason.

Tires claw, the engine accelerates in a rising whine as the car tears away into the night. Pascual is left in the sudden quiet, drafts whistling about his ears again, to sort out his senses. There were two of them, he thinks, and I did not close them out, I closed them in. The car was in the stable; I must have brushed it in the dark. There is a knot on his head where the chair hit him.

Pascual sits pressed against the wall until the open doorway begins to grow light. He has finally realized the significance of the scraps of plastic bound with tape. His right hand cramps around the handle of the knife; there will be no more ambushes tonight.

14

Pascual steals out of the crumbling *masia* at first light, leaving the suitcase just inside the door. The rain has abated. He sees no signs of human life. He figures his chances at fifty-fifty: if he has scared them off, the car is his salvation and he will find Katixa there; if not, returning to the car is suicide. Pascual decides he must at least look. He has only a vague idea of the topography, but in the growing light he is able to find the rock face marking the turnoff. The rest is mere physical toil, a hard slog uphill. Anxiety for Katixa torments him at every step.

He approaches warily, scanning the woods, stopping to listen, knowing his precautions are laughable. He sees and hears no one. The car is empty. He gets in and starts the engine; if he is not dead yet, it is probably safe and he considers sounding the horn but decides against it. He has no better choice than to drive and hope to find Katixa on the road. He descends the track, finds the *masia* and throws the suitcase in the trunk.

Pascual drives out of the hills without finding Katixa. There is light traffic: a car or two, a road-hogging tractor. Pascual finds the road to Vic and rolls on to the valley floor. He considers trying to find the villa but decides that if he is right about who came at him in the dark, the villa must be off-limits.

Pascual speeds back down the N152. He is back in Barcelona by noon. The mud on his clothing has dried enough so that he can brush some of it off, but the *conserje* at the residence nonetheless gives him the look reserved for street rabble. Father Costa is not in, which Pascual has anticipated; he leaves the car keys with the *conserje*. The five million francs are still locked in the trunk.

Aware that his judgment may be clouded, Pascual decides that he must risk a quick stop at the pension. He is becoming habituated to fear. The Metro takes him to Liceu and in a couple of minutes he is on Avinyó again, having doubts and looking behind him every three steps.

The widow Puig is speechless with terror at the sight of him. She has grown older in a handful of days. The floors and walls have been scrubbed clean of blood. Pascual finds a new door with a new lock on his room. He confronts the widow Puig.

"I thought you were never coming back," she says, backing away, blanched and trembling.

"I'm paid up to the end of the month."

"The police told me you wouldn't be back. I thought they took you to jail."

"Did you rent my room?"

"Just this morning. Forgive me. I didn't know."

"I'm not going to hurt you, for Christ's sake. Where are my things?"

"One moment." She scurries into her private quarters. She

reappears dragging Pascual's overstuffed duffel bag along the floor, staggering like an exhausted mule in the traces. "There are two boxes, too. The books and tapes."

Pascual takes delivery of his possessions. "You owe me a refund."

"Yes, yes. Only I don't know what I have on hand. I'll have to see." Pascual has no idea if she is legally bound to refund his money but realizes she would lick his shoes clean to be rid of him.

"I'll settle for two thousand pesetas and a chance to take a shower."

She agrees. Clean, shaven and changed, Pascual consolidates his estate. "Keep the books. Start a library. Anything in this box you can have." He is taking a few clothes, toiletries, his tape player and a few chosen cassettes. The widow Puig is standing with banknotes fanned out like a poker hand. Pascual folds them away and stands up. A notion strikes him. "Has anyone called for me?"

The widow Puig looks at him in shock and her mouth flaps silently for a moment. "Yes. There was a call. Montse, she said."

"Montse."

"Yes. She'd read the papers and was worried. I told her you'd disappeared. How was I to know you'd come back?"

"Nobody else?"

"Nobody else." Under Pascual's glare she sags onto a chair. With the duffel bag over his shoulder Pascual abandons ship.

In the Manhattan the post-lunch crowd is working up enthusiasm for the coming siesta. Pascual stows the bag under the table, has a *carajillo* and asks Manolo if there have been any calls for him.

"Only one. You did better twenty years ago when you had fuzz on your lip."

Pascual is giddy with relief. "One will have to do, I suppose. Any message?"

"She'll call back between four and six. She wouldn't leave a number."

"I suppose I'll have to be here, then."

"You'd better be. The *patrón* is tired of playing switchboard."

"Tell him I'm sorry. My phone was disconnected."

Manolo nods at the bag under the table. "Moving?"

"Going on a little trip."

"Nice time of year for it." Manolo smiles, looking out at the street, where litter scuds along the pavement under a dishwater sky.

Pascual limps across the road and through the gate of the Industrial School. Inside the residence the *conserje* beckons him over to the desk. "Are you a resident?"

"No." So far Pascual has managed to dodge the question, tuning entrances and exits so no one realizes he has spent the night. "I'm paying a call on Father Costa. Is there a problem?"

"What's in the bag?"

"Books for the padre. Call him up and ask him yourself. Tell him Pascual's here." He nods at the phone. With a look that betrays profound doubts about the priest's judgment, the *conserje* waves him up the stairs.

Father Costa is just making coffee. He greets Pascual with a certain amount of reserve. "And how are things with the uncle?"

"Could be better. His health's going." Pascual dumps the bag on the floor.

The priest gives him a thoughtful look and pours the coffee. "And when do you leave for France?"

"Ah, well. Any day. I have to look into bus schedules and things, tie up a couple of loose ends. Any chance I could stay another night or two?"

Father Costa gives him his cup and makes a ceremony of sugar and spoons. "I suppose so, if you're discreet. You may revive a few scandalous rumors, but I daresay my reputation will survive. Can I offer you a *copa?*"

"Please." Pascual looks into his coffee. "Ah. I left a bag in the boot of your car. Some books and family papers and things from the uncle."

"I brought it up for you." The priest inclines his head toward a corner, where Pascual sees the canvas suitcase, smeared with mud.

"Ah, thanks." Sweat breaks out at his hairline. "Sorry about all the impositions. I'm greatly in your debt. Someday . . ." He is mumbling into his coffee cup.

"Don't mention it." Father Costa sets a snifter of cognac on the table at his elbow and retires to his armchair across the room. "You're exhausted."

"Didn't sleep much. You know these drafty old farmhouses. Cold as the devil. Impossible to heat; just throw another two or three blankets on the bed. Sorry I didn't make it back last night, by the way. The weather turned nasty and I felt sorry for the old man, up there all alone. It seemed a pity to dash off, especially after he was so decent about the money."

"Yes. Enough to get you to France, is it?"

He knows, thinks Pascual. "Enough."

Father Costa sits in his armchair, legs crossed, relaxed, sipping his coffee, looking at Pascual with a totally opaque expression. He is waiting for Pascual to say something, but Pascual has nothing to say. Pascual sets down the coffee and takes the cognac. He cups the snifter in two hands, staring into the amber liquid in desperation.

"Pascual," says the priest.

"Yes?"

"One of the great pleasures in my life over the past year has been to assist in your . . . rehabilitation."

"Very kind of you. I'm in your debt."

"Not at all. It was quite an interesting process. And I think we're nearly there."

Pascual drinks. "Nearly, eh? So what remains to be done?"

The priest's chin rises but his eyes remain fixed on Pascual. "Here's a first step. Adopt, just as an exercise in structure, a few of those rules that we have evolved to make human coexistence bearable on this execrable planet. You note that I am being careful to avoid putting it in theological terms, out of respect for your atheist sensibilities." Pascual nods. He can feel the noose tightening, just as he could always feel it in class, with the black-robed Jesuit coming slowly down the aisle toward his desk, each sentence irrefutable, inexorably exposing his miserable ignorance, sloth, inadequacy. Father Costa smiles. "I think you will find with practice that these . . . strictures give your life a certain tautness you may find pleasing, just as physical exercise gives the body a pleasing firmness."

Pascual raises his eyebrows in expectation. "May I suggest a rule to start with?" says Father Costa.

"Please do."

"Stop lying."

Pascual nods slowly. He stares into his glass. He wishes he could go to sleep. He takes a drink, looks at the rug. He looks at the patch of sunlight in the next room. "If I lie, it's to protect someone else," he says finally.

"I see. This all has something to do with your Arab?"

Pascual looks up, startled. "No. Nothing. This began before that."

The priest's square-jawed face is blank for a moment, then contracts in thought. "All right," he says. "I'm not going to interrogate you. Instead I'm going to give you a moral lecture." Pascual nods in acquiescence. "These rules I mentioned are what confine the unruly animal spirit into a shape that can be called human. Despite centuries of sophistry the rules are very simple. Thou shalt not kill, thou shalt not steal. Thou shalt not lie. Flout these rules at your peril. End of lecture."

Pascual tosses off the last of his cognac. He sets the *copa* down carefully on the table. "She's a fugitive," he says. "From the police and from her colleagues. She needs me." Pascual looks at the priest, aghast. He has said it.

Father Costa is intent, heavy brows low over the piercing eyes. For a long moment there is silence. "And I suppose you need her?" the priest says.

"Like air, like water," says Pascual. "Like the blood in my veins."

"There was another call for you," says Manolo. "Not the local talent, this one. Sounded foreign, English maybe."

Pascual stops dead. He has forgotten about the CIA. "Any message?"

"A number to ring. The *patrón* wrote it down somewhere. What can I serve you?"

Pascual orders a *fino* and sits on a bench along the interior wall, near the pinball machines. Darkness has fallen and just enough fear remains to make him cautious about sitting in brightly lit view of the street. Manolo brings the sherry and a slip of paper with a telephone number on it. Pascual takes one sip of the drink and considers odds for and against. He finally decides that in his present uncertainty another possible ally cannot hurt. He gets change at the bar and descends to the telephone on the lower level.

He punches in the number and waits. "Hello?" says a female voice in English.

"Pascual here."

"That was prompt. I wasn't sure you were still with us."

"You have news?"

"I've got something. Want to talk?"

"I'm listening."

"I'd rather do this face-to-face."

Pascual closes his eyes. "I'm not moving. I've had a rough twenty-four hours and my leg hurts and I'm going to sit right here. Come and have a drink with me. You can get a Coke."

There is a brief pause. "OK. Where's there?"

Pascual tells her how to get to the Manhattan and hangs up. He goes back and nurses his *fino*. He is working on his second when she appears. Today she is a little less conspicuously yanqui, in black jeans and a maroon sweater. "Charming," she says, sitting opposite him, turning to look at the mural over the bar with the faint tentative smile of the tourist. "That's New York, isn't it?"

"Hence the name. What can I get you to drink?" Manolo is approaching, studiously casual, wielding his towel.

"I may have that Coke, but I think I'll have him pour a little rum in it." She orders a Cuba Libre with perfect assurance and Manolo clicks his heels and gives a little bow, an absurd performance Pascual has never seen before. He taps his glass with a finger and Manolo retires.

"Do you have a name?" asks Pascual.

"Sure. You can call me Shelby."

"First name or last?"

"Take your pick."

Pascual shrugs. "What's the news?"

She settles with her elbows on the table, fingers laced, all business. "Well, there's not much, really. All I've been able to do is start a few balls rolling. I have to say, you're not exactly current business."

"Meaning?"

"Meaning nobody much gives a damn about you."

"There's been a lot of water under the bridge since they wrote me off, I'm sure."

"Wrote you off is right. 'So what?' was the main response I got when I told people what happened."

"They did tell me they couldn't make any promises. But aren't they even curious about how the PFLP penetrated a CIA cover?"

"Well, the main school of thought seemed to be that these things happen. There's a hell of a lot of Arab traffic through here, and some people said you probably just got spotted on the street. But I did get one person interested enough to start following a few trails. It may take a while. But he did seem to share your curiosity. He said it would be a nice little intellectual exercise."

"That's reassuring. If you talk to him again, remind him his little brainteaser bleeds."

"I'll do that. Did you ever wonder why they put you in that pension?"

"No. I guess I should have."

"Rome probably went through the locals to find it. Everybody's got a pet landlady or two."

Pascual remembers instances of the widow Puig's indulgence with regard to late rent; he always put it down to the fact that she liked him. "She's got some Africans, too. She told me the city pays her."

"That may even be true. I doubt she knows anything more than that somebody called her and asked about you, or told her you were coming, and that she could expect a little break on her property taxes or something. Why did you stay? You could have split, gone some-place else, and we wouldn't have been any wiser."

"I don't know. Inertia. Fatigue. I trusted them. God knows what I was thinking."

"It's not a mistake you're likely to repeat, I gather?"

"No."

Shelby smiles. "I did one other thing."

"What's that?"

"I talked to the people who are most likely to be interested in your old Popular Front playmates. I talked to the Israelis."

The telephone behind the bar rings.

Pascual watches the boss answer it. "Ah," he says absently. "Anybody there still remember me?" The boss says something to Manolo, who points at Pascual. The boss glares at him and gestures with the phone.

"Excuse me," says Pascual, rising. He pushes his way to the bar and takes the phone.

"Pascual," comes the distant voice, and Pascual goes weak with relief.

"What happened to you?" he says.

"Where is my luggage?" This is Katixa's no-nonsense voice.

"Don't worry. Your luggage is safe."

At the other end of the line there is an audible exhalation.

"You have it with you?"

"Yes."

"We have to meet."

"Fine. Are you all right?"

Something like a puff of laughter comes over the line. "Never better. What about you?"

"I've seen enough of the country for a while. When can we get together?"

"Now."

"You're in Barcelona?"

"Of course. Where's an easy place to meet?"

Pascual has turned his back to the bar to avoid the owner's sour look. Now he can see Shelby watching him over her shoulder. "When?"

"Now. As soon as possible."

Pascual rubs at his brow. "How about Sants station? Know where it is?"

"Sure. Where?"

"Out front, facing the plaza. I'll be waiting, say, at the far end of the pavement closest to the parking garage."

"Fine. I'm in a blue Audi 100. How soon can you be there?"

Pascual calculates and says, "Give me forty-five minutes. I'll have to shake some people here."

He returns to the table, slowly, and sits down. "Bad news?" asks Shelby, who he realizes is staring at him.

Pascual makes an effort to rally. "Nothing. Having trouble finding a place to sleep, that's all. Sorry. You were saying. About the Israelis."

"Yeah. Well, I got a call back from a man named Dan."

Pascual tries to focus. Too much is happening too fast. "Ah yes. The thousand-year-old man."

"The man of a thousand cigarettes anyway, judging from his voice."

Pascual fumbles for a cigarette. "He was my special friend in Israel. I was his project."

"He remembers you well."

"I don't suppose he wishes me well, too."

"Not that he particularly mentioned. He did say you might be worth a trip to Barcelona."

Pascual freezes with the match halfway to the cigarette. "He's coming here?"

"He was making noises about it. He's going to get back to me."

Pascual gets the cigarette going; he feels that the current is getting a bit strong and he has lost his paddle. In the silence Manolo arrives with the drinks. Pascual raises his glass. "Cheers," he says without cheer. He focuses on the baby face across the table and says, "How long have you been in this line of work?"

Deadpan, she says, "A couple of weeks. If I keep you alive they'll let me answer the phone next month."

Pascual blinks at her. "You're a riot," he says.

15

Pascual stands in front of the broad glass facade of the Sants terminal, looking for Katixa. Cars jockey for position along the curb. When the blue Audi swings over, Katixa at the wheel, it takes him by surprise. Pascual leaps in. "Where'd you get this thing?"

As he slams the door she is already pulling away. "Where the hell's the money?" Katixa does not look her best this evening; she is pale and her eyes betray fatigue and tension. "Relax. It's perfectly safe."

Katixa honks, swerves, accelerates. "Why didn't you bring it?"

"You didn't say to."

"Christ, do I have to spell everything out?"

Pascual stares, wounded. "Are we ready to sail tonight, then? I had the impression there were a few things left to arrange."

Katixa slows abruptly and parks at a corner. She puts on the hand brake and heaves a sigh, hands resting on the wheel. "Forgive me." In her face Pascual can read twenty-four hours of high-level stress. "It's a hell of a lot of money," she says, turning her face to his.

Pascual hooks an arm around her neck. "My love," he says. He brushes her lips with his, pulls her tighter. She twists on the seat and her arms go around him; he can feel her trembling.

Against his throat she breathes, "What happened to you? I had visions of you lying in the hills with a broken leg, freezing to death."

Pascual releases her, his hand lingering to caress her cheek. "And I was worried sick they'd got you."

"Who?"

"Your old friends. They missed you, eh? Good thing."

"What the hell are you talking about?"

"There was an old *masia* a kilometer down the road from where we turned off. I found it and ducked in out of the rain and somebody slugged me in the dark."

She frowns at him and says, "What makes you think it was etarras?"

"Somebody had visited the cache and drawn some weapons. The wrappings were on the floor."

There is a deep line of anxiety between Katixa's brows. "They let you go?"

"I put up a fight. I drew a little blood, I think."

Katixa is having trouble believing it, he sees. Finally she says, "God, they're close."

"I think there were two of them. They must have been watching the cache. Or planning to, only the weather kept them indoors. Anyway, it worries me. How did they know we were coming?"

She works on it for a few seconds. "Maybe they didn't. Maybe they're just watching likely spots. Bordagorri must have told somebody else about the place, or left another map."

"They took off in a car. I was afraid they'd see you on the road."

"No. I waited at the car until daybreak but you didn't come. Then I started walking and got a lift. I waited at the villa. Finally I walked into Vic and got a train."

"I was afraid to go back to the villa. I thought they'd know about it, too."

"Christ, and I thought it was safe." She closes her eyes for a moment, lets her head loll back against the headrest. "To hell with it, it doesn't matter now. What have you done with the money?"

"It's with a friend. Sitting in the corner of his room."

She vents a little whiff of laughter. "Somebody you trust, I hope."

"A priest."

"A priest? Good God."

"Don't worry. If it's not safe there, then where?"

"He doesn't know what's in it?"

"I told him it was family mementos," says Pascual.

Katixa looks doubtful. Her eyes flick away out the windscreen, into the mirror. Finally she says, "Fine. Is it all right there for a couple of days?"

"Maybe a couple. What's going on?"

"I need a little more time. I'm working on our ride to Morocco."

Pascual digs for a cigarette and matches. "The Frenchman?"

"Yes."

"Don't tell me about it," he says, lighting the cigarette.

"I'll give you a ring in a day or two. Then you can come and join me and we'll be off."

Pascual gives her Father Costa's number. "Phone during the day." There is a pause. Pascual smokes, watching cars pass, listening to the city. He puts his arm around Katixa again; she sags against him. Pascual stubs out the cigarette in the ashtray, half-smoked. "Spend the night with me," he says. "We'll get a room."

Katixa lays her head on his shoulder. Pascual closes his eyes, fingers in her hair; he will never let go. "Not tonight," Katixa says.

"Why?"

"I have to return the car."

"Ah. And whose is it?"

"Our mark rented it to gad about in while he's docked at Palamós. I gave him a story about needing to see my lawyer. He thinks I'm a textile heiress sorting out an estate. We're meeting for dinner tonight."

After a long moment Pascual says, "It's going well, then, is it?"

Katixa raises her head, pulls away. "Pascual, anything that happens is just business, remember that."

"What might happen?"

"Listen, imbecile. I'd fuck King Juan Carlos if it got us out of the country together, safe." She softens, looking into Pascual's stunned face. "It won't come to that. Have faith in me." Pascual nods. "I won't betray you." Katixa kisses him, and Pascual would rip out his heart and hand it to her if she asked.

Pascual downs a fried egg and chips in a bar across from the Clinical Hospital. The cook stands behind the bar with a cigarette dangling from his lips, surveying the light crowd with the hopeful look of a much-beaten dog when the whipping stops. Pascual nurses his *tinto* and worries about Katixa, worries about the money. He decides that whether or not the priest peeped, for the moment there is no better place for it than in his quarters.

He limps out into the night, sore and tired and reluctant to sleep on the priest's couch. Pascual has no desire to fuel unsavory rumors, even less desire to submit to Father Costa's scrutiny. Suddenly and with great force he feels the pull of the port; if he is going to spend the night on the streets, there are no better streets to do it on than the Ramblas and their tributaries. He will find friends; he has money to stand drinks until dawn. Tonight the odds against a marauding Arab finding him seem long.

The Metro delivers him to Liceu. The Ramblas are thinly peopled, only the bars still open. He is most likely to find familiar company in the Plaça Reial, but it is too open, too populated, the most likely spot for chance exposure. Pascual has a favorite dive in Carrer Nou, in the Barrio Chino. It is small, smoky, dark, comfortable, too daunting to attract a tourist clientele. Sometimes there are prostitutes at the bar, remnants of the once-thriving Barrio Chino trade that has mostly moved out to Pedralbes. There are sausages hanging from the ceiling, sawdust on the floor, *cante jondo* on the jukebox. There are tables along the wall and at one of them Pascual spots company good enough to start the evening with.

Ferran is a junkie, a mummified ectomorph with the eyes of a pawnbroker, eternally appraising. He wears a voluminous woolen sweater to hide his arms and a blue kerchief to keep his matted locks out of his face. His long fingers are entwined in a goatee that reaches to his chest. He is the wrecked progeny of a respectable clan of the *haute bourgeoisie* and the most erudite person Pascual has ever known outside the confines of a university. Across from him sits Anna, in a fox stole, looking about twelve years old despite lipstick and mascara. Pascual has heard it bruited about that Anna turns tricks for those attracted to the prepubescent, but to him she has always insisted she is a student and even produced a thesis to prove it, handfuls of closely scribbled and impenetrable prose she carries in her bag. Her age is indeterminate but at least twenty-five, he judges; her stature and enormous brown eyes are deceptive. Her relationship with Ferran is the subject of speculation; Pascual presumes it is platonic, as they are both still alive. He sits next to Anna and orders a cognac from a silent barkeeper intent on his own miseries. Ferran watches Pascual with narrowed black eyes that glitter. "He moves, he breathes."

"For the moment."

"How did the police treat you?"

Pascual shrugs. "The way the police always treat people. I'm famous now, I suppose?"

"You've had your fifteen minutes, let's say."

"Rumors are rife," says Anna.

"And what are the rumors?"

"Drugs, espionage, a *crime passionel.*"

"Espionage?"

"Don't worry, nobody believes it. The consensus seems to have settled on a vendetta of some sort. Possibly involving a woman."

"Do they mention any names?"

"Mine. But only because I've been carefully putting it about."

Pascual laughs. There is a brief silence and Ferran says, "And the truth?"

"I don't know. A case of mistaken identity, I think."

On the jukebox a gypsy is pining for Granada. Pascual braces for further questions but this company is used to discretion. "Well then, I'm off," says Ferran. He rises from the table, gaunt and creaking at the joints. "I have work to do."

Anna blows him a kiss. *"Ciao.* Remember, tomorrow at the Òpera. Six o'clock."

Pascual watches Ferran slink out. "What kind of work does he have to do at midnight?"

"Something involving a syringe and a rubber hose, I believe."

"Ah, of course."

They listen to the music. "They haven't caught the man, have they?" asks Anna.

"No."

"Are you frightened?"

"Not here. Not now. Ask me in ten minutes."

The talk moves on. Anna speaks volubly, incessantly, with the zeal of the true logorrheic. She has a friend who has just come back from India with hepatitis and a firm belief in reincarnation. Pascual orders two more cognacs. Anna has always believed she was Hungarian in a previous life. Pascual says nothing. He drinks cheap cognac and stares into the ashtray, thinking of Katixa.

Anna slides a hand through his arm. "Come home with me tonight." Her face is a hand's breadth from his: round, smooth, dominated by full lips and the huge brown puppy eyes. Pascual has wondered what it would be like to sleep with her but has never succumbed.

"I love somebody else," he says. He watches as tears begin to well at the corners of those devastating eyes.

"Come anyway. You can close your eyes and think of her."

Here is a place to spend the night offering itself; Pascual wonders only if the price is too steep. A variety of things flash through his mind: the long haul till dawn; Anna's sexual partners; Katixa in the arms of a Frenchman. "All right," he says.

The foot traffic in the dark narrow streets of the Barrio Chino is the usual: men in pairs or alone, the occasional whore. Anna marches at his side, clamped onto his arm, high heels clicking on the paving stones. She is babbling again. Pascual pays no attention; he is trying to evade the image of Katixa, now no longer encumbered with the Frenchman. He begins to waver.

Anna slows, steering him toward a doorway to one side of a bar. Pascual can see that the place is still open. "I'm hungry," he says.

"Hungry?" The thought is enough to stop her in midsentence. Pascual opens the door of the bar. There is a long narrow room brightly lit by fluorescent tubes, with tiled walls, high stools along a zinc counter, half a dozen bottles behind the bar. This is a bar for the poor, spare and functional. Nighthawks look away from the TV high in the corner by the door long enough to watch them come in. The barman is old and soured by the world but he knows Anna and greets her. There are a few meager *tapas* on the bar, some olives, some mushrooms, a handful of prawns. They sit at the end of the bar, where someone has been chopping squid with a cleaver. Pascual asks for the prawns and a glass of *tinto*. He turns to meet Anna's gaze.

"I'm sorry," he says.

"For what?"

"I really do love her."

Unblinking, Anna says, "Then why aren't you with her?"

"She's far away tonight."

Anna caresses his cheek with the back of her hand. "So stay with me. Listen, if you don't want to fuck me, don't fuck me. Hold me in your arms and whisper her name in my ear. Don't worry, I'm used to it."

Pascual holds her hand, looking into the suddenly much older eyes and trying to calculate the odds of remaining celibate until morning. He wishes Father Costa were here to watch him exercising his morals. The barman puts the prawns and a few slices of bread in front of him. He finds he is not hungry after all. He takes a drink of wine. When he looks back at Anna his eye is drawn over her shoulder to the doorway where a man has just entered. Anna sees him freeze and turns to look. Pascual watches the man come down the bar toward them, hands in the pockets of his gray suit coat. "Anna, get lost," says Pascual. "Run away. Fast." He sets the glass on the bar.

Anna wheels back to him. "Who is it?"

Pascual lifts her bodily off the stool. "Go." She stumbles and goes, brushing past the man. Pascual nods at him. *"Ahlan wa sahlan,"* he says. "Brother Hisham. I thought it might be you."

The man smiles, coming to a halt a meter away. "Pascual." His Arabic makes a *b* of the *p*.

It's true, Pascual finds; your life really does flash before your eyes. "You're going to kill me, aren't you?" he says.

Hisham takes the stool Anna vacated. His hands remain in his pockets. He still has the soulful eyes, softening the lantern-jawed face with the thick mustache. Hisham looks like a girl's favorite horse. "Of course," he says. "For Khaled, Mustafa, Zeid, Farid, all the others."

Pascual's heart is knocking painfully in his chest. All he can think of is to talk; he wishes he had Anna's gift. In desperation he says, "You won't kill me here, in a room full of witnesses."

Hisham looks over the bar, lazily and without concern. "I see six people. And I have eight rounds in the magazine."

"Just tell me how you found me." Pascual's Arabic flows masterfully, rusty or not; Pascual could recite the Koran if it would keep him alive.

There is a hint of contempt in Hisham's look. "You should never trust a drug addict. He will sell anything, anyone, anytime."

"Ferran?"

"Find a likely source and cultivate it. Remember when they taught us that?"

Pascual just has time to absorb this shock when the right hand begins to slide out of the pocket. He reaches over and puts the tips of his fingers on Hisham's forearm, just enough pressure to stop the movement. "But how did you know to come to Barcelona? How did you know I was here?"

"They sold you," Hisham says. "That's justice, isn't it?" His hand moves under Pascual's fingers.

"Hisham." Among the images that flash like lightning is one of himself and Hisham on a balcony somewhere, Aleppo perhaps, on a cool fragrant evening, Hisham's mournful eyes gazing into his. "Why do you think I never told them about you?" It is a desperate lie; Hisham was among the first Pascual coughed up. The eyes widen and the movement stops; Pascual can see his instinct is true. "I never dared tell you," he says, and sees Hisham freeze; he will do nothing until he hears what Pascual never dared to say. Pascual clutches the lapels of the gray suit coat, as if to plead. Instead he pulls with both hands as he whips his head forward and butts the Arab on the nose with great force. Stunned, Hisham reels and, without letting go, Pascual jerks the jacket down over his shoulders, pinning his arms to his sides. By the time Hisham has rallied and realized that the quickest solution is to bring up the gun and fire through the pocket, Pascual has reached across the bar and snatched the cleaver.

His first swipe is across the face and it catches cheekbone and nose cartilage, enough to flick blood onto the white tiles and knock the Arab off the stool. A shot blows out the pocket and brings general commotion but hits only the wall, and Pascual hacks again, a jarring, glancing blow that nearly severs an ear and lays bare a patch of clean white bone. Hisham fires again, toppling barstools as he falls, twisting to protect his head, with no idea of where the muzzle is pointing. Pascual has his feet on the floor now and brings the cleaver back down with fear and fury and gravity behind it. The blade disappears into Hisham's skull with a noise like the cracking of a giant egg and a splatter of blood. There is a tumult of voices.

Pascual picks up speed going along the bar until he is running as he reaches the door; in the street he passes Anna, frozen on the pavement, and her look haunts him as he flees. He runs through narrow streets until he sees the bright lights of the Parallel ahead and then slows, knowing no policeman can let him pass in this condition; he walks in shock toward the sea until he is capable of further thought and then makes for the dark mass of Montjuïc, looking for shelter. Father Costa is right; he is an animal.

16

A cold and bedraggled animal makes its way through the gates of the Industrial School. A night huddled in bushes on the slopes of Montjuïc has done nothing for Pascual's limp. He has washed flecks of blood from his hands and face at a fountain, but his fear of death has been replaced by fear of arrest on sight. He wants to wash and he wants to sleep. He wants a place to hide. He wants Katixa.

Father Costa is on the verge of leaving for the school, shoving books into a briefcase. "What have you done to your forehead?" he asks, peering at Pascual.

"Eh?" Pascual puts fingers to his head and feels a tender spot.

"That's quite a bruise. Been fighting in bars again?"

"The other fellow started it," says Pascual. The priest's look lingers and once more Pascual is convinced he knows everything. He flops on the couch. "One more day. Twenty-four hours."

"Until what?"

"Until I leave you in peace."

The priest closes and latches his briefcase. "You found your friend?"

"I'm waiting for her call. With your permission, I'd like to lie here and sleep. Take a shower, perhaps."

The priest considers, impassive. "Very well." He dons a coat and scarf. Carefully doing up the buttons, he says, "We'll go somewhere good for dinner tonight. You look as if you could use a good meal."

Damn him, Pascual thinks after the priest has gone. He goes to the suitcase in the corner and looks for signs of tampering. He opens it; there are the stacks of five-hundred franc notes, undisturbed. Damn all Jesuit deviousness, thinks Pascual. From the telephone on Father Costa's desk Pascual dials the number the CIA woman gave him last night at the Manhattan.

"Yes," says a man's voice in English.

"Let me talk to Shelby," says Pascual.

"Can't do that. I can have her call you."

"All right. Have her call Pascual at the following number." He reads the priest's number off the phone. "Tell her I ran into an old friend last night and the friend got the worst of it."

"She'll know what that means, will she?"

"No. But it ought to pique her curiosity."

Pascual lies on his back on Father Costa's couch, the little cassette player on his chest, earphones on. A shower and a little feverish sleep have restored him physically, but psychically he is a wreck, a six-car pileup. His wrist is sore; he can still feel the impact of the cleaver on Hisham's face, jarring him to the shoulder. Until the past week, he realizes, he was a child. So far, adulthood terrifies him. In desperate search of solace, he is listening to *Wachet auf*. Pascual has never been partial to the organ but this piece with its perfect grace has always eased his heart. Even the title calls to him; he is a sleeper struggling to wake.

The telephone in Father Costa's study rings. Pascual tears off the earphones and flies off the couch. "Pascual?" says the faint southwestern twang.

"Yeah." He sinks onto a chair, heart pounding.

"Found yourself a new phone, huh?"

"I killed Abu Imad last night."

There is a pause. "Say again? Who?"

"Hisham Al-Khalili. *Nom de guerre* Abu Imad. Responsible for the 1987 Barajas attack. I killed him last night in a bar in the Barrio Chino. Doesn't anybody in your office read the papers?"

There is a faint distant click of the tongue. "I did wonder. What I saw said two Arabs."

"Well, the cops know better than that. They'll have talked to the bartender, and he'll have told them who I was with just before, and they'll find her and she'll tell them who I am. I don't have much time."

"Mm. Well, I'd better come and get you then. We'd like to talk to you."

"Who's we?"

"The gentleman I mentioned yesterday."

"Good God, that was fast."

"You ever heard of airplanes? Apparently he's still interested in you."

"That's good. He owes me now, too. A medal, at least."

"If you can be at the Manhattan in half an hour, I'll try and get you to the ceremony on time."

■ ■ ■ ■

Pascual drags himself across the road, a beetle making for the nearest rock. He stands exposed waiting to cross Urgell, waiting for the
squeal of brakes, a squad of policemen piling out, guns drawn. Inside
the café nobody gasps or points at him. Manolo brings him a ham
bocadillo; Pascual imagines he detects a sardonic light in the old waiter's eye. Furtively, he picks up the *Vanguardia,* expecting to see his
own photograph. The incident is recorded on page three: *Riña en el
Barrio Chino resulta en asesinato*. Skin crawling, Pascual reads.

Having fed, he watches the street and sees Shelby pull up at the
corner in a Honda Accord. He is moving before she has time to get
out of the car. "Where are we going?" he asks as she pulls out into the
perilous traffic on Urgell.

"You know what a safe house is?"

"I've spent half my life in safe houses."

"Well, this is one of ours."

Shelby drives like a yanqui, carefully and with tight-lipped disapproval of Latin bravura. Nonetheless she is skillful, and if she
appears at first not to know where she is going, Pascual realizes
that she merely wishes to be sure nobody else does either. The safe
house turns out to be in a narrow sloping street off the Parallel at the
foot of Montjuïc. Shelby parks the car just off a tiny plaza with two
benches and a tree, a mere widening of the street, and leads him to
a nondescript entrance like ten thousand others in Barcelona. It is
a newish building and there is plenty of light in the stairwell from a
skylight far above.

The apartment is cramped but airy, with the echoing quality of
concrete and tile construction; light streams in through French windows above the street. Shelby leads Pascual back to a dining room in

the rear, where there are more windows giving a view over rooftops all the way to Tibidabo. The furniture looks as if it came yesterday from the Corte Inglés. At a table sits Dan, cup and saucer in front of him.

Dan is unchanged; faces like his have reached the limit of aging. In Barcelona he could pass for an ill-used and worn-out Andalusian laborer. He smiles, but there is no warmth in it. "Well, well," he says. "El Cid Campeador, slayer of Moors."

Pascual nods. "I don't suppose it was for my sake that you got here so fast."

"Not really, no." Shelby plays hostess, ushering Pascual to a chair and ducking into the kitchen. Dan shoves cigarettes and a lighter across the table toward Pascual. "But we're certainly interested in your old friends, and it was thought a good idea to send someone out to have a talk with you. And now I get here and find you seem to have killed one of them. I must say, it makes a pleasant change from the last time I visited your fair city, when we'd just had two men killed here and were desperately trying to find out why. This time it feels almost like a vacation."

"They've identified him, have they?"

"Not yet. But they displayed a heightened interest when we had a little talk with them. Al-Khalili's one of the ones we're lucky enough to have fingerprints on, and as soon as they can be transmitted we should find out whether you're telling the truth. Have a cigarette."

Pascual takes one and lights it. Shelby reappears with a bottle of sherry and three glasses. Pascual watches her pour. "If they arrest me, will you have another little talk with them? For my sake?"

"Good God, you can't possibly believe we have any influence with the Spanish judiciary."

"I need influence before it gets to the judiciary. Don't tell me you can't put a word in the right ear."

"Possibly. But I can't make any guarantees. In any event, apparently it was self-defense. Surely any decent lawyer could keep you out of jail."

"A trial would be as good as posting my face on a billboard and pasting a target on my back."

Dan shrugs. "Then I'd stay out of sight if I were you." He sips sherry and says, "Did you have much of a chance to chat?"

"Not much. I asked him how he found me."

"And?"

"He said, 'They sold you. *Ba'ouk.'* Just like that. They sold you."

"Who sold you?"

"He didn't get to finish."

Dan smiles. "Well, it wasn't us."

"And I suppose it wasn't the Yanks, either."

Shelby at least pays him the courtesy of a frown. "Why would we?"

Pascual laughs bitterly. "Because somebody made you an offer. I have no illusions about my status or about the intelligence business."

Dan says, "It couldn't have been us, because we had no idea where you were. We passed you off to her bunch and that was that. Whoever sold you had to have you first. My guess would always be the Spanish."

"Who would know to ask the Spanish?"

"Maybe the Spanish shopped you around. They needed something from somebody and you were the only currency they had."

Pascual looks the Yank in the eye. "Can you find out?"

"I don't know. I can try. If that's who sold you out, there's not a lot we can do for you."

Pascual smokes. A number of thoughts have crystallized. "I don't think there's a lot you can do for me, whoever sold me out. In fact, I think there's a pretty good chance that when you find out who did it, you'll do your best to forget all about it."

"Oh?"

"Well, my first guess is always going to be Uncle Sam, because that's who thinks he owns me. And I don't think you're going to rock the boat."

"Not if they had a good reason, no." She smiles, and in the smile there is nothing left of the coed.

Pascual nods. "OK. Like I said, I have no illusions. The only reason we're here right now is that we all want as many PFLP killers out of action as possible. And that's it. Other than that we have no interests in common. Now I just gave you one dead *fida'i*. Chalk it up in my credit column. And don't help them. If somebody in Rome or Washington or Tel Aviv decides they want me dead, the only favor I ask is that you don't actively help them. Just let me disappear. Deal?"

The American woman shakes her head. "I think you're paranoid."

"OK, I'm paranoid."

The Israeli is smiling. "It feels like hell, doesn't it?"

Pascual sucks on the cigarette. "Yes, it does."

"Don't worry. It won't last forever. Someday you'll step into a car, turn the key, and BAM! You won't feel a thing."

"Thank you, that's very evocative."

Dan's smile broadens; for an instant Pascual thinks he is about to slap him heartily on the shoulder. "Now you know how Yossi Peled felt."

All Pascual can do is nod. "Now I know."

■ ■ ■ ■

Pascual finds that fatalism is the easy choice when it allows one to eat well. He can think of no better cover for a wanted man than the company of a priest; further, if he is going to be arrested, it might as well be over a lavish meal. One of the perquisites of associating with Father Costa is the priest's gastronomical expertise. Tonight the priest has chosen a modest establishment on Viladomat that he says is the best place for seafood in the Eixample. On the white linen tablecloth in front of Pascual is a zoological adventure: mussels, prawns, eels, *cigalas, percebes, centollas, ostiones,* other things he has no name for, things he would never guess were edible, the underside of a reef on a platter. To wash it down Father Costa selects a white Rioja so crisp it bites. The priest is in a different element here; in a corduroy jacket over a beige sweater, relaxed and expansive, pressing wine and delicacies on Pascual, he looks less like a grand inquisitor and more like a favorite uncle. For the first hour he talks about nothing but food, wine, travel. Father Costa has sojourned in Americas North and South, the colder regions of Europe where German is spoken and, of course, Rome. They compare notes on the Eternal City; somehow Pascual finds himself telling tales of Beirut and Aden. They are seated in a nook where none can overhear but the waiter on his occasional visits. Pascual is aware that he is recklessly spilling secrets but the constraints are gone tonight, perhaps loosened by the grilling Dan put him through in the late afternoon.

When silence falls Father Costa orders cognac. Plates disappear and two *copas* materialize. The priest swirls the radiant liquid gently and says, "And do you have a destination in mind, you and your fugitive friend?"

Pascual takes a careful sip. The cognac is even better than the priest's private stock: silken and ethereal, the color of amber. Suddenly he is frightened at the extent of what he has revealed. Without looking at the priest he says, "No."

Silence reigns for a while; Pascual watches the comings and goings in the main dining room. He feels like a maiden lured into an old man's parlor and plied with Madeira.

"Note that I do not ask where," says Father Costa. "Nor do I ask what is in the suitcase that has sat in the corner of my room for the past two days."

Pascual finally looks at the priest, who sits with his long face propped on a thumb and forefinger. "You've guessed, have you?"

"I've speculated."

Pascual takes a deep breath in lieu of more cognac. "What do you want, then?"

"A frank discussion of your prospects. I would think that it might be mere prudence to share your plans with one who has your well-being in mind."

"They're not mine to share."

"No. But consider that you are not likely to find a more discreet confidant. I am under no obligation to treat any of it as confidential. But perhaps out of habit, I am prepared to do so."

Pascual twirls the stem of his glass, watches a fat man across the room downing oysters with the devotion of a starving child. "We're going to go somewhere a long way away, start all over." In the ensuing silence the words sound puerile, even to Pascual.

"Very well. I wish you the best. Are you prepared to spend the rest of your life as a fugitive?"

"Money can buy a lot of security."

"It's your money, is it?"

Damn him, thinks Pascual. "It belongs to her."

"She earned it, did she?"

Pascual has no answer. His brain is fogged by alcohol; at moments like these the simplest syllogism is a mystery as deep as the universe. "I don't know. What I know is that we have it. Nobody's going to starve if we use it to set up a new life."

"Ah. That's all right then. The things we can justify, just because nobody starves."

"Look." Pascual leans across the table, intent. "Be happy we're not using it to buy guns. We're through with politics. Be content with that."

Father Costa stiffens. "Good God, boy. Who's talking about politics? My concern is for your immortal soul."

Pascual leans back on his chair with dignity. "The soul is a myth."

The Jesuit's face hardens. "Call it what you will. Call it your personhood, your individual consciousness, which presumably you will admit exists. Eh?"

Pascual opens his mouth, closes it again. "Go on."

The priest shifts on his seat, preparing for combat. His lowered brows terrify Pascual. "Listen to me. You spent your youth denying that personhood is worth the slightest consideration. You were prepared to obliterate the personhood of others for the sake of a particular disposition of power. And you obliterated your own personhood with it. For you, the only being that mattered was a mythical beast called society. You located all consciousness there, all right and wrong. You imputed to it a soul. That is what politics is, the care and feeding of the mythical beast. Politics was your creed, and it required you to deny the reality of the person. You ignored the vital evidence of every waking minute that the cells of this mythical beast are what suffer and dream and sin and sacrifice, not the beast itself, which exists only in the imagination of fools. And while you saw through the myth, you have yet to take seriously the evidence of your senses, to admit that you exist, to recognize your soul."

Pascual scowls across the table at him. "I just want to be human."

The priest slaps the table. "Wonderful. We have arrived at a term we can agree on. Fine then—be human. If you can. To walk on two limbs and solve differential equations is not enough."

Pascual has nothing to answer. He drinks and stares at the table-cloth. Father Costa asks for the bill. Outside the air is crisp, invigorating. Pascual cannot face another night on the streets. Suddenly he is totally dependent. He follows the priest to his car. They drive in silence, the priest working at the gears with savage efficiency. Pascual watches lighted windows go by and wishes he were behind them, safe in front of the telly.

Father Costa says nothing to the *conserje*, who averts his eyes as they pass the desk. In the priest's suite Pascual waves off the offer of another *copa*. He senses that he has one more chance to make himself clear before total alcoholic disintegration sets in. "I'm trying," he says.

"Trying what?" The priest pauses in the doorway to his room.

"To erase all that." Pascual totters, steadies himself on the wall. "You cannot imagine how I loathe myself." He feels that as long as he remains standing he holds an advantage. "And there is no excuse. I was not ill. I was not insane. And I can never escape that person."

Pascual's sense of space has gone haywire. Father Costa is two steps away but seems to be speaking from a great distance. "That person can be forgiven."

"Yes. I can be forgiven." Pascual raises a finger; this is the crucial point, if he can only get it out. "I can be redeemed. By love. She loves me, she came back for me. Do you see that? She is my redemption, and if she is not a saint, who am I to reproach her?"

Icily calm, Father Costa says, "It is not in her power to redeem you."

Pascual stares at him. "With respect, Father. Your theology I don't doubt. But what do you know about human love?"

Something has hit the mark; the priest glares, stiffens. "You have drunk too much," he says. He disappears into the inner room and closes the door. Pascual leaves the suite in search of a bathroom. He finds one at the end of the long echoing hall. Returning, he passes two residents who give him a wide berth and a suspicious stare. They look over their shoulders as he lets himself back into the suite. Pascual curses them and their imaginations. He strips to his underwear, douses the lights, and lies on the couch under the blanket the priest has lent him. His brain swims but he cannot sleep.

Sometime later the door to the inner room opens with a creak. Pascual lies rigid as Father Costa comes softly across the carpet toward the couch. No, he thinks. Not this, after all. The tall shape of the priest comes into view, dimly, at the foot of the couch. Pascual can make out a dressing gown and slippers. He has clenched his fists under the blanket. Father Costa sinks onto the couch, his thin flanks touching Pascual's leg. Next will be the hand on the thigh, thinks Pascual, and then I will try not to hit him.

In the dark the priest says, "You asked what I could know about human love."

To show he is awake Pascual says finally, "Yes."

Seconds pass. "If your mother were here, you could ask her," says Father Costa.

There is a long silence. Outside Pascual can hear night traffic, remote and free. Down the hallway someone laughs and a door slams, reverberating. Pascual understands obscure things suddenly but has the discouraging sensation that every bit of knowledge multiplies his ignorance a thousandfold. After a time he says, "I'm sorry."

"Your mother could neither redeem me nor destroy me. I hoped for the one and then feared the other. But all she could do was hurt me, poor lovely creature, and time healed that. Be careful that you do not put too much faith in what the love of a woman can do for you."

Pascual has unclenched his fists and put his hands to his face. His fatigue is bottomless. "I'm trying, Father. It's hard."

"Of course it's hard. Truth is a harsh master, honor a cruel discipline. And love is the cruelest of all."

"I don't understand you."

The old priest stands, wanders back toward his room. "It's late and we've both drunk too much. I ply you with drink and it's my own mouth that runs away with me. Sleep well."

17

Pascual is going mad in a shuttered room. Stress, mayhem and roiled depths of memory have taken him into uncharted regions of post-alcoholic malaise. The suitcase lies open on the couch; Pascual hoped the sight of five million francs would hearten him but it is merely colored paper. He resists the temptation to plunge his hands in and strew bundles of currency about the room. He closes the case and replaces it in the corner. He dares not leave the phone but the room is growing smaller by the hour. He is nearly ready to bolt for the open streets when the phone rings. Katixa's voice is water in the desert, instant revival. "I'm on my way," she says.

"Where? Here?"

"Where else? Do you have the luggage?"

"It's right here."

"Meet me at Sants again. Can you be there in half an hour?"

"Less." In twenty-three minutes Pascual is standing on the pavement in front of the station, his duffel bag and the black Pullman bag at his feet. A *guàrdia urbana* rolls by and his heart kicks: he will run, fight, hurt somebody before he lets himself be arrested. This time he sees the blue Audi a hundred meters away and has the bags in his hands before it has stopped rolling. Katixa emerges to open the boot and help him stow them away. Today she is in jeans and leather again, her hair tucked under the beret. She is a healthy feline predator.

Pascual folds himself painfully onto the passenger seat. Katixa peers at him. "You look like hell."

"I killed Abu Imad the night before last. The police are looking for me."

Katixa stares, starts the car, pulls away. "I have a feeling life with you is going to be exciting."

Pascual tells her the story. For reasons he cannot put his finger on, he does not mention his talk with the spies. "I'm a fugitive now," he says.

"Well," says Katixa. "The two of us, a matched set. What fun."

"It was a near thing. He almost killed me."

Katixa negotiates traffic in silence. When she stops at a light she turns to him, caresses his face. For a moment she appears about to speak but instead leans over to kiss him. Pascual grabs her and holds on until horns sound behind them. "It's all right," says Pascual. "I'm fine, never been better."

The weather has cleared. The drive up the coast shows a sea of lambent aquamarine beneath a turquoise sky. Blanes, Tossa, Sant Feliu: the tourist towns of the Costa Brava, emptied of Germans, have the look of disused stage sets. Above the winding highway, pines cling to rock.

In Palamós there is brisk sea air and a lot of empty beach. Katixa parks on the Passeig del Mar and she and Pascual stand on the long treelined seawalk in silence. Pascual was here once as a child, when it could still almost lay claim to being a Catalan fishing village. Now the broad sweep of the bay is encrusted with empty hotels. The Costa Brava has become a Spanish Disneyland, a continuous strip of fast-food joints, amusement parks and time-share condos. In the autumn chill Palamós is an overgrown town with a scattering of high-rise apartments and empty streets. "So where is he?" asks Pascual.

"Probably still at lunch." They walk a few steps. "The boat will be in the marina on the other side of the point. He sleeps there. But he spends his time at the Club Nàutic, with the wealthier local lay-abouts. Or anywhere he can drink and cruise for women."

Pascual scans the harbor, the long wharf where a freighter is moored, the buildings of the old town huddled up on the point. "Why here? This isn't exactly St. Tropez. I wouldn't think there was enough entertainment to keep a man of sophisticated tastes here for long."

"He's done St. Tropez. He's done Portofino and Corfu, too. You run out of places after a while. But at the moment I believe I'm what's keeping him here."

Pascual has resolved to let nothing shake him. "So when do I get to meet your new boyfriend?"

"We're meeting him for a drink at four. You are, by the way, my brother."

"Your brother."

"Yes. Who has decided that Morocco may be good for what ails him."

"What about you?"

"I haven't quite got to that yet. If need be, I'll break the news to him when we hit the surf off Tétouan."

Pascual frowns out to sea. There is a wind in his face and he is beginning to be conscious of things he has left behind. "I'm hoping I'll have a better feel for the brilliance of your plan after I meet him."

Katixa turns back toward the car. "Come on. I'll show you the boat and then we'll get you a room."

Pascual trails her. "What's wrong with yours?"

"Remember who you are. Even I draw the line at incest."

"For God's sake, that's taking verisimilitude too far." Pascual trails Katixa, watching her haunches in the jeans.

"You want people to remember us as a couple?"

"We are a couple."

"You want the cops looking for you if they happen to get me?"

"Whatever happens to you, I want to be there."

"You've forgotten how it goes, haven't you?" Katixa turns; she is smiling slightly but her eyes are blazing. "You've lost those reflexes." Pascual has no answer. Katixa starts the car and follows the street around the point, passing steps that lead up to the old town. The *puerto deportivo* is a small harbor enclosed by a concrete breakwater. There are only a handful of boats moored along the dock. The largest is a sleek white twelve-meter cruiser with a large foredeck, an open bridge and a swept-back, rakish look. Even at rest it looks fast. "What do you think?" says Katixa.

"It ought to get us to Morocco. Can he drive it?"

"He seemed to handle it pretty well when he took me out yesterday."

"Showing off, was he?"

"So was I." She puts the car in gear. Pascual glowers through the windscreen. "It's a drama," says Katixa, "And we're actors. Put on your makeup."

She drops him at the hotel and goes to park on the seafront again. The hotel is a modest three-star job a street back from the sea. Like all out-of-season hotels it gives an impression of lassitude and indifference. The slight avian woman who wanders to the desk from unknown regions after Pascual rings the bell could clearly live happily without another guest until spring. Pascual takes his key and his bags to a room on the second floor, four doors down from Katixa's. The room is painted white and has a tiled floor and a view of the sea between buildings. Pascual can hear voices faintly from remote chambers, echoing through uncarpeted halls. He sits on the double bed, remembering precisely this feeling in hotel rooms from Sofia to Hamburg: out there is the hostile universe, in here is only sterility and despair.

A short time later he hears Katixa's step in the hall. When her door closes he steals out of his room, suitcase in hand, and pads down to her room. She takes the case and sets it on a luggage stand. She opens it and stands staring at the bundles of bills. "Feel better?" says Pascual.

Katixa zips the case shut. "Much. Let's go have a drink with a Frenchman."

Pascual hates Thierry Rey on sight. Rey is a big man, handsome, well-turned out, with expensively tended black hair and lively dark eyes. He has recently shaved; there is a faint whiff of cologne and the dark jaws are too smooth to have gone since morning without a scraping. Rey wears a denim baseball cap and a sailing jacket with an ostentatious brand-name logo. His Castilian is perfect and his charm undeniable.

"You're the big brother," says Rey.

"I'm the chaperone," says Pascual, shaking hands.

Rey laughs, without a hint of discomfort. To Katixa he says, "I can't say I see a resemblance."

"Pascual is the postman's child," Katixa says, lighting a cigarette. They are in a faithful re-creation of an English pub some genius has installed a couple of streets back from the seafront; the light is dim, the chairs upholstered in maroon plush, the beer no doubt warm. Rey orders them Scotch from an unmistakably Catalan bartender who looks annoyed by the business and fades through a doorway as soon as he has served them.

"You don't sound French," says Pascual.

Rey gives him a cool smile. "My father was a Franco refugee. He struck it rich in Lyon but always considered himself a Spaniard. He never spoke anything but Spanish with us."

Pascual will not be outdone. In French he says, "Well, we're all Europeans now, they tell us."

"So they say. Where'd you learn your French?"

"Mostly in Paris. I got kicked out of so many schools here they had to send me north where the headmasters were a little more tolerant."

"Not in my experience they're not."

In Spanish Katixa says, "I knew you two would get along. Can we do this in a language I can keep up in?"

Pascual shrugs. "That's quite a boat you have over there in the harbor."

"Ah, you saw it? It's a beauty, isn't it? It's an Italian boat, a Cranchi, top of the range. Three-eighty horsepower twin diesels. I'll take you out for a spin."

"How far would it take us?"

"As far as you want to go." There is a pause. "Your sister tells me you want to go to Morocco."

"I've heard it's quite a place."

"Never been there?"

"Never. Though there are parts of Paris that might as well be there."

"Well, you'll find almost everyone speaks a little French in Morocco." Rey sips whiskey, looking at Pascual with an amused gaze. "There are lots of ways to get to Morocco. Why do it on the sly?"

"Let's say I'd just as soon not have to show my passport to the Policía Nacional on the way out."

"I see." Rey has not quite lost the amused look, but he is tapping his lips with a finger. "You're not an international drug baron? A terrorist?"

Pascual laughs. "No. There's a little matter of military service I never did. Compounded by several failures to appear in court and a lawsuit or two."

"There's a limit to the amount of tolerance Papa's money could buy," says Katixa. "Pascual's dedicated his life to finding that limit and he's finally done it."

Pascual drinks whiskey with a sheepish look. "Well, I'm certainly not one to cast stones," says Rey. "You think Morocco's better?"

"I think Morocco's a start. I hear they're still bribable down there."

"They're bribable everywhere, in my experience," says Rey. "It's just that the price scale varies."

"Well, I'm out of credit here."

Rey nods, thoughtful. "You know what you're getting into? To really do it without getting caught might mean a bit of a swim, a bit of a hike. Some money. And some luck. In many ways it's not a hospitable country."

With a shrug Pascual says, "This is not a hospitable country for me anymore."

"There are lots of Europeans in jail down there who thought it was a little more easygoing than it really is. Why Morocco? The way Europe is now, you can slide over borders without any difficulty."

Katixa says, "We're hoping to get him out to a place where he can live on the cheap for a while, while I get the inheritance sorted out. Then I can send him enough to get started in something. Something other than debauchery."

Pascual gives her a stony look, playing the part. Katixa says, "He's a wonderful brother, but as a role model he's a fucking disaster."

Pascual has to laugh again. Rey drains his whiskey and says, "I'll give it some thought."

They walk Rey back to the Passeig del Mar, where he folds himself into the Audi. He has to shove the seat back because he is so much taller than Katixa. "Did you leave me any petrol?" he says.

"Sorry. I didn't think to fill it."

Rey's indulgent smile cuts Pascual deep; he himself has smiled just this way at women he has designs on. "Never mind. Supper tonight, then? How about that place just around the curve up there, what's it called, Can Joanet? They do a great *arroz negro.* We'll have a *cremat,* get a little drunk. See you there at ten?"

"Sounds good. *Ciao.*"

"You played him perfectly," says Katixa as they watch him drive away. "He'll bite. Tonight at supper we'll have him."

"Perhaps we can discuss sleeping arrangements on the boat."

"Oh for God's sake, stop it." Her patience is at an end. He puts an arm around her shoulders but she shrugs it off. "I'm going back to the hotel. You go for a walk and try to remember what it takes to run an operation."

Shamed, Pascual kicks his heels on the seafront. Old men walking dogs steer clear of him. A clean cold wind is coming across the broad bay; the sun is setting over the hills to the west. Pascual wonders if he will be able to sit through a meal with Thierry Rey. He heads back to the hotel. He taps softly on Katixa's door. She opens; she has let down her hair and taken off the sweater. A thin cotton shirt hugs her figure. Pascual closes the door and reaches for her. "I'm sorry," he says. "I love you too much."

"Tell me about it when we're free. Then you can tell me everything." Katixa holds on, her breath on his throat. Pascual knows that her rigid emotional control is a survival tool but now he would give blood for a touch of her tenderness. He kisses her. With one arm around her neck and the other around her waist, mouth to mouth, he knows there will be no despair as long as he can hold on to her. The kiss goes from hungry to tender, from tongue and teeth to a pulsing of lips, and Pascual draws back far enough to say, "I didn't know."

There is alarm in the ebony eyes. "What?"

"I never knew what *querer* was. I never knew wanting could hurt this much." Pascual is at her mouth again. She makes a soft moaning noise and writhes in his embrace. He reaches down to grasp her crotch through the jeans. She gasps. Pascual stoops, pushing his hand on through her legs to grab the back of a thigh and sweeping her off her feet with the other arm around her neck. He carries her to the bed in three swift steps and lowers her onto it, falling on top of her. He is working at the button of her jeans when she clasps his wrists.

"No. I've got my period."

"I don't care." Pascual strains against her grip.

"Stop!" Pascual freezes and then releases her. The note in her voice has stunned him.

Katixa falls back onto the pillow. "Not now, please. Come." She is holding out her hands to him. Bewildered, Pascual lets her pull him down on top of her. "Hold me," she says. "Just hold me. It's not the time. Not now. I feel like hell and I need to be held."

Pascual holds her, breathing the scent of her hair, feeling her tremble. He holds her and listens to the faint noises from floors below, the slamming of a door, laughter. He is striving against feelings of humiliation. Beneath him Katixa stirs. "Turn out the light."

Slowly, Pascual rises and obeys; the shutters are closed and little of the declining light outside penetrates. Pascual hears Katixa slipping off clothes. He sits on the bed and removes his shoes. "Come here. I'll take you in my mouth," says Katixa.

"No." Pascual rolls toward her, gathers her in. She has kept the shirt and her panties on. Pascual kisses her gently. "When you give the word, I'll make love to you like you deserve." Pascual is in turbulence and knows only that holding her will calm it.

Against his throat she breathes, "There's time. We'll have years."

They lie on the bed in darkness. The tension subsides in Katixa's body. "Katixa," Pascual says.

"What?"

"The money." Her breathing stops.

"What about it?"

"Who does it belong to?"

Time passes before she answers. "Us, now."

"By virtue of what?"

There is another long pause and Katixa rises on an elbow, face above his in the gloom. "Don't tell me you're having pangs of conscience."

Pascual heaves a great sigh. "I thought that was what this was all about."

Calmly she says, "If you want to be precise, the money belongs to Alonso Itarroiz's insurance company. You want to give it back?"

"No. I suppose not." Pascual waits a beat and says, "What if we gave it away? I mean, not all of it. We'll keep enough to make a start somewhere, give the rest away. I'm not sure I want to be rich."

He stares at the ceiling, afraid to look at Katixa. Nobody is more surprised than he that he has blurted this out now. Suddenly he is desperately afraid and snaps a look at Katixa. She is contemplating him, absorbed.

"You're afraid the money's more important to me than you are," she says.

Pascual puts a hand over his eyes. "Yes."

There is silence while Pascual counts heartbeats. She brushes hair off his brow. "Imbecile. I could have run with the money all by myself." She kisses him lightly. Pascual searches the black eyes. "But I came for you."

Pascual nods. "Tell me we've learned something."

Gravely, tenderly, Katixa caresses him, fingers dragging lightly over the stubble on his cheeks. "I've learned I need you."

Pascual could lie like this forever, looking into eyes as black as midnight. "I'll work for a living. I'll hold down a job. We'll have babies. We don't need five million francs."

Softly, Katixa says, "At this point, there is no giving it away. It's either leave it in a bin somewhere or run with it."

"I don't want to be an outlaw. I don't want to spend my life running, lying to people."

"Get used to it. It's harder to stop than to start."

"But that's one reason I need you so much. I don't have to lie to you. You're the only woman on earth who knows where I've been, because you've been there too."

Katixa makes no reply. She lowers herself into the crook of his arm. After a time, just audibly, she says, "And a hell of a place it was, too."

They lie in each other's arms; Pascual dozes. When he wakes he has lost all sense of time; the lamp is off, but with the shutters closed he could not say if it were noon or midnight. He is in a hotel room and there is a pulsebeat of anxiety under everything but Katixa is in his arms, breathing softly and regularly against his neck. Pascual is calmed; has he ever been happier than here on this bed? He eases his arm from under Katixa; she stirs but does not open her eyes, then rolls onto her back, her lips slightly parted. Pascual rises, goes to the bathroom. When he returns he leaves the bathroom light on and stands looking at Katixa on the bed. He feels a carnal need that will not be deterred by Katixa's biological cycles. He wants to burrow to the dark convergence of Katixa's legs and take the warm moist tissues of her intimate self gently into his mouth. He kneels on the bed and grasps the waistline of the panties and tugs gently. The black triangle of hair appears and Pascual freezes, uncomprehending.

Katixa jerks her legs up to her chest, rolling away from Pascual. She slides off the side of the bed and staggers against the wall as she pulls up the panties. Her eyes are fierce with the alarm of the abruptly awakened. Pascual is immobile on the bed, in shock. When Katixa steadies, Pascual's eyes flick to her hands, which cup her crotch as she sags at the knees, sliding slowly down the wall. "Mother of God," Pascual says. He knows now what he has seen; shaved flesh and a line of stitches holding together the edges of a very ugly wound in a very tender place.

18

Katixa is crying. She is huddled in the corner, arms folded around her knees. Pascual is not quite in touch with his limbs, which seem to be strangely weakened; moving with care he has managed to make it to the armchair. He has broken into a sweat. Beneath the shock Pascual's mind is working, somehow, and all the cylinders have clicked into place. In a hollow voice Pascual says, "I did that." He remembers with great clarity the force of the slash and the snick of the blade as it caught Katixa in the dark.

Katixa nods. "Twelve stitches," she manages to say. "You nearly disemboweled me."

Pascual cannot speak for a moment, seeing it. This horror is the worst of all he has suffered. Finally he says, "You've been lying all along."

"Yes."

"You never left them, did you? You're still an etarra."

She shakes her head violently. "No. You don't understand."

Suddenly the world goes red with rage; Pascual is off the chair and on his knees before her, hands clamped onto her arms. Her face is distorted, turned away from his. "Then what the fuck were you doing there?"

She cries out and Pascual releases her. She buries her face in her hands and vents a single sob. More cylinders click and Pascual stands and crosses the room, slowly. He opens the suitcase and sees the array of five-hundred-franc notes. He removes a bundle to see another beneath it. He digs further and sees text on newsprint. He plunges his hand deep into the case and withdraws a stack of banknote-sized strips of newspaper, text in Spanish, held by a rubber band. Pascual picks up the case by the handle and flings it against the wall above the bed, strewing its contents out across the room. The suitcase flops empty on the bed and there is a scattering of small packets of newsprint on the bed, the floor, the armchair, only lightly seasoned by rare bundles of genuine French five-hundred-franc notes.

Pascual sweeps dummy currency off the chair and sits again. He is nauseous. Katixa's sobs are ebbing. "Talk." In the wake of the rage Pascual feels a magisterial calm settling on him.

"I had to." This is a Katixa Pascual has never seen; she is an orphan, braced for a whipping.

When Katixa's breathing is under control, Pascual says, "I'm listening."

Katixa wipes tears with both hands. "They made me," she says.

"Who? Your pals, what do you call them, Goikoetxea and Arrieta?"

"No, no, you've got it all wrong. The other side."

"Who?"

"I think they're from CESID. The GAL again, maybe. Who knows what they're calling them this year?"

"The Spanish?"

"Of course. Who else?"

Pascual reels. "I don't get it."

"They caught me, for God's sake. They're running me. It's an intelligence operation."

Pascual is falling, into an abyss. "They turned you."

"They forced me. I had no choice."

"So it was all lies. From the start."

"No." She shakes her head. "Only since I got to Barcelona and started looking for you."

"What happened?"

Katixa covers her face with her hands. "Wait," she says. After a moment she rises and goes into the bathroom. Water runs; Pascual hears a gentle breathy moan. When Katixa comes out she is as composed as one can be with a face mottled by tears. She pulls on the jeans and methodically gets a cigarette going. Pascual has not moved a finger. Katixa shoves the empty bag on the floor and sits cross-legged on the bed. Pascual is looking desperately for the old Katixa but sees only a strangely diminished version, eyes downcast and voice subdued. "They caught me the day after I hit Barcelona. With the money. Everything since then, they've been running."

"Good God." Pascual passes a hand over his face. "How did they find you?"

"My papers must have been compromised. They came to my hotel room at six in the morning. I opened the door to a gun in my face and they've been with me ever since."

"Christ. Everything we've done, they knew about?"

Her eyes meet his. "Pascual, everything we've done they set up."

He has to close his eyes for a moment to take that in. "All that up in the hills?"

"All of it. Newspaper in the bag, just enough real cash on top to fool you. They took me over the ground the day before, showed me where the contact would be if things went wrong. We knew there was a risk of confusion in the dark. We never expected you to come blundering into the house."

"Christ, I almost killed you."

"I thought you had. They patched me up in Girona."

When the horror passes Pascual looks at her again. "Why didn't you just show yourself, tell me you'd stumbled out of the rain as well?"

"How was I going to explain the car? Not to mention the man lurking in the corner."

"So it's all a CESID operation? You never killed Bordagorri, never took the money?"

"No, no, no. I told you, all that was real. I was running, I had the money and I was looking for you. But they've taken the whole thing over."

Pascual closes his eyes, hands at his temples. "I don't get it. Not a thing. For what, for Christ's sake?"

"We're bait."

Pascual stares. "Bait?"

"To catch etarras."

"Explain."

Katixa draws on the cigarette. The hotel has fallen silent and smoke curls through the light of the single lamp by the bed. "Bordagorri's group has always been target number one for the

Spanish security forces. Nobody's stayed alive and operational longer than we have. If they can smash what's left of the group they'll have crippled the most effective arm of ETA. Bordagorri's death wasn't enough—they've seen him surface after hearing rumors of his death before. I think they're convinced this time, because they caught me with the money and they know he wouldn't let it out of his sight. But they're not satisfied. They want everyone. The whole ETA-Militar command structure. And they know the money will draw them."

Pascual wants a cigarette himself but is seized with paralysis, watching the outlines of the catastrophe emerge. "I see," he says, without conviction.

"They want us to draw out the rest of Bordagorri's group, and any other rivals for power. Grabbing me was a big coup for them. They could have put me on trial, paraded the money in front of the cameras, made a political success of it. But somebody started thinking. With Bordagorri dead, they know there's going to be a succession fight. Goikoetxea and Arrieta are just the start. As word gets round, other group leaders will see a chance to get in on the feast. And the Spanish see a chance to root out the whole structure before anybody gets the upper hand. Somebody did some quick thinking and realized that the remains of Bordagorri's outfit would do just about anything to get the money back. That's where we come in. They decided the best way to lure the wolves out of the woods was to set us out in the clearing, tied to a stake. They want us to try and cash it in and see who shows up to kill us."

Pascual has reached his limit for the moment. He holds up a hand to stop her, rises, gets a cigarette going. He smokes and paces, not looking at Katixa. "What's the idea, you start flashing the money around Biarritz or something? How the hell will the money draw them?"

Katixa speaks patiently, quietly. "Laundering cash is always the big problem. There are a limited number of ways you can do it, a limited number of reliable people you can turn to. And the Spanish have run some of them down. They've got their hooks into a banker in Venezuela who's dealt with ETA money before. The deal is they won't bust him if he cooperates on this. We take the money to him and he sees that word gets back to Bordagorri's people when it shows up. And they'll have to come and take it back."

"Hang on," says Pascual. "Why not just toss you in jail and plant the money themselves? Why do they need you?"

"Verisimilitude. Goikoetxea and Arrieta know I stole it."

Pascual stands still, looks Katixa in the eye. "And me? Why the hell do they need me?"

"They don't. But they suggested I might like you to take the fall."

Pascual sucks on the cigarette until sparks fly. "Explain."

"That's a pretty dangerous role, the goat out there tethered to the stake. To make the choice to cooperate a little more attractive, they offered me you as a companion."

"Why?"

Katixa cannot bear his gaze. "We turn up together but I go off on a mysterious errand while you hang around Caracas waiting for the bank to call. And one morning a couple of etarras kick in your door. Ideally CESID puts the cuffs on them before you get too badly hurt, but then things don't always go ideally. You were to be my insulation from that risk." Katixa has delivered this with eyes downcast; only at the end does she look up. In her face Pascual reads desolation.

Intent, he says, "Did you tell them about me?"

"No."

"So how did my name come up?"

"They knew all about you, Pascual. They knew about us. They knew we'd been in Aden together. They knew about Brussels. From the start they were asking about you. Had I contacted you, had you contacted me, when was the last time I saw you? I was afraid I'd compromised you by coming to Barcelona and I did what I thought would protect you—I told them I'd had no idea where you were, I knew you had betrayed us six years ago, and the only reason I would look for you would be to kill you." Katixa's voice wavers. "I thought I was protecting you but I think that's what gave them the idea. The evening of that first day, they came back with the plan. We'll give him to you, they said. And you can let him take the bullets."

Pascual resumes pacing, from the door to the window and back, passing the bed. The shadows are deep and the air is stale. Pascual feels a desperate conviction that many things depend on his concentration for the next few minutes. He stubs out the cigarette.

"Two questions," he says. "Why didn't you just run? You had a car, for Christ's sake. You get into some traffic, ditch the car near a Metro stop, four hours later you're in France."

"I can't run," says Katixa.

"Why not?"

She raises her face to his and there are tears again, tracking down her cheeks. She opens her mouth but nothing comes out; Pascual has been holding himself on a tight rein and is on the verge of seizing her by the hair when Katixa says, "They've got my daughter."

The photo is small enough to fit in the palm of a hand, bent, creased, fuzzy at the edges and perhaps a little faded. It shows a girl who could be five or six years old, with dark straight hair covering the forehead and large, very serious dark eyes. There is something about the face, perhaps the eyebrows, that distinctly suggests Katixa. Pascual has absorbed so many shocks that this one has merely plunged him into a mute fatigue. "What's her name?" he says.

"I called her Idoia, after my mother."

Pascual looks at the photograph a minute longer and hands it back. "And who's her father?"

"A dead etarra named José Manuel. Not a great passion. There wasn't much to do in Algiers, what can I tell you?" Katixa stares at the photo. "I never thought about ending it. I never told him, either. In six months he was dead, shot in an ambush on an operation in Guipúzcoa. I got her to my mother in Bilbao when she was six months old and she's pretty much raised her. I've spent as much time with her as I could, which hasn't been enough. I promised her I would come and take her away someday and finally I did."

Pascual has the sensation of infinite ignorance, endless vistas of unsuspected presences opening at every turn. He remembers sex with Katixa at the Méridien; did her motherhood make a difference? Was he too dim to perceive it?

"How did they get her?"

"I brought her with me to Barcelona. She was sleeping when they came and got me. She woke up and started screaming. They had a hell of a time getting her down the stairs without waking the hotel."

"Christ."

"They've let me see her three times. They seem to be treating her decently but she cries when I leave."

Pascual wanders to the window and pulls the shutter open slightly to see a stretch of lamplit street. Out in the night there are secrets, so many his head swims. "Where are they keeping her?"

"I don't know. When they let me see her it's in a car. The last three times it's been here, at a campsite between here and Calella. I think they're keeping her in a villa somewhere close. My handler takes me in the car, another car drives up, Idoia gets out. We have half an hour together with three men watching us, they take her away. It's hard."

"What can they do? They can't just hold her forever."

Desolate, defeated, Katixa says, "They'll kill her if we don't do what they say."

"They wouldn't do that. They can't."

"Of course they can. You think a little scandal has put an end to the way they do business? You've forgotten a lot, haven't you?"

Pascual stares at her. Wearily, he returns to the chair. "I had a second question, remember?"

"What?"

"Why didn't you tell me all this at the start?"

"I was afraid you would run. And if you bolted, I'd have to do it all alone."

Pascual shakes his head. "When would you have pulled all this out of the hat?"

"When it was over, if we were still alive. Or when I found a way out."

Pascual finishes his cigarette at the window, stabs at an ashtray. "What's with your boyfriend, then? Who the fuck is he?"

"He's a CESID agent. He's probably one of the ones they send over the border to hunt etarras. I told them he'd have to be pretty damn good to fool you, but it didn't seem to concern them. How his seamanship is I don't know, but they really do intend to get us to Morocco by that route. They want to have control of us the whole way. In Morocco there'll be someone else."

New horrors occur to Pascual. "So they killed Prieto?"

She nods. "They couldn't let us out of their control."

"Did you help them?"

"No. I knew they would spoil the deal somehow, but I didn't expect that."

Pascual shakes his head. "What happens tonight?"

"We go to dinner, we keep working on him. He pretends to be taken in, agrees to run us down there. In a couple of days we go."

"Lovely. I'm feeling clever for running the scheme on him and all the time you two are running a scheme on me."

"That's the way it's supposed to work."

Pascual reaches for the photo, eases it from Katixa's fingers. "What happens to her in all this?"

"They keep her until I've done my part in Caracas and then she can visit me in jail while I wait for my trial. They've promised me a reduced sentence for my cooperation. Of course, I don't know if we can trust them. Not even to keep us alive."

Pascual feels a great bitterness building. "We're fucked then, aren't we?"

"All three of us," says Katixa.

19

Pascual wakes from a restless doze, sticky with sweat. The room is dark, the air is stale. Katixa is no longer beside him. There is a rustle of cloth at the window and he struggles to rise.

Katixa has opened the shutter a crack, looking out at the night. Pascual wraps his arms around her, kisses her through the hair behind her ear. Once before, they stood at a window like this. Pascual closes his eyes; he will not let her run again.

"He's expecting us," says Katixa. "It's past ten."

Pascual is astonished that it is so early; it feels like the depths of the night. After a time he says, "We're following their script, then?"

"Do we have a choice?" In the silence she turns, nestles her head against his throat, locks her arms around him. Pascual feels her shake. "Forgive me," she breathes. "I don't trust people. It's too hard."

When she is quiet Pascual puts a hand under her chin, raises her face to his. "I forgive you everything. Forever, always. Now tell me how we're going to get Idoia back." She stares at him, blinking, looking for signs. For Pascual something has crystallized.

"Call the bastards," he says. "Make an excuse, tell them a story.

I refuse, I'm too tired. Anything. Reschedule for tomorrow and we'll spend the night thinking."

"Thinking about what? I take no risks with Idoia."

"I know. But there may be some leverage somewhere."

"We can't run, we have nothing to bargain with."

"All I want is some time to think. I couldn't go over there and play a role now anyway."

Katixa remains still for a long moment, then nods abruptly, pulling away. "I'll have to go and talk to Rey."

"Make sure you're composed. Don't give anything away."

She is wiping tears, casting about for clothing. "I'll tell him you're jealous and refuse to let me go on romancing him."

"Perfect."

"That'll freeze them for a day or so, make them think about other schemes."

"Good. There's got to be a pressure point. As long as they don't know that I know, we've got an advantage."

Katixa dresses, spends some time in the bathroom. Pascual gathers packets of fake currency, repacks them in the bag with the real money on top. Katixa emerges, hair swept back in a ponytail and face clean.

She pulls on her jacket. "I'll tell them you're threatening to bolt and they should wait to hear from me."

"We quarreled. I accused you of sleeping with him."

"You threatened to catch the bus back to Barcelona but there isn't one until tomorrow. You stormed off to your room. No. That's not you. You found the nearest bar. There's one just around the corner on the seafront. Camp there and drink. They may have people watching, so make it look real. Brood a bit, complain about women. I'll drop in on my way back and we'll make up, publicly."

Pascual nods. It is Brussels again but this time there will be no farewells. He puts his hand to the back of Katixa's neck and pulls her close for a rough kiss. "We'll beat them," he says.

The bar is spacious, decorated in a hypermodern style full of chrome and glass, with an expansive view of the beach just across the road. In summer this is the place to be in Palamós. Now it is a place where a stranger so badly misinformed as to come here out of season can perch on a stool and drink, unmolested by the barman and his two companions silently slapping cards onto green felt at the other end of the bar. Pascual stares into the mirror behind the whiskey bottles and broods as instructed, though not on women.

With nothing but straws to grasp at he remembers a telephone number in Barcelona. There is a phone in the back by the toilets and Pascual gets enough change from the barman for a call down the coast. Receiver to his ear, he pauses with the first coin on the lip of the slot. Katixa will never agree, he thinks. Nonetheless it is a straw and he drops the coin. The phone rings twelve times at the other end before a man answers. "I have to speak to Shelby," says Pascual in English. "Extremely urgent."

"Who's this?" says the voice, brusque and American.

"It's Pascual and it has to be fast. Can I give you a number for her to call me at?"

"Shoot."

Pascual reads the number off the pay phone. "I've got maybe fifteen minutes," he says.

"Don't go away." There is a click.

Pascual goes into the toilet and pisses, washes his hands, stares into the mirror. He needs a shave, needs a comb, needs a weapon. He comes out just as the telephone rings and scoops it off the hook. "Yeah."

"Where the hell are you?" says Shelby.

"Never mind. Listen. If I could deliver a top ETA commando who wants out but doesn't want to go to a Spanish jail, could you muster enough resources to get us out of a CESID trap?"

"Whoa, slow down a second. What in the hell have you been up to?"

"Just listen. We're in a tight spot and the Spanish are out for blood. If I can get the other party to agree, will you come and talk to us?"

"I'm getting a strange impression you haven't been exactly frank with me."

"That, from an intelligence agent, is pretty goddamn funny. Fine, I'm begging. Will you help us?"

Seconds pass. "I can't go poaching on the Spanish."

Pascual's forehead is against the cool tile of the wall. "Listen, my neck's on the line here. This is as dirty as they come. There's a hostage involved, a child, and the scenario calls for me to wind up dead. Now I know I rate pretty low on the agency's priority list, but I'm offering you quality goods here. Somebody who did the same Mediterranean circuit I did and can fill in some more gaps for you. A prime source, and all you have to do is lean on the Spanish a bit."

"A top ETA commando sounds like a Spanish matter all the way. And I'm not sure there's much we could do if we wanted to."

"You're the fucking CIA, don't tell me you can't do it."

Shelby's voice comes coolly over the wire. "You really don't know what we can and can't do, do you? I'd have to know a hell of a lot more and talk to some people in faraway places."

"Talk to them tonight. Look, this is a career-maker. You bring in the person I'm offering, they'll let you do a lot more than answer the phone."

"I am touched by your concern for my prospects, Pascual, I want you to know that."

"Fuck, what do I have to say to you? Will you at least tell somebody upstairs what I'm proposing?"

"Tell 'em what? Does he have a name? This source of yours?"

This is the moment; Pascual must betray Katixa and he can hear her screaming no. "One of her names was Claudie Leroy. She was involved in an Action Directe operation in Brussels in '87 and she can give you plenty of good stuff on Libya-based networks involving various groups."

"I thought you said she was ETA."

"She is. You get her real name when I get some kind of guarantee."

Pascual can hear Shelby thinking and he is starting to hope. "I'll get on the phone," says Shelby.

"I'm in pretty deep here. If you hear from me again it'll mean my time's just about up."

"Let me give you another number. One that will get me direct."

She reads off a number and Pascual repeats it. "OK. Got it. Thanks."

"Anytime. Hey listen, I have a message for you."

"A message?"

"Yeah. From Dan. He says blame the French."

"What the hell are you talking about?"

"Remember the French consular official who went missing in Beirut last year and then turned up again?"

There is a pause while Pascual labors to catch up. "So?"

"So it seems the Israelis talked to some of their sources and found out you were the main currency in that transaction."

Pascual rubs at his brow, trying to shift gears. "What?"

"The French swapped you to the PFLP in exchange for their influence in getting their guy released. That's how your old pals found you."

Three or four seconds pass. "The French? And how the hell did they find me?"

"Good question. I'm still working on that. But I'd say it's starting to look like your hometown guys did you in."

Pascual exhales into the phone. "And I wanted to come home."

"You've become a national resource, pal."

Pascual slams the phone down. Suddenly he needs fresh air. He pushes out into the night and crosses the road. There is a stiff wind and a roar of waves coming across the sand. Pascual smokes for a while, his back to the town. He hopes he has bought a little insurance but is haunted by the thought that all he has done is betray Katixa. He turns and scans the seafront. A car rolls by. Somewhere, he is sure, somebody is watching him.

He walks toward the old town. There is a garden at the end of the seawalk, pines and palms and flowerbeds. Beyond it the street curves, lined with restaurants. Can Joanet is a sizeable place with a menu board on the pavement and a brightly lit enclosed terrace, mostly empty tonight. Pascual stands in the shadow of a beachfront kiosk, looking across the street. Through glass he can see Katixa sitting across a white tablecloth from Thierry Rey.

They have the look of two lovers, leaning toward each other across the table, except that these lovers are quarreling. Pascual is too far away to see facial expressions, but he can see body language. He can read the tension from here. Katixa talks, Rey listens, arms folded. Rey speaks, stabbing a finger at her. Rey rises, disappears into the main room of the restaurant. Katixa remains at the table, head sagging. Pascual wants to cross the street and start upending tables.

Instead he walks back down the seafront to the bar and orders another cognac. He oscillates between despair and a curious elation: for Katixa he will ride into the teeth of the guns. The card game ends in an outburst of laughter and Pascual listens to the men talk, men with homes, men with wives. Men with no conception of what is going on around them.

Sometime later the door creaks open and Katixa comes in with the wind from the beach. Pascual turns and stares as she approaches him, hands in her jacket pockets, hair tousled and black-eyed gaze leveled at him. The show is partly for the benefit of the men at the end of the bar, whom he can feel watching, but the tension is real. Eye to eye they stand, and finally Pascual puts a hand to the back of her neck. The kiss brings a heavy silence to the bar and a slow incendiary glow to Pascual's loins.

In pitch darkness they make love, in sweat and desperation. Pascual has waited all his life for this. This can ease hunger, fear, pain. Katixa is a dark heat radiating from the loins. Katixa is the musky smell of secret places, the comfort of flesh. Katixa comes at the summit of a long dark uphill journey, a pillow stuffed in her mouth to muffle her cries, thrusting her sex against his tongue. He wipes her tears and holds her; he is willing to forgo his own pleasure to save her wound but after a time she rolls, rises to her hands and knees, guides him into her. Pascual loves her in the dark, collapses in exhaustion with his face buried in her hair.

When Pascual wakes, there is no mistaking the depths of the night. He lies and listens, and becomes certain that Katixa is awake beside him. "I can think of a way," she says. "If we have the balls."

Pascual lies on his back, staring into nothingness. "Tell me."

"Can you still shoot?"

Pascual runs cold in the entrails. In Aden he could shoot but he has never fired a shot in anger. "At close range."

"This will be close. But with luck you won't have to shoot. If you're quick enough, you'll take a couple of prisoners."

Pascual's heart is a drumbeat. "Tell me."

Katixa rises, opens a shutter so that lamplight from the street falls on the floor and shows the ghostly outlines of the room. She finds cigarettes in the dark and lights one, her face glowing orange for a second or two. Perched on the side of the bed she says, "You look like him."

"Who?"

"Rey. There's a resemblance. You could pass for him with a little help."

Seconds pass. "What are you thinking?"

"I'm thinking that we either take some chances or we let them take us further away from my daughter. I'm thinking that the last thing they will expect is boldness."

"You're not thinking of loosing off shots with Idoia in the room, are you?"

"Listen. Both times when they've let me see her, there have been three men. Rey and me in one car, two men and Idoia in the other. They let Idoia out and she runs over to me, Rey wanders over and the three of them smoke while we sit on the playground. They're not at a high stage of alertness."

"What are you thinking, I drop out of a tree and disarm the three of them with a sharpened stick?"

"No. You are the third man."

Pascual watches her cigarette glow. "I don't get it."

"I said there's a resemblance. You're both tall, dark-haired, same general type. His hair is shorter but you can cut yours. And there's the cap and jacket."

"That's not enough. They'll see right through it."

"They'll see the man they expect to see. They'll never get their hands out of their pockets. You get out of the car, they maybe squint at you as you approach, the next thing they see is the muzzle of your gun. I'll have Idoia on the ground, covered up. You disarm them, we lock them in a car trunk. Then we take the other car and run. North, to France."

Pascual shakes his head in the dark. "Madness. To begin with, where do we get the cap, the jacket? The fucking gun, for that matter?"

"We take them from him."

"You are mad."

"No. There's a way to do that, too."

20

With morning light beginning to creep through the gap between the shutters, it stands up to Pascual's scrutiny, if barely. He is at the window watching the world turn gray, his back to Katixa on the bed. "A hell of a lot can go wrong," he says. "Somebody moves too fast, feels like a hero, shots fly."

"You'll have the drop. Just make sure that if somebody gets hurt it's them."

"If we kill CESID people, they'll turn the country upside down to get us. The borders will be sealed tight."

"Work it right and nobody will get hurt. Even if things go bad, we'll be over the border before they find any traces."

"Then what?" Pascual wheels to face her. "Have you thought about what comes next? All the money we have is that top layer in the suitcase. We'll have a six-year-old girl on our hands. We'll be on our own, no money, no resources."

"Except one."

"And what's that?"

"Our story."

Pascual scowls at her. "I'm not following you."

"Prieto, Idoia, the whole thing."

"And how does that help us?"

"That's our leverage. Once we have Idoia back, we're in a terrific position to deal, because they can't let the story out. Give it to TF1 or the *Nouvel Ob* and it'll light up Europe. They'll deal to prevent that, you know they will. Look, the GAL scandal nearly brought down the government, and there they were at least trying to kill etarras. What'll happen when it comes out that they murdered a shipping agent and held a six-year-old girl hostage to work one of their schemes? They'll deal."

Pascual nods, slowly. "And what do we ask for?"

"Immunity. A little cash. A word to the French that they wouldn't object if we flew to, say, Martinique."

Pascual takes a deep breath, whistles it out. "It could work."

"It could, yes. It all depends on you."

Pascual returns to the window. "Let's put Idoia first," he says. "What happens to her if we do nothing, go through with the plan?"

"I wind up in jail, you wind up penniless in Caracas, maybe dead, Idoia winds up a ward of the state, sharing a bunk with an eleven-year-old gypsy prostitute."

"All right. I'm just thinking of the risks. Flying lead is not good for six-year-old girls. Or their parents."

The bed creaks as Katixa rises. She pads across the floor to stand at his shoulder. "It's no disgrace to be scared. I was always scared. Every time."

Pascual can see foam on the beach, luminous in the growing light. "I just want to be sure we have no better choices."

Katixa turns him, puts her arms around him, rests her forehead on his cheek. "We have no good choices. And we don't have much time to decide."

Pascual kisses her, lips tensing against her soft warm temple. Outside, an early riser speeds down the seafront road, the sound of the engine dying away to nothing. "I've already decided," he says.

"They're on the fifth floor," says Katixa over the sighing of the waves. "As far as I can tell, the building's mostly empty. It's the off-season, it's a good place to put a safe house. I don't know how many people they have in all, but I've seen three different men up there. There's a phone and that's my contact." They are on the beach, looking inland. Winter is coming and the gulls have retaken the beach. Pascual shivers in the wind.

The building is a ten-story apartment complex on the Passeig del Mar, long balconies with a view of the sea, prime real estate. "What if they refuse?" he says.

"They won't refuse. I'll tell them you've taken off, I'll insist on seeing Idoia before I agree to discuss the next move. I'll get female and hysterical if I have to."

"You're sure they'll tell you to come to the apartment?"

"That's their base. Where do you think they've been keeping me? The hotel room was for show. It was all a fake. The first thing they'll do is haul me back there."

"What if they send somebody different with you to see Idoia?"

"That's a risk we run. So far it's always been Rey."

"What if the outer door's locked?"

"It won't be. When I go over there I'll tape the lock, prop it open, something. I'll find a way. You'll get in. Sit on the first landing and you'll hear us when we come out of the apartment upstairs. Remember, don't move unless you hear me say something. If there's more than one of them, or some other reason to call it off, I'll keep my mouth shut."

"What if we can't find the car?"

"We'll find it. There's always parking on the seafront somewhere close to the door. Anyway, with a gun to his head, he'll tell us where it is."

"What if they're watching me?"

"They may be, I don't know. But if you get on that bus I don't think they'll follow. They've depended on me all along to track you and I don't think they'll change. In any event, make the bus in a last-minute dash and they won't be prepared."

They trudge a few feet along the sand. Pascual has not felt this deep inner tension, this focused alertness, since he made his break in Athens. He is feeling for reflexes, skills and habits long discarded.

Wind whips hair about Katixa's face. "The bus leaves from the plaza just up that street there. I'm not sure what time. There's a bar there. We'll go and get a coffee and you can find out about the bus. The haircut may be the hard part."

"There's got to be a barber in this town."

"Try to find one fast. The timing is hard to predict. I'll call them and tell them you've split, go over there, throw a fit, demand to see Idoia. If they're in an agreeable mood I might have to stall them and if they're irritable I might have to use all my feminine wiles to get them to agree. With one thing and another you should try to be in place by ten and you might have a hell of a wait. How are you for cash?"

"Down to pocket change."

"I'll give you enough for the bus and the haircut."

"I assume we don't bother to check out of the hotel?"

"It's a good bet somebody there is under orders to report on us. I'll retrieve the francs. Is there anything in your room you can't bear to abandon?"

Pascual shakes his head. He scans the horizon. "You're sure we can take him? How fast is he? How good is he?"

"Remember how you felt with that *moro*'s knife at your throat? He won't move. Once you've got the gun, he's ours."

They have talked through it a dozen times, in the wee hours, watching the streets grow light beyond the shutters. Every operation Pascual was ever on was like this: contingencies, fallbacks, places and times; what-ifs with no answers, the risk factor that cannot be removed. At some point you must leap. "What if they change the meeting place and don't tell you?"

Katixa tosses her head angrily, a light of desperation in her eyes. "Then we'll have a hostage to bargain with. It's not the best-case scenario, but it beats getting on that boat."

Pascual nods, thinking of the insurance he holds in the form of a Barcelona telephone number, insurance that might just possibly mitigate the worst-case scenario.

Gulls wheel and cry, waves expire on the sand. The sun is breaking fitfully through ragged clouds. Pascual is at the lip of the precipice; with Katixa he fears nothing. Inside his coat pocket his hand closes around the handle of Katixa's knife. "Let's go get that coffee," he says.

■ ■ ■ ■

The bus is nearly empty: one old man has boarded before him and there are a couple of passengers from further up the line. They stare at him without interest as he presents his ticket to Sant Feliu and makes his way down the aisle to the rear. He finds his assigned seat and stares at whitewashed walls as the bus creeps through narrow streets. Tonight, thinks Pascual, we will be in France. Tonight I will have a family. Tonight, perhaps, I will be in jail.

There is no longer any open space between towns; it has all been filled in with hotels and miniature golf courses and German restaurants. In Sant Antoni de Calonge the bus stops and Pascual bolts to the front. "I have to get off; I forgot something." The driver tries to dissuade him; his fare is not refundable. Pascual leaps off and makes tracks.

Now he is launched; he is a stealth missile, off the radar screen. Pascual's heart beats rapidly; in the crisp morning air he is the man who confounded the police of Europe for six years. He is invisible and he is deadly and this time he is right.

He has landed in a no-man's-land of shut-up restaurants and empty vacation colonies. He hikes until he finds where the natives live. In a sleepy café he has a coffee and asks after a barber.

His locks fall as he watches in the mirror. Rey wears his hair fashionably full but without the tresses that spill ten centimeters below Pascual's collar. Hiking again, Pascual stuffs Father Costa's old woolen coat into a rubbish bin, transferring the knife to the sleeve of his sweater. He is stripped down for action, a little cold in the breeze but generating heat with the exertion of walking. He stops in a chemist's shop and with the last of Katixa's cash buys a pair of cheap sunglasses.

He is back in the center of Palamós before he realizes it, stumbling into the plaza where he caught the bus. He orientates himself and heads toward the sea.

He spots the blue Audi parked on the Passeig del Mar. Ten stories of balconies rise above him. Pascual cannot approach the site of an opposition safe house without hair rising on the back of his neck. Casual, he remembers, the hardest thing on earth: to walk on enemy ground without sending out panic signals. He moves into the shadow of the buildings, making it harder to be spotted from above. An old man on a Vespa putters down the street past him.

He mounts the steps and pushes; the heavy outer door opens. There is a tight fold of paper jamming the latch in the disengaged position. The foyer is empty. The elevator is at the back of the hall, the stairway to the right. Pascual pads softly up the steps, into the gloom.

Off the radar, primed and locked on target, Pascual waits.

In the quiet of a deserted apartment building late in a drowsy morning, Pascual is at peace. He has leaped and is in midair; this is the airy suspension that precedes the shock of landing. Pascual closes his eyes. Tonight another life begins; he is already thinking of Paris, potential allies, places to hide. He wants a cigarette but will not risk it.

He has lost track of time when a door opens somewhere above. Footsteps echo in the stairwell, more than one person, shuffling, stopping. The door closes with a mild reverberation. Distinctly Pascual hears Katixa say, with acid in her voice, "Don't touch me."

As the elevator hums, Pascual descends the stairs. He waits at the side of the elevator door, knife in hand. When the doors open, a step sounds inside and Pascual swings into the car and presses the knife to Rey's throat. "Don't move," Pascual says, slamming him against the rear wall of the elevator. The surprise is so complete that Rey's face registers no expression. Katixa is on Rey in an instant, reaching inside the jacket and coming away with a black automatic, dancing back again and stabbing at the button to close the elevator doors. "Take off the jacket," she says, gun leveled at his head.

Pascual has already snatched the denim cap from Rey's head and put it on his own. He holds the point of the knife at the tender skin just under Rey's right eye, at arm's length. Pascual gives the tip of the knife a twitch. "Now," he says. "Or you lose an eye."

The doors ease shut. Rey blinks, shock giving way to a cold assessment of his position. He wriggles out of his jacket, the knife hovering in his face. Katixa has located the switch that shuts off the elevator and tripped it. Pascual snatches the jacket, slips the knife into a side pocket, and pulls it on. "Trousers," says Katixa. "Fast, fast." Rey hesitates and her arm goes rigid, the automatic hovering at forehead level. He undoes his belt buckle. *"Vamos,"* says Katixa. "If it was for my sake, you'd have them off by now." The look in her eye is deadly.

"They'll shoot you like dogs," Rey says, unzipping.

"You'll die first," says Katixa.

Pascual has kicked off his boots and is stripping off his jeans. Rey's trousers come down and Pascual snatches them, tugging them clear of his feet, making him stumble. They go on without trouble; Pascual zips and buckles. He pulls a ring of keys from the pocket, identifying the key to the Audi. Rey is pulling on Pascual's jeans. Katixa punches the button to open the elevator doors. She gives Rey a shove. "Move. Grab the shoes. You can put them on while he brings the car." To Pascual she says, "You found it?"

"I found it." Pascual has laced up his shoes and is heading for the door.

"Pull up in front." Katixa is herding Rey toward the foot of the stairs, gun to the back of his skull. Rey holds his elbows away from his body, hands slightly raised. "Your girl's going to miss her mother," he says.

Pascual pushes out onto the street. He pulls the cap low over his eyes, surprised at the brightness outside. It is a relief to move his limbs after the long wait. The keys are in his hand; he has to restrain himself from breaking into a run. Until this moment he has not quite believed they could pull it off. Now they must get Rey into the car. Quick down the steps, Katixa with the gun at his back. There is no one to see anything. Pascual does not believe Rey will risk a shot through a kidney. On the passenger seat, with Katixa and the automatic in the back seat behind him, he will ride quietly up into the hills, where they will transfer him to the trunk.

The hundred meters to the blue Audi are an endless march. Pascual is running cold now, convinced there is a CESID team watching his every step, undeceived. He reaches the car at last and jabs clumsily at the lock; he swears at himself, exhales, slips the key in. The lock pops and Pascual opens the door. He folds himself into the seat, slams the door, and finds the ignition. The key goes in and he pumps the accelerator once, twice. His legs are cramped; he gropes for the seat release lever between his legs. He finds it, pushes back, adjusts the seat to his liking, reaches for the key again.

Pascual looks out over the beach to the bright blue sea and takes a deep breath. He has done it; he is another man now. Why then can he not turn the key?

Rey is as big as Pascual or bigger; the seat was adjusted for a shorter person. The certainty that Katixa was the last person to drive this car clicks into place. And yet that is impossible. Pascual knows the clock is ticking; there will be time for questions later. And yet he cannot turn the key.

He depresses the clutch, pumps the accelerator, and starts to exert pressure with thumb and index finger, unable to understand but hearing the clock ticking. He has broken into a sweat and his hand will not obey. Why would Katixa have driven the car this morning? Pascual stomps on the clutch and wills himself to turn the key. Suddenly he hears Dan saying, "Someday you'll step into a car, turn the key, and BAM! You won't feel a thing."

Absurdity. He tries again to turn the key but his hand will not move. Pascual has bottomless faith in Katixa, and he will show it by turning the key. There is an explanation. Still his hand will not obey. Doubt is a serpent stirring at the back of his brain. Pascual tears the door open; he will take doubt by the throat and slay it. He jerks the hood release lever and strides to the front of the car, the electric whine telling him the keys are still in the ignition. He tears open the hood and looks. Long ago Pascual was taught how to kill in this fashion. He looks for the telltale wire, the clip on the ignition wire to the distributor or the starter. He can make nothing of the unfamiliar engine of the Audi; he is no mechanic and he sees only a jumble of machinery. Sweat creeps into his eyebrows; he begins to see, to navigate his way around the engine. There is the distributor. Everything seems in order. But there are other ways to booby-trap a car.

Pascual closes the hood, very gently, and drops to his knees, then his stomach, the thin electric keening from the open door scraping at his nerves.

Under the car he sees nothing. There are no explosives taped to the undercarriage, no pendulum waiting for the car to move in order to close the contact, and his relief is immense; he is merely giving in to nerves, and Katixa is waiting. He is about to rise when he sees the thin black wire, winding along the exhaust pipe toward the rear of the car. For three seconds he is paralyzed. This is a wire that should not be there. This wire seems to come from the vicinity of the fuse box. Pascual scrambles to his feet, rips the keys out of the ignition, and makes for the trunk. He fumbles with keys, finds the right one, opens the trunk.

An ocean of Semtex fills the trunk. Pascual gapes at the brick-sized packets of plastic explosive, black lettering stenciled on greasy paper. He can see no detonators, but they will be underneath, where the wire comes up through a small hole, easily drilled. There is enough plastic here to make a crater of this end of the street, blow out windows all over town and atomize the man who turns the key.

Pascual is adrift in a sea of icy sweat. In shock he closes the trunk, with infinite gentleness. In shock he turns and looks back up the street, appealing to Katixa. He sees only the figure of a man, standing alone on the fifth balcony up, a hundred meters away.

In shock Pascual begins to run.

What is this emotion? Pascual wonders. Is this grief? Is this rage? Is this merely an emotional breakdown? He has been in the confessional for hours, his eyes growing accustomed to the dark, at long intervals hearing old women whisper, moving quietly about the church. The shock has worn off and he has had time to think.

In reality he was thinking even as he ran; the cap and the jacket went into the first rubbish bin he passed and he laid a false trail through the back streets of the town before scaling a wall and dou-bling back to the small church, the first likely refuge he spotted, the confessional standing empty and inviting in a corner. The irony of his hiding place is not lost on him; Pascual has always lacked faith. He lacked faith in Katixa, and that is why he is still alive.

He has worked it out, desperate for a way to believe in her but finding none. Pascual teeters again at the brink of the abyss. In order not to plunge he must go very cold, as cold as during the dark years. Cold and iron-hard: Pascual begins to plot his steps in the coming hours.

His craving for a cigarette signals to him that he is returning to the land of the living. Switching trousers was a masterful touch, as Rey's papers came with the switch; no clever forensic technician would ever piece together the real identity of the scattered bits of charred flesh left by the explosion.

Cold, glacier cold. Pascual stirs and pushes open the door of the confessional. On stiff limbs he emerges into the light of the central nave and freezes. Standing by the altar, staring at him in surprise, is a white-haired priest. Pascual stares back; the priest says, "Did you want to confess?" in a dubious tone.

"No, father." Pascual approaches him, seeing apprehension in the old priest's eyes. "But I am terribly cold. I would be grateful if you could lend me a coat."

Priests and overcoats. Pascual wonders if every old priest has a closet full of them. This one is good; it keeps him warm and changes his outline. Night has fallen and no one else is abroad. Pascual believes he understands but knows who he must talk to.

This time he approaches from the other direction. Under the streetlamps he can see that the blue Audi has disappeared. Had he had his wits about him, Pascual could have disconnected the wire and driven it away himself. The key is still in his trouser pocket. Perhaps there was another one; otherwise he has no doubt Katixa knows how to hotwire a car. Looking up at the fifth-floor balcony he sees light behind curtains.

The label next to the button by the number 5A reads "Dupleix." Nobody has unjammed the latch and Pascual pushes the door open. He makes directly for the stairs. On the fifth floor he finds 5A and raps on the door. Silence, muffled footsteps, a voice. "Who is it?"

"Your neighbor. I have to talk to you." Seconds pass and Pascual wonders if he has chosen the wrong formula. Neighbors are evidently thin on the ground in winter. Finally locks click and the door swings open. The man who stands peering at Pascual is short, bald, chubby, with glasses like the ones men wore a hundred years ago, tiny oval lenses in wire frames. Judging by the look on his face he harbors grave doubts. "A man came to see you today," says Pascual.

"Who are you?" The little bald man eases the door shut by a few degrees.

"He wore a cap and a sailing jacket. He came to you a little before eleven and he left about twelve o'clock. He might have had a woman with him, or she might have waited in the hall. After he left, you stood on the balcony and watched him walk down the street and get into a car. Then he got out again, looked in the trunk and ran."

The door closes another few degrees and Pascual slides his foot into the gap. The man says, "Please remove your foot. You're not my neighbor and I have no idea who you are or what you're talking about." His Castilian is fluent but accented.

Pascual slips into French. "You know damn well what I'm talking

233

about. And I know who you are. I'm not the police, either French or Spanish, but if you don't talk to me they'll be hearing some ugly rumors. Now if you'll let me in we can talk like civilized people." Pascual is keeping his temper on a tight rein, but he is ready to batter the door down if need be. There is a standoff lasting a few seconds and then the man steps back, opening the door wide. Pascual walks into a living room furnished with mismatched sticks of flimsy modernistic furniture and lit by a single floor lamp. He turns as the door closes and stands with his hands in the pockets of the borrowed overcoat.

His host circles warily along the far side of the room. "So who am I?"

"You're Alain Dupleix and you look just like your photos. I haven't read anything under your byline for some time but left-wing *engagé* journalism must be a decent living, to judge by this place."

"Book royalties mainly, and not all that decent." Still frowning but apparently gratified, he says, "Can I offer you something to drink?"

"You could offer me a cigarette if you have any."

Dupleix shrugs and walks to a low table at the end of a sofa. He produces cigarettes and a lighter from a drawer and watches as Pascual gets one going. "All right. You know me, but I still don't know you."

"I'm the man who walked to the car and then ran away."

"No, you're not."

"I assure you I am."

Dupleix opens his mouth to speak, thinks better of it, turns his head slightly, narrows his eyes. He is an ugly little man but, Pascual can see, a very sharp one. A long moment goes by as Pascual smokes.

"That's extremely interesting," says Dupleix. "And what happened to my visitor?"

"I have no idea. But I would find it extremely interesting to know."

"And what was in the trunk of the car?"

"Enough *plastique* to have you sweeping up glass for the next two days."

After a frozen moment a slow smile stretches Dupleix's thick lips. "Perhaps you'd like to sit down and start at the beginning."

Pascual shakes his head. "First I want to know his name."

Dupleix's chin rises. "That, I'm afraid I can't tell you."

"Then you won't get the rest of the story. Thanks for the cigarette."

"Wait." Dupleix stands with arms akimbo and makes his calculations. Seconds pass and he says, "His name was Ignacio Bordagorri."

Dupleix brings cognac. Pascual has not stirred from the chair. He wants nothing more than to sit here for eternity, staring into nothing. He looks up when Dupleix waves the bottle at him. "You're surprised," says the Frenchman, pouring.

"No, I knew it all along." Pascual takes the glass and drinks, grimacing. Smoke and spirits; he will not need food for hours yet. "I should have known it, anyway."

Dupleix gives himself a generous splash and sets the bottle on the table. "Who are you?" he asks.

Pascual has begun to think again and does not reply. "What did he tell you?"

Dupleix seats himself on the sofa and peers across at Pascual. "Until I know who you are I say nothing more."

Pascual tips his glass to him. "All right, I'll guess. He told you he wanted to come in from the cold and he wanted you to mediate. You've done it before—you were the go-between when Awwad Marwan gave himself up to the French in '89. And you've written about the Basques before; you probably talked to Bordagorri at the time. Today he gave you the old story about being tired and wanting to deal. Something along those lines. He probably also told you the Spanish were intent on killing him. He said he'd be in touch and he left. You went out to the balcony to watch him go, maybe because he told you he might be under surveillance and he knew you would look for it. And you were supposed to see him die."

Dupleix has not moved, his frown deepening. "And then?"

"And then when you have picked the splinters of glass out of your face you take up your pen. You write outraged articles about how you witnessed this act of state terrorism, the GAL catching up with Bordagorri at last. There's no corpse left but there's you to swear it was Bordagorri—you knew him. You make it a *cause célèbre* and the Spanish finally stop looking for Bordagorri because on the one hand they're really convinced he's dead now, something they've never been before, and on the other they're so busy defending themselves before the outrage of the world that they can't spare the attention. And our friend Bordagorri, after a quiet couple of months, slips out of the country and takes up somewhere new, free at last of an identity that had grown a bit cumbersome."

Dupleix drinks, a sour look on his face. "I'm not ready to take your word for all this."

"He set you up, comrade. He came this close to making you his pet scribbler, a dupe for the ages."

"Dupe? State terrorism is no myth, friend. Look at Goikoetxea and Arrieta."

Pascual gapes. "What? What about them?"

"Haven't seen a paper today, eh? They found them yesterday near Durango, shot, half-rotted, the initials GAL carved into their foreheads."

Pascual stares, and then he laughs, shaking with it, spilling cognac. Dupleix glares at him. Calmer, Pascual shakes his head in pity. "Bordagorri killed them, don't you see? He killed them and took the money."

"What money?"

Pascual drains the cognac and stands. "Do you have a car?"

"Why?"

"Because if you do we'll go and find him and he can answer all your questions himself."

"I thought you said you didn't know what happened to him."

"I have an idea where to begin looking."

Things are moving too fast for Dupleix; he has the ghastly look of a child whose matches have started a conflagration. "But if you're telling the truth, he won't be exactly glad to see us, will he?"

"I should say not. But you're a journalist, aren't you? What's he going to do, shoot you?"

Dupleix manages to croak out, "Where, then?"

"Barcelona."

■ ■ ■ ■

Dupleix's car is a natty little BMW. The Frenchman is silent until they are clear of Palamós and then the questions begin, the right ones, the key ones, the ones Pascual will never answer. He lets his head loll to one side, feigning sleep. Dupleix waits for answers, begins to grow irritated. Abruptly the car slows. "Listen. I really must insist. I deserve a little more consideration, sticking my neck out like this. I don't even know who you are. Either I get a little more frankness or our collaboration is at an end." The car grinds to a halt on the rocky verge. Pascual opens his eyes, gropes for the door handle, tumbles out. He takes two steps, doubles over, retches. Cognac burns back up his throat and dribbles onto the ground, the pungent odor rising. Behind him he hears Dupleix leave the car, come warily around to the rear. "What's wrong with you?"

Pascual moans gently, breathily, slightly dazed. Until the nausea actually hit he intended only to fake it. He waits for Dupleix to come within range and then whips a hard left upward into the soft belly. Dupleix makes a sound of great exertion but is suddenly incapable of movement, bug-eyed in the moonlight, bending forward. As he sags to his knees Pascual nips the keys out of his hand.

He stops at a tavern on the outskirts of Sant Feliu for directions, and a rousing discussion ensues, complete with tattered map. There is no direct route from Sant Feliu to Vic and he must choose a winding road through the hills or a lengthy detour on better roads. He buys the map at an inflated price and departs. The route through the hills is shorter and there is little traffic. Pascual drives just beyond the edge of prudence, cornering with a squeal and passing with abandon. The world is reduced to white lines and lights sailing in the darkness;

as a burned limb shies from the flame, there are things Pascual's mind simply cannot approach.

He rolls into Vic late in the evening and has to ask for the road to Sant Julià. The streets are deserted; Pascual makes a wrong turn or two before finding the villa. He rolls past and parks around a corner. On foot he explores; after a glance around he scales the low wall. He half expects to see a blue Audi parked at the side of the house but there is nothing there and no lights showing. At the rear of the house Pascual punches in a pane of glass and unlatches a window into the kitchen.

The house is empty. Pascual storms through silent rooms, turning on lights, looking for clues. He finds a desk in a study; there are papers in a drawer. Ticket stubs, old letters, a bill or two. Three of the envelopes bear a Barcelona address. Pascual notes it and switches off the lights. He leaves by the window. He has nothing but this hunch to go on but this cold dark rage will carry him for days.

By midevening he is crossing the Besòs and wondering how to get where he is going. He blunders about in the city traffic, finally finding the Diagonal. *Av. Pearson* said the envelopes; that is a street up on the heights above Pedralbes, rarefied air for the wealthy. Pascual turns off the Diagonal at Pedralbes and climbs, heavy on the accelerator.

In the rearview mirror he can see lights strewn out across the flat coastal strip behind him. He turns onto Pearson, still climbing. There are consulates here, exclusive schools, the homes of the wealthy. Pascual cruises, watching the villas go by. There are walls with locked gates. He reaches a hairpin turn and crawls around it; there are more villas. The numbers are hard to spot; Pascual slows, creeps along in second gear, looking for the house.

When he finds it he drives on by, counting houses. He heads up the hill at speed. There is a hairpin bend and suddenly there are no more houses, only empty hillside above. Pascual pulls to the side and parks. He opens the trunk of the BMW and roots around until he finds the tire lever. Closing the trunk softly, he stands for a moment and then begins to walk.

22

The city spreads to the sea below, a vast scattering of lights. There is a cold wind. From a gap between two villas Pascual can look down over a scrub-grown hillside into the back gardens of the houses below. He counts houses again and steps off the road and begins to descend. He takes it slowly, placing his feet with care, avoiding noise. There are garden walls to either side of him, a few trees on the slope. In a minute he has reached the back wall of a villa with a *porte-cochère* at the side. He stands for a moment listening and watching. The upstairs windows are dark and he cannot see the ground floor. The wall, however, is only head high. Pascual feels carefully for broken glass on the top of the wall and, finding none, lays the tire lever on top of it and pulls up for a look. There is a small garden and a French window opening onto a terrace. Through the window Pascual can make out a dark room with light spilling through a doorway. He listens for a second or two and scrambles over the wall, dropping down on hard-packed earth. He listens for a moment and takes down the tire lever.

The Audi sits under the *porte-cochère*. There is light behind blinds at the side of the house and he treads softly to the window to stand on tiptoe. He can see nothing and hear nothing. He makes his way to the back of the house again and steps onto the terrace. Standing at the

French window he can make out a room full of furniture, seen dimly in the light coming through a doorway. Pascual steps off the terrace and explores the other side of the house. Here there is a window just above his head, and through it Pascual can see the upper reaches of a tiled wall. It is a single-glazed window and Pascual can hear voices now, along with the scrapes and clinks of kitchen noise. He cannot make out words but he would recognize Katixa's voice in a hurricane.

Pascual has a plan in the way that a wolf has a plan when he descends on the sheep; prudence plays little part in it, fear none. He has no firearms and they will have several; all he has is surprise and the ruthlessness of the damned. He returns to the Audi. He gives it another five seconds' thought, not hesitating but rehearsing, and inserts the tire lever into the crack of the door on the driver's side.

He gives it enough of a wrench to set off the car alarm and then moves swiftly back along the side of the house as the electronic whoop fills the night. He hops onto the terrace and steps to the French window. He waits out an excruciating half minute or so before the car alarm shuts off. In the silence he hears careful footsteps on the drive. The room beyond the French window is still dark. He works the tire lever into the gap between the doors and pulls hard as he exerts steady pressure with shoulder and hip. The latch gives with a crack and the door swings open.

If Pascual is working on a tactical principle at all, it is *do what they don't expect*. Instead of going in, he pulls back onto the terrace and makes for the corner of the house. He can hear Katixa now, somewhere inside, calling to Bordagorri. Nobody is panicking; these are people who have lived in crisis for years.

Pascual hugs the wall at the corner of the house and hears

Bordagorri coming fast, back toward the terrace to take the enemy in the rear. Pascual is making it up as he goes along and nearly pays for it as Bordagorri comes around the corner fast, low and too far away for a clean whack on the head. Pascual has to lunge and hack to catch the wrist as it brings the pistol up at him. Something breaks but Bordagorri makes no sound; he merely goes for the gun with the other hand as it clatters onto the flagstones. He fumbles it and Pascual kicks him square in the face, breaking his nose and knocking him away from the gun.

The gun is a CZ 75, a Czech automatic Pascual has fired many times. Pascual flings the tire lever away over the garden wall and hauls Bordagorri to his feet by a handful of hair. He jams the muzzle in his ear and shoves him off the terrace on boneless legs toward the *porte-cochère*. They go in at the side door and there is Katixa, coming out of a room at the end of a hallway, low and looking for targets, two hands on her weapon. Bordagorri is sagging back against Pascual but still moving, and Katixa freezes in her crouch as she reads the situation, one knee on the floor.

"Drop it," says Pascual. "Yesterday."

Katixa sights down the barrel of her automatic but Pascual can see that she knows it will take a better shot than she can guarantee. Still she hesitates and to encourage her Pascual takes the gun out of Bordagorri's ear and presses it to the top of his scapula. Bordagorri's body makes an effective silencer, and blood and bone blow out the front of his shoulder with no more than a loud messy pop. Bordagorri stiffens and then something like the sound of water going down a drain comes out of his throat. "Now," says Pascual, moving the gun back to the ear. "On the floor and send it this way."

Katixa lowers the pistol, goes into a kneeling position, and slides the gun along the tiles toward Pascual. Pascual gives Bordagorri enough of a shove to start him on his way down and scoops up Katixa's gun. "Back through the door," he says as Bordagorri slides down the wall, wide-eyed, ruining the paint.

Pascual drives Katixa back into a living room filled with bright heavy furniture no one has ever sat on, a showplace room with no signs of life: no books, no ashtrays, no stray wineglasses. A single lamp lights the expensive desolation. To the left is a dining room in shadow and beyond it the lighted kitchen. Pascual sees enough to satisfy him that no one is waiting in ambush and slips the second gun into the pocket of his coat. Katixa is still backing away and Pascual stops her with a jerk of the gun. She is calm but watchful, a coiled spring.

"You're the queen of the liars," says Pascual. "You're an artist. And I'm your masterpiece."

Katixa raises her chin. She opens her mouth and then closes it again. In one instant Pascual sees her as she is, lovely and deadly and utterly alien, and himself as he was, duped, an imbecile, on the other side of a chasm. Now at long last he is wise. "You're a snake," he says.

"I'm a fighter," says Katixa.

"You're a whore."

"Ah. That's the best you can do, is it?" Katixa will never stop challenging him, that ghost of a smile on her lips.

Pascual's arm is tiring. Lowering the gun to his hip he heaves a long sigh and says, "Along with everything else you're a genius. My compliments."

"It was his idea." She juts her chin in the direction of the hallway, where Pascual can hear Bordagorri slithering and groaning.

"No. It has you written all over it. The whole thing from the start was for Dupleix, wasn't it? From the very start."

Katixa shrugs. "Of course."

"Seems like a lot of trouble, but then an eyewitness confirmation of Bordagorri's death was worth a lot, wasn't it?"

"About five million francs."

"What was the scenario before I found your wound?"

"We had two or three to choose from. That was the least of our worries. You're easy."

Pascual nods, despairing. "I've always believed anything people told me. Throw in the occasional blow job and I'm a dog on a leash."

"You said it, not me."

"So where were you heading? I doubt Venezuela was really on the itinerary."

Katixa hesitates. Her eyes flick to the CZ 75 and Pascual can see her estimating chances. "Manila," she says. "Money can still buy anything out in that part of the world."

"It's the Wild West, they say." Pascual, too, wants to talk forever; when the talking stops, the hard part starts. "Who was the girl in the picture?"

"A niece. A nice little girl in Bilbao."

"You're a quick thinker. And an actress, Christ, what an actress. You almost made me believe you loved me."

Katixa is trying; Pascual can see how hard she is trying with that sad-eyed look. "I did," she says. "Until you sold us out."

"Everybody but you."

Katixa's eyes are fixed on him; she smiles, and in spite of everything it tears at his heart. Bordagorri is no longer slithering; these

are firm steps behind Pascual. He wheels in time to see him come
through the doorway, death's-head eyes wide above the crushed
nose dripping blood, one good arm clawing at him. Pascual dodges,
Bordagorri catching the tail of his coat, teetering on unsteady legs.
Pascual caves in teeth with the butt of the automatic, sending him
to his knees; Katixa is moving fast. With Bordagorri hanging onto
his coat like a legless beggar Pascual spins to freeze her with the gun
before she can come over the top of the sofa; she halts as if yanked
by a string and slides back to the floor. Bordagorri releases Pascual's
coat suddenly and sprawls away on his back, fumbling one-handed
with the gun he has pulled out of Pascual's pocket. Pascual puts two
quick shots from the CZ 75 through his chest, nothing silencing
the CRACK CRACK of the automatic this time. Pascual sights on
Katixa's forehead as she backs into a wall. *"Tranquila,"* he says. She is
breathing deeply, watching her lover on the floor.

Bordagorri is dying. Wet noises of profound distress are coming from his throat. He is on his back, trying to rise, the eyes in the
wrecked face intent on Pascual, wide with panic. He gives up the
effort and his head hits the tiles with a dull crack. Pascual advances
on Katixa, pistol leveled at her. She has never looked more beautiful
and he nearly shoots her just for that. He sees no fear in the midnight
eyes, only a preternatural alertness. She is three steps from the arch-
way into the dining room and her shoulders turn slightly.

"Move and I'll kill you," says Pascual.

Katixa freezes. "You're going to kill me anyway," she says.

"No. Much worse. I'm going to turn you in."

For the first time Katixa wavers; her eyes betray her. Katixa is
afraid. "You know what they'll do to me?"

Her fear gives Pascual strength. "Nothing you don't deserve."

She sags against the wall. "So, after all, you're nothing more than a run-of-the-mill informer."

"No. I would have gone to the ends of the earth with you, you know that. I loved you."

"And I loved you. Until you betrayed us. Sometimes I love you still."

"You tried to *kill* me," Pascual says, voice edging up the scale.

Katixa shakes her head. She is weary, infinitely weary. "It was his idea."

"You tried to talk him out of it, did you?"

"No. But I was sorry."

"You were sorry?"

"Pascual."

"How could you love someone and do what you did to me?"

"Pascual. The money."

Pascual cannot believe his ears. "The *money?*"

"It's yours now. The way out is all ready. Papers, tickets, everything. You take his place and in three days we're in Manila with five million francs."

"You can stop now."

"The money's in a suitcase in the front bedroom, under the bed. The papers are in the top dresser drawer. Your passport's there too. We're booked on a flight out of Madrid tomorrow afternoon."

"You're mad."

"Then forget me. Let me go out the back way, over the wall, and you've got the money."

"I don't want the *money.*"

"Don't you? Five million francs, Pascual."

"I want you!" Pascual's scream puts everything on hold. He still has the gun trained on her chest. Katixa is frozen, her look genuinely surprised, like a woman whose cat has lashed out and scratched her.

Pascual lets the gun fall to his side. "But that's only because I'm a slow learner," he says, quietly.

Katixa begins to tremble. She raises her hands to him. "But Pascual," she says. "Now you can have me."

"You're mad."

"You own me now. Don't you see?"

"Stop it."

"Bordagorri owned me, but you killed him. I belong to you now. Haven't you understood yet? I'm a whore, remember? And what does a whore need more than someone to own her?" Katixa's hands fall to her side and abruptly Pascual sees the thirteen-year-old girl, hearing her father's breathing at the door. Pascual watches her shake and thinks no, no, never again. And still he takes two steps toward her. "Katixa," he says. "You're not well. You're sick. We can heal you, my love."

Her kick drives straight to his groin. Pascual doubles up in agony and feels the gun wrenched out of his hand. He has just enough left to grab her wrist with the other hand. She nearly knocks him off his grip with an elbow to the face but through stars and the extraordinary trauma in his nether regions he manages to hang on, with both hands now, fighting the twist of the muzzle toward his face. She splits a lip with a right cross to his mouth but desperation is making him strong. Pascual has never left his feet and his move is instinctive; he pulls and turns with all his weight, bringing Katixa's much lighter body with him. Like a hammer-thrower, he pivots, sailing her across the dining room, gun in hand, to skim across the table and fetch up against a cabinet on the far wall with a rattling crash. She bounces onto the floor but she still has the gun; now it is a race. Katixa has made it to a sitting position, cobwebs clearing and the gun coming up, as Pascual rolls clear of Bordagorri's body with the second gun in his hand. In the light from the kitchen Katixa is sighting the CZ 75 on his forehead with both hands, eyes black as the night and wide as creation, when Pascual squeezes off a shot from his knees that kicks her onto her back. She fires into the ceiling as she falls.

Pascual rises, totters, and stands over her. Blood seeps from a hole in her chest. Katixa's eyes are open and she is trying to raise the pistol. On her face is a look of intense concentration. Her arm shakes but the automatic rises until it is trained on his breast. Pascual spreads his arms. "I forgive you everything," he croaks.

Katixa looks him in the eye and time is suspended and then her face distorts in pain and her arm falls, the gun thumping on the floor. Katixa coughs, sending a spray of blood onto his trousers, and he can see from her eyes that she is finished.

He screams then, turning away, wheeling across the room, sustaining the vowel of the single word NO at the top of his lungs until he hits a wall. Eyes squeezed shut and gun muzzle digging into the soft flesh under his jaw, he can already feel his own brains soaring, skull and gray matter and flecks of blood blown high into the night; all he has to do is pull the trigger and it ends: rest at last for the weary and he will not have to live with having killed Katixa.

When he opens his eyes there are two dead people on the floor. The house is quiet. He takes the gun away from his throat. Pascual knows that his sanity is teetering on the brink. He does not understand the psychic mechanisms, but he senses that an effort is required. He tosses the pistol on the floor near Bordagorri's hand.

The bedroom is where the living has gone on in this house; the sheets and blankets lie rumpled. The money and the papers are exactly where Katixa said they would be. Pascual reappropriates his passport but leaves the tickets. The suitcase is not locked and there are no packets of newsprint, just Pierre and Marie Curie all the way to the bottom. Five million francs in cash is a heavy load to carry.

Hauling it down the stairs, Pascual feels that only now has he finally grown up; only now has he touched bottom, learned the dimensions of this cold little box we live in, learned what Katixa knew. Pascual finally understands what wealth is all about; with five million francs he may be able to buy some warmth.

He knows time is short; the shots must have been heard, police will come. Out the back and over the garden wall; he can hear neighbors' faint worried voices, but nobody can see him. He is spitting blood and the sick sour pain in his testicles robs him of strength. He toils up through scrub to the road, watches for a moment, hauls the suitcase to Dupleix's car, sweating. Airport, he thinks. First flight out. No, there are fewer controls by train. Estació de França, then. Ditch the car, be in France by morning. In Paris he will disappear.

He hears sirens and passes a police car coming up on Pedralbes. The city is exposed below him as he descends, a carpet of lights sweeping to the black sea. Leaving Barcelona is a nightmare that will not end. The Diagonal, downhill. Traffic, an alien city lit by neon. With five million francs Pascual will survive.

Rambla de Catalunya, down toward the sea. He circumnavigates the Plaça Catalunya and now he is on the Ramblas, pressing down through the heart of the old city. Why in God's name has he come this way? The traffic is a madhouse and there are memories that bruise his heart. On the Ramblas young girls are laughing under the plane trees, arm in arm. Columbus on his column now, tires squealing as he turns toward the Estació de França and thinks about a place to leave the car. He must find something near the station; five million francs is a lot to carry. Ahead he can see the arcade; once again there will be a train to take him away from this place.

Abruptly Pascual turns, toward the Barceloneta. A great lassitude has come over him. He drives past restaurants on the Passeig, where unknown people sit under lights too bright to bear. Pascual follows the road around the port and out onto the long breakwater. He will drive until the breakwater ends and plunge off the edge into the cold dark water. On his left now is nothing but the sea, restless in the dark.

In a stolen car with five million francs in unmarked bills Pascual drives, passing parked cars sheltering lovers in the dark, until he can see the city shining across the water. He pulls over and switches off the ignition, and he has run as far as he is going to run. He can see Montjuïc rising against the night sky. He can see the long strings of lights climbing into the far hills. Pascual senses that he has arrived at a choice: he can keep the five million francs or he can keep this.

And what is here but grief and pain, he asks himself, and has no answer. And yet he finds as he sits and gazes across the harbor that with all its grief and pain it terrifies him less than the cold little box that Katixa showed him, and where her soul now resides, he fears, forever.

23

In Yemen there was a welcoming committee of *ashbal,* cub scouts from some Leninist nightmare, a ragged line of dark unkempt children in red kerchiefs with crudely carved toy Kalashnikovs and a Palestinian tricolor on a crooked stick. The little knot of Europeans stood where the bus had disgorged them, silent, wary, dazed by the heat. Pascual scanned the wide expanse of bare rocky earth laid open to the merciless sun, looking with sinking heart for something that looked like habitation. In the distance were crags that had not held vegetation for a million years.

After the ceremony, devoid of enthusiasm on either side, they were greeted sourly in English by a deeply tanned East German who took them to tents at the far side of the camp. The women disappeared and Pascual was left wiping his brow on a camp bed across from his tent mate, an Englishman from Manchester whose humor had taken on increasingly desperate tones as the journey from Beirut had progressed. "I was hoping for something a little closer to the swimming pool," the Englishman said, blue eyes wide in the gloom of the tent, sweat beading on his upper lip.

They saw the women again at the first meal, an unsavory mess featuring some unknown type of bean, served on dusty trestle tables in a large open-sided tent. The German did not appear; young bucks in olive drab, gold teeth shining, pistols at their belts, crowded the edges of the tent, gawking. There was some subdued conversation; the atmosphere was one of dawning dismay. Pascual, at the end of his table, looked across the aisle to the next table down, at the girl with the cropped brown hair, who chewed doggedly while sweeping the men outside the tent with a fierce glare. She was no more than a girl and even without hair she was drawing most of the attention. Pascual had overheard her speaking French and identified her accent. *"¿Española eres?"* he said when he caught her eye.

"Try again," she said, fixing the glare on him.

Pascual put up his hands, appeasing. "Euskadi? I should have known. Forgive me."

Pascual and the girl exchanged a long look, and he could see her making the rapid assessment that friends were going to be a precious commodity in this place. "At least you've heard of it," she said finally.

"Never been there, I'm afraid."

"I'll show you the country sometime. If we ever get out of this place." The girl smiled, and if it was only for the sake of appearances it was magnificent nonetheless.

"I could have saved you a lot of trouble," says Shelby. "Of course, then you wouldn't have bagged the top two on the Ten Most Wanted list."

Pascual shrugs, a slight movement of the head. They sit at a gray table in a gray room. Pascual has been here for hours, unmoving, and his entire world is gray. He is a killer now, at last, an accomplished one, and it has turned his heart to ash. Shelby is expecting him to speak, so he says, "Let me guess. She initiated the whole thing."

Shelby nods. "ETA-Military had a sleazeball named Ordoñez on their hands. Normally when one of their people gets out of line they just shoot him, but she found a use for him. The French wanted him for things he'd done on their side of the Pyrenees and ETA was fed up with him because he was a drunk and a rapist. So she gave him to the DST, in exchange for a line on you. They came to us, and somebody remembered where we'd parked you."

"I was tailor-made for the role."

"They must have been planning to cut and run for some time. That was a hell of a scheme they had worked out."

"She never forgave me for selling out."

"I guess not." Shelby is in adult garb today, a sober dark-blue suit. There is a silence and she says, "They still don't know quite what to make of you. I mean, what you've done in the last week would be a good two years' work for the average counterterrorism task force. Come clean and they may be willing to keep you out of the papers. It may be hard, because this is going to explode. Since the GAL scandal the Spanish are sensitive about this kind of thing."

Pascual shrugs. "I've been here before."

"Except this time not everybody wants a piece of you. Old Dan's back in Tel Aviv, just happy you got Hisham before he got anyone else. You're a Spanish national and this is an internal Spanish matter. As far as I can read things here, there are two schools of thought.

Some of them want to fry you for aiding a fugitive at the very least and three homicides at the most, but there are others who are willing to grant you a few points for your delivery of five million francs in ransom money and two top-grade etarra pelts. Even so, I'd say there's only an even chance you'll wind up back out on the street."

Pascual stares at the tabletop. He is thinking about one of those top-grade etarra pelts and how it felt under his hands, his lips. He will go to his grave wondering if Katixa didn't shoot him because she couldn't or because she wouldn't. He looks up at Shelby.

"Fair's fair," he says.

There is a pause. "We might be able to help, you know."

Pascual stares back at her. "But there's always a quid pro quo."

"Of course. You'd have to do a few things for us now and then. There'd be monetary considerations."

Pascual needs a second, maybe two, to look at it. "I'd rather rot in my chains."

Shelby's eyebrows rise, then fall again. She unclasps her hands. "I'm afraid you're going to have to take your chances then."

"I can live with that."

She nods, vexed but hiding it. "Well, I tried."

"At least you kept me alive," he says. "They'll let you answer the phone now."

She smiles, pushing away from the table. "Actually they're transferring me out of here."

"Promotion or demotion?"

"More action, anyway. Someplace far away and in turmoil."

She extends her hand and Pascual shakes it. He says, "Stick with the casual look. You could walk into the Ministry of Defense with a camera and a mobile satellite hookup and nobody will ever believe you're CIA."

"CIA?" she says, pausing at the door, innocence writ large on the round open face. "Somebody's been jerking your chain." Pascual listens as the click of her heels on the floor fades away.

They have put him in a room with a bunk bed. There is a high window with wire mesh over it. Pascual was brought here by night and has only a vague idea of where he is. Outside he can hear the rumble of traffic. He is feeling for a state he mastered in the long months in Israel, a suppression of deeper concerns by concentration on the small pleasures of the moment. His injuries have been treated, he has been fed, the room is cool and quiet, there are no claims on his attention. The past is an open sore, so when Pascual's mind wanders it wanders to the future: the planet is vast and someday, somewhere, there will be a chance to be Pascual in a new way. There may even be a chance to beg forgiveness of people he has betrayed in large ways and small. He can name them all. Pascual wonders how many more screens he must burst through, how many scales must fall from his eyes before he will know what ordinary people seem to know.

There are footsteps and the door swings open. His keeper is a close-cropped tavern brawler with a jaw to light matches on. "Come on," he says. "Your godfather's here. Bring your coat."

Pascual gapes. "Who?"

"Don't ask me. I don't move in such exalted circles."

Pascual follows him along an echoing hallway, down a flight of stairs. He is ushered into an office where a man stands at a tall window looking down on the street. Pascual is startled to see that it is nighttime again. The door closes behind him and the man turns from the window. He is tall, gray, heavy, draped in a black overcoat. He has pitiless eyes behind square lenses and a firm, censorious mouth. "Pascual Rose," he says.

Pascual understands nothing. "That was my name. They gave me a new one."

The man waves the statement away with the hat he holds in his right hand. "That's what he calls you."

"Who?"

"Esteban." The man in black is moving toward the door.

Pascual follows him into the hall and to the head of another staircase, spooked, remembering Father Costa's first name. "What does he have to do with all this?"

"Absolutely nothing." They go through a door and they are in a courtyard, in the cold night air. The man dons his hat. A black Mercedes stands idling on the cobblestones. A man with the unmistakable look of a senior noncom in civilian dress hastens to open the back door. "And," says the man in black, as he settles on the seat beside Pascual, "you will never ever dare to connect his name with any of it. Understood?"

Pascual nods. Doors slam. "Understood," he says, understanding nothing. The car eases out through a high vaulted gate onto a busy street, a sentry snapping a salute as it passes.

"Where am I taking you?" asks the man. Pascual stares at him blankly. "Look, it's not a trick question. Where do you want to go?"

Pascual blinks at him. "I'm free?"

"For God's sake, don't make me change my mind. Now where do I drop you off?"

After a couple of seconds Pascual says, "The Ramblas, I suppose. Who are you?"

"Nobody. All you need to know is that the padre vouched for you."

"But how did you know to call him?"

The man shakes his head impatiently. "He called me. Four days ago. Told me you needed watching out for. When you turned up last night and I got the report, I saw what he meant. This is a favor to him and you'd better not make me look bad. His word has always been good enough for me and I don't say that about many people."

Pascual's head lolls back, his eyes closed. He remembers rumors, whispers of Father Costa's connections, a secretive and very Catholic society. Pascual never believed the rumors. *"Gracias,"* he says.

"Don't thank me," says his deliverer, but Pascual is thinking *gracia,* grace, is this what they mean?

At Plaça Catalunya the Mercedes pulls over and disgorges him into the crowd. "Go and see Esteban," says the man in black as Pascual slides out, and then the black car oozes away.

Standing at the head of the Ramblas, Pascual is weak with freedom, dazed by grace. People jostle him as he stands, looking seaward down the long gentle slope where he will find friends, a drink or two, someone to lodge him for the night. He is broke and nearly broken, but there is suddenly a hint, a whiff, a distant intimation of something more than grief and pain. This is what he has, these streets, these people, and as Pascual takes his first steps homeward, he senses that it may, perhaps, just be enough.

Dominic Martell was born in the United States and has spent most of his life there, but he has lived and traveled extensively in Latin America, Europe and the Middle East. He has worked as a teacher and a translator. *Lying Crying Dying* is the first of three novels originally published in the 1990s featuring repentant ex-terrorist Pascual March, chronicling his quest for atonement in the chaotic early years of the post–Cold War period. A quarter of a century later, in the transformed landscape of the even more chaotic post-9/11 digitally connected world, Martell began to wonder what had become of Pascual and brought him out of retirement in a new novel, *Kill Chain* (Dunn Books), the first of Pascual's twenty-first-century misadventures.

about the type

The main text of this book is set in Hofler Text Roman, an old-style serif font designed by Jonathan Hoefler Foundary, released in 1991. A versatile font designed specifically for use on the computer that is suitable for body text, it takes cues from a range of classic fonts, such as Garamond and Janson.

Hoefler Text raised awareness of type features previously the concern only of professional printers. *New York* magazine commented in 2014 that it "helped launch a thousand font obsessives."

10-6-20